In memory of Phillip Kigusiutnak, Jimmy Muckpah,
and James Tagalik—what I learned from you
is written in between the lines.

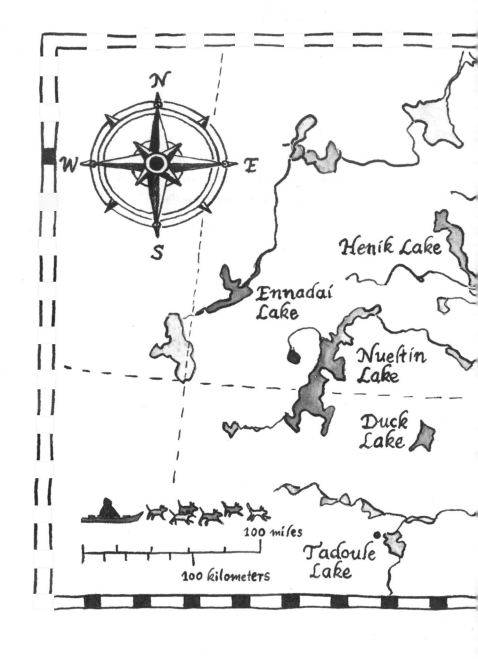

N

W   E

S

Henik Lake

Ennadai
Lake

Nueltin
Lake

Duck
Lake

100 miles

100 kilometers

Tadoule
Lake

CHAPTER 1

The train rattles through an increasingly dull landscape of ... nothing, really. Not a road, a house, or any sign of human life. Just trees, snow, train tracks.

And a telephone line—at least, I think that's what it is. The wires are held up by rotting poles, leaning low to the ground as if they knew they didn't belong here.

I sigh. Kitty looks up from her VIA Rail magazine as if my sighing is an invitation to talk. Which it isn't. Kitty, by the way, is the person that through the unavoidable fact that she gave birth to me is legally entitled to be my mother. And yes, don't tell me that no halfway normal adult still goes by the name of Kitty at age thirty-three. I know that.

"Emmylou ..." Kitty leans forward, trying to make eye contact. I look out the window.

"What?" I want to say, but I haven't talked to her since we left Calgary, and that's 46 hours and fifteen minutes ago—not counting the time change. The longer we don't talk, the harder it is to break the silence.

"Are you hungry?" she finally says.

It's a loaded question. If I say yes, we can go to the dining car and pretend that all is normal. But I'm tired of pretending.

"Come on, Emmylou. You have to talk to me eventually." She reaches over to ruffle my hair. I duck away.

"If you have to be like that, go ahead. I'll be in the dining car if you change your mind."

Kitty throws the magazine on the seat next to me and slips on her shoes. She flings her hair out of her face, straightens her shoulders, and walks down the aisle. She's lost weight in the last few weeks and she looks smaller, but that didn't stop her from packing up our stuff and dragging our suitcases down the stairs of our apartment building and into a new life.

I stretch my legs out onto Kitty's seat. It's still warm. I flip through her magazine and then—because there's nothing better to do—I count the telephone poles. It has the same effect as counting sheep. When I wake up, I wonder if they've secretly backed up the train while I was sleeping. Same muskeg, same patches of snow, same telephone poles.

The Muskeg Express. That's what the people here call the train. I'm not kidding. There is nothing "express" about this train. I could ride my bike faster if there was a road to ride a bike on—which there isn't. No road goes in or out of Churchill. Just one long, lonely, never-ending train track.

I scan the landscape for anything alive. Not even a bird is sitting on the shrubs on the edges of the frozen ponds. Stunted spruce trees huddle together, tiny islands in an ocean of drifting snow. Gray clouds are hanging so low, they're almost touching the ground.

I imagine myself out there, walking alone in the bog. What if I met a bear, casually walking toward me while I'm desperately trying to get unstuck from the muck?

I turn away from the dreary landscape and catch a movement a few seats ahead of me. A boy's face is reflected in the window. He's about my age, I'd say. I wonder if he, too, is being dragged to a place where he doesn't want to be. I try to study his face, but it's hard to see in the faint reflection of the glass. His hair is dark, his cheeks are round, but not like a child's. His face has more edge to it. He looks like someone from a different country. Maybe … Oh, no, I'm so stupid. I bet he's Inuit. Inuit? Is that how you say it? He's not the foreign one. I am. That's when reality totally sets in—we are actually going to the Arctic. I never really thought about it that way because it's still Manitoba, after all, but why else would there be polar bears in Churchill?

I shift in my seat, trying to get the light just right, so I can see the reflection of the boy more clearly. I wonder what he sees when he looks out the window. Does it look different when you grow up here? Does he notice things that I don't see?

The boy turns his head. For a split second, our eyes lock and I quickly turn away. Best not to make friends. I know we won't stay for long.

It's only three days ago since I said goodbye to Maya, but it already feels like years. "Drifters," Maya called us, as I tried to cram all my belongings into the two worn-out, oversized suitcases.

"You know what you are? You and your mom? You're drifters," she'd said.

Drifters. I kind of like how it sounds. I stopped packing and let myself flop onto my mattress, picturing myself adrift on a blue ocean, my bed a raft carrying me toward a faraway horizon.

"Earth to Emmylou! Are you listening at all?" Maya plopping next to me.

Me opening my eyes, blinking. Above me, not the sun, but the glaring fluorescent white of the naked light bulb that illuminated my room for eighteen months, two weeks, and five days. A new record.

"You are going to stay in touch, right?" Maya leaning over me.

"Right." Me wiggling away. I never do. Stay in touch, I mean. Truth is, we're not drifting. We're running. No, not we. Kitty is running—I just don't know from what.

"Here, you must be starvin', Marvin." Kitty passes me an egg salad sandwich and a small carton of apple juice. The kind that kindergarten kids have in their lunch boxes. I sigh. Only two more years. Two years, one month, and eight days, to be precise. Then I'm eighteen. Stupid thing is: I am starving, and apple juice has always been my favorite. The PA crackles and the conductor's voice fills the train car.

"Ladies and gentlemen, we will be arriving at our final destination shortly. Welcome to Churchill, Manitoba. The local temperature is minus nine degrees. Have a wonderful stay and thank you for traveling with ..." The PA crackles and the conductor's voice is cut out by the screeching of the brakes.

My palms are getting sweaty. All of a sudden, I don't want this train ride to be over. Don't want to walk out into yet another train station, not knowing where we'll go from here. Waking up in the morning, confused. Where am I? Why am I here? I guess the "why" is the easy one to answer: wherever Kitty goes, I go.

No questions allowed. Final destination? Not in her vocabulary.

"Emmylou! Look! A polar bear!" Kitty presses her hand against the window.

My heart tries to jump out of my chest, even though I'm sitting safely in a train.

"Where?" I ask, forgetting that I wasn't going to talk to her.

A white shape is moving at a quick pace along a gravel road, just on the other side of the train tracks. It takes me a few seconds before I realize it's not a bear.

"That's a dog, Kitty." A big white dog, the kind you see in movies about polar exploration. Real furry and with standing-up ears.

"Well," Kitty grins, "it *could* have been a bear. Churchill, Manitoba, Polar Bear Capital of the World. Come on, Emmylou, it's gonna be fun."

"What? Getting eaten by a bear? If you want to get rid of me, there's easier ways, you know." I stare at her. It takes her a second before she realizes what I'm talking about. But when she does, her smile disappears.

"That wasn't you. That was all that girl's idea."

"Maya."

"Huh?"

"My friend. Her name was Maya."

"Yes. Maya." The way she says her name makes it sound like Maya had done something horrible to her. All we did was look up "emancipation" and what we would have to do so I could live on my own.

"I can tell you right now, your chances of getting eaten by a bear are greater than me signing those papers. For better or worse, you're stuck with me. Up to you what you make out of it. Wanna make things miserable? Fine."

"Me? Who's making things miserable, Kitty? Things were going okay until …" I try to think back, but there isn't anything there. All I know is, one day things were okay and then they weren't. But I don't know when or why. Things just started sliding until there seemed no way out.

"It's gonna be great, Emmylou. We can have a new start, leave all those old problems behind. Heck, nobody even knows anything about us here—no assumptions, no judgment, just a fresh, clean start. It will be good, you'll see."

The train comes to a stop next to a building with wooden beams and old-fashioned-looking rooflines. A small sign dangles from the overhanging roof. *Churchill*, it says. Nothing else. I glance out the windows on the other side. Through the falling snow, I can make out the river pushing gray, slushy ice past a gigantic industrial-looking building toward the icy ocean.

★

A woman in a huge red parka rushes toward us the minute we step out of the train. Her face is hidden by the fur trim of the parka's hood. *Please don't make me wear dead animals around my face*, I silently plead to whoever might be listening out there.

"Are you Kitty?" The woman holds up her hood with one hand and reaches out to Kitty with the other.

"Yes. You are ... Walter's wife?" Kitty shakes hands with Dead-Animal-Face.

"No, gosh, no!" The wind sweeps her hood off and I realize she's only a few years older than I am. "Walter is my boss. I just work 'ere for the polar bear season. I'm Marie."

She's got an accent. French?

"Walter is out with the Tundra Crawler. That's all your luggage? Come with me. The van is out front." She grabs the heavier of my two suitcases. A cold, wet, fishy-smelling wind whirls around me as soon as we step out of the wind shadow of the building.

"What's your name?"

"Emmylou."

"Nice name. You speak the French?" She pulls her hood up.

"No."

"Too bad. Nobody except me speaks the French, so I have to look after all the French guests. Your first time waitressing?"

"Sorry?"

"You come to work 'ere, no? Walter tell me to pick up the two new workers."

"I'm just here with my mom." I turn around to look at Kitty.

"Well, actually … now that you're homeschooling and not on a fixed schedule … Besides, the lodge only offers accommodation to their staff, so …" Kitty says.

"So? I'm here to work as a waitress?" I feel a lump in my throat and I'm immediately mad at myself. Why does it still hurt? Don't I know her by now?

"Does it matter at all to you what *I* want, Kitty?" My voice too loud, the volume control gone.

"Of course. Always," Kitty says, but they're just words. Hollow and empty.

"Why are we here then? I liked Calgary. Even the school wasn't too bad, but you …" Just then I see the boy from the window. He's struggling to carry a hockey bag, while at the same time trying to lift four cardboard grocery boxes. An old man with a well-worn blue coat and a red and white toque approaches the boy. The old man takes two boxes and the boy picks up the other two. They leave the platform, walking along the train tracks. It happens so quietly, so naturally, as if they were in a world of their own.

"Ahhh … 'ere is the van." Marie slides the passenger door open. *Sleepy Bear Lodge*, the sign reads in bold black letters. "Don't worry, you will like it. You meet people from all over the world. And lots of bears around the town right now. This is the premier place for adventure." She smiles at me. I don't smile back. In one sentence, she has mentioned the three things I could completely do without: people, bears, and adventure.

As the van pulls out of the parking lot, the boy and the old man are crossing the train tracks toward the river. Where are they going? I can't see any houses over there. Just shacks of different sizes and colors. Surely they don't live there? I crane my neck until I lose sight of them between the buildings of town.

"This 'ere is the best bakery in town." Marie points to a building with red metal siding. In front of it sits a wooden fishing boat stranded in the concrete parking lot; a plywood polar bear is propped up inside the boat.

"And this is where to buy souvenirs, carvings, prints, and T-shirts." She points out galleries and restaurants and tourists shops along the main road as she's driving. I hear her talk but I'm not paying attention. Neither is Kitty; she's staring out the window, not saying a word. Her way to make me feel bad.

Marie pulls up in front of a two-story log building. Hand-painted wooden signs dangle between the posts that are holding up the porch roof. *Sleepy Bear Restaurant. Soups. Salads. Muskox. Arctic Char.*

"'Ere we are," Marie says and grabs two of our bags. She holds the heavy wooden door open and shuffles us past the reception counter and up a staircase. What an odd place. Not a tree in sight, and everything in this building is made of logs. The stair treads are made of massive trees cut in half, and the railing is made of smaller trees sanded smoothly, but not so smooth that it hides the little channels chewed by bugs when the tree was part of a forest. If I wasn't so mad, I might actually like it. Once upstairs, we pass an alcove with two log chairs and a small bookshelf. We walk down the long and narrow hallway right to the end, where the light appears dimmer and the doors are closer together.

"This is your room." Marie points to a door with a wooden sign. *Aurora*, it says. "They don't 'ave numbers 'ere. So you just 'ave to remember your room name." She pulls the wooden door latch open. The ceiling is sloped and a dormer window overlooks the street below. A small table with a single chair sits by the window. Two beds are squeezed against opposite walls. Definitely too close. Kitty plunks her suitcase onto the bed closest to the door and turns to Marie.

"Thank you ... what was your name again?"

"Marie," Marie says. "I'll let you settle in first and show you around later ... *d'accord*?" She doesn't wait for an answer. Can't get away fast enough. I guess there's one thing we have in common.

CHAPTER 2

"Geez, Emmylou. There are only guests at four tables. How can you get their orders mixed up?"

Kitty looks at me as if I couldn't tell a glass of milk from a Coke, which obviously I can. I just can't remember if the milk is for the kid with the snotty nose by the table right next to the stone fireplace, or the girl with the fancy blonde braids by the table in the back corner.

"How am I supposed to remember who ordered the Arctic char and who asked for the fish'n'chips, and who wanted Caesar salad with extra bacon, and who didn't want any bacon at all?"

"Write it down." Kitty pulls the notepad out of the apron she's wearing over her black mini skirt, size extra-short.

"If you're so much better at it, why don't you do it, then?" I pull my notepad out of my jeans pocket and toss it to her. The pad is empty except for a few unintelligible scribbles on the first page. I can't write as fast as the people are talking, and if I'm writing, I miss what the next person is saying. So I thought it would be easier just to remember, which it isn't.

"You could at least pretend you're trying."

"I *am* trying." I glance at the clock on the log wall. Only twenty more minutes and then I'm off my shift and Kitty's will officially start. "I never signed up for this job," I say as I untie my apron.

"So that's it? You're playing stupid to punish me for getting you a job?"

"I'm not playing stupid!"

"So what, then? Are you telling me you are stupid? It's waitressing, Emmylou. Surely you can figure out how to take a couple of orders?"

"That's totally beside the point!"

"What is your point, then?"

"The point is ..." I say, but I don't know what it is anymore. It's always like that. She turns things around in my head until I don't know any more what I was feeling. It's driving me so crazy that sometimes I don't even know if I *am* actually crazy.

I storm out of the dining room and bump into Walter at the reception.

"Hello, young lady—how's your first day?" His voice is outgoing, sociable, and a lot younger-sounding for someone with almost white hair—just like you'd expect of a lodge owner. Friendly to everyone. But I know he doesn't really care. Just wants things to run smoothly.

"Fine. Thanks," I mumble.

"Good, good. Uhm … anything wrong with that black dress I gave you?" Great. Just what I need. Another adult that knows better what I should be wearing and what I should like.

My new boss looks me up and down, and I see myself through his eyes—wild messy hair, shaggy jeans, a baggy sweater that's more cozy than stylish.

"No, it's great. Perfect." I'll trade it for your cargo pants, I want to add but, instead, I just flash him a fake smile and walk past him.

★

Back in our room, the ceiling feels too close, the walls too tight. I sit on my bed and pick up my phone. I wonder if Maya has tried contacting me. No coverage. I scroll through old text messages.

Text me when you get there. Don't let her drive you insane. That's the last one.

Too late, I text back and press the send button.

Message not delivered, comes the reply.

The air is stuffy and suffocating. I put on an extra sweater and then my purple winter jacket on top. It's tight but it'll do.

A cool wind blows wet snow into my face. I pull my scarf tighter over my ears and nose while I'm walking down the wooden steps of the lodge. For a second, I think of going back to my room to get the red parka Walter had loaned Kitty and me. The other part of my new uniform: red down parka with dead animal around the neck for outside. The black dress with nothing around the neck is for inside. I'm not going to wear either.

I tie my hood as tight as I can around my face, stuff my cold hands in my pockets, and keep walking down the main street. Seems like I'm the only one walking. Converted school buses transport tourists to where they need to go. Where are they going? I wonder. There are barely more than a dozen streets in this town, so what's there to see other than the polar bears— wherever they are? Not here, I hope.

For a town this small, there's a lot of vehicle traffic out there. Bears would avoid that, wouldn't they? I look around— no bears.

Then suddenly I hear snow crunching behind me. My heart pounds like crazy and I feel my palms getting sweaty. I jump to the side, ducking away from the attack.

"Whoa, young lady, I didn't mean to startle you." A man

grins as he walks past me, wiping snow/snot/slush off his beard.

"Sorry," I say, both relieved and embarrassed. I resist the urge to follow close behind him. The scare is still in my bones. The man turns around.

"You shouldn't walk out here on your own. Bears will come right into town, you know."

"Thanks," I say, not sure if he's playing on my fear or if he's dead serious. After all, *he's* walking on his own. Either way, I look back more frequently. I even take off my hood so I can see what's coming from the side. I'm spooking myself. I have to quit that or I won't survive here. Mentally, I mean. I need to be able to get away from Kitty. Even just for short breaks.

If Maya were here, she'd make me forget my fear. I imagine her screaming, "BEAR!" right behind an unassuming tourist, and then running as fast as she can, scaring the living crap out of the poor guy. With Maya, walking down a street where polar bears could be lurking around the corner would have a certain thrill, could even be fun. Alone, without her, not so much.

I read the signs of the businesses as I stroll down the streets: *Polar Bear B&B, Polar Bear Tours, Bear Country Inn* … It's a tourist town. Tips should be good here and that's all Kitty really cares about.

There's a commotion at the end of the street. A bunch of tourists are coming off a white bus, another group waiting to board. *The Tundra Crawler Adventure*, the sign on the bus reads. It boasts the picture of a polar bear looking into a giant off-road vehicle. The tires alone are as big as the bear. The Crawler isn't here, though. The tourists have to get to the crawlers by bus. Good. That means the polar bears are somewhere far away. The driver sees me and waves. It's Walter, my boss. I wave back and turn off the main road, avoiding him and the crowd of people.

Seems like I've reached the edge of town. There's houses on only one side of the street; bare, treeless land on the other. Further down, toward the river, loom the harbor buildings. They look rundown and shabby, as if no one bothered to keep them up. There's no sign of ships or any other activity. A gravel road leads out of town and past the port. Should I turn right and back to town or left onto the gravel road and follow the sign to *Cape Merry*? Neither option appeals to me. Possible run-ins with Kitty or possible run-ins with polar bears? I turn left.

The air smells more fishy here. Like the ocean. Snow clings to my scarf, turning into a mushy slush from my warm breath.

The damp air crawls under my jacket and there's nothing I can do about it.

The road winds its way up through shrubby bushes, brown leafless branches reaching into the dreary sky. Huge rocks are strewn across the land as if someone had dropped them there a long time ago. I guess someone had. Weren't those boulders left by receding glaciers? I dimly remember something like that from my last geology class. Oh, well, no more geology class for me— or any other class. That was the one condition Kitty had agreed to: No more switching schools. No more being the awkward new kid that has been everywhere but belongs nowhere. From now on, I homeschool myself. Goodbye teachers, hello Google.

On my left is the river, the water far out in the channel. It must be low tide. Boulders of all shapes and sizes, that must be under water at high tide, are now exposed to the air, ice clinging on them to form bizarre sculptures. Mist rises from the river and is absorbed by the low-hanging sky. On my right is the ocean with a beach of shattered ice, like broken pieces of glass. Overlooking the river and ocean are the ruins of an old stone wall, gray stones on gray rock. Cannon holes stare like hollow eyes across the river from an old fort on the other side.

On the low land toward the coast are two old houses, dwarfed by the size of the boulders strewn about. Suddenly, I feel like I am being watched. I turn around. There's something large and light-colored. A bear? I stop dead in my tracks. The white shape doesn't move, and I have no inclination to stand there and wait till it does. So I run. I run back toward town as fast as I can. When I look back, the white shape blends in perfectly with the other rocks around it. No sign of a bear.

A black truck comes up from behind me. I walk off the road to let it pass. The truck stops next to me. The driver's door opens and a tall man in the obligatory down parka jumps out. A rifle lies on the passenger seat.

"What are you doing out here all by yourself?" the man says.

"I'm not by myself ..." I mumble, even though it's quite obvious there's nobody with me. I try not to glance at his gun.

"Didn't you see the sign?"

"What sign?" I ask.

He looks around. "Here. Give me a hand." He bends down to lift up a green metal sign. "It must have fallen over in the storm."

POLAR BEAR ALERT

STOP

DON'T WALK IN THIS AREA

"There really is a bear?" I look around but see nothing move.

I glance at his gun. He opens the back door and stores it in a gun case. That's when I notice the green Manitoba Conservation sticker on the side of his truck. He's a conservation officer!

"Jump in. I'm not supposed to give tourists rides, but we just chased a bear off the cape. He was swimming across the river when my patrol relief came."

"Patrol?"

"Polar Bear Patrol. Hop in. Never know where he'll come ashore again."

"I'm not supposed to hop into vehicles with strangers," I say as I'm already halfway onto the passenger seat. "But in this case ..."

"Where to?"

"Hm?"

"Where are you staying?"

"Oh. Sleepy Bear Lodge."

"Good place. You like it there?"

"That bear, did he attack anybody?" I ask, evading his question.

"No, no, no. We haven't had an attack for three years now."

"Oh." Great conversation, Emmylou. There's a guy who just chased off a polar bear and could tell you about a bear attack three years ago, and all you have to say is "Oh."

"He's just been hanging around too close to town. That's been his second warning. If he doesn't watch out, he's going to jail."

"Jail?" He's kidding me, right?

"Yep. Polar Bear Jail. Just out the other end of town."

"Oh! Really? Cool."

"No, it's not all that cool. They keep 'em there until they can helicopter them out onto the sea ice. No food. Just water. Wanna make their prison stay as uncomfortable as we can, so they won't come back. Off you go."

"Hm?" I hadn't realized the truck had stopped. We're back at Sleepy Bear. "Thanks." I climb out of the truck. "One more question: Can I go see the polar bear prison?"

"No. Nobody's allowed in there. They try to minimize the human contact. That's the whole point."

There are a million questions I want to ask him, but his wheels are already rolling and I quickly shut the passenger door.

Right next to Sleepy Bear's entrance is a black chalkboard. *Next Tundra Crawler Tour leaves 4 PM.* The board is surrounded by pictures of bears standing on their hind legs and peering into the monster truck's window. There's one picture that shows a whole train of trailers pulled by one of those crawlers: *The Tundra Crawler Hotel.* In the foreground, a mama bear with two cubs walks across the tundra. In the background, a hint of Northern Lights. What was it the conservation officer had said? "Minimize human contact?"

I slip through the door and make a beeline for the stairs.

"Emmylou, is that you? Hey." Kitty pokes her head out of the restaurant door. "How is your day?" she asks.

"Fine." I try to put as much sarcasm in my voice as I can muster. I'm about to tell her that there's NOTHING in this town to do but wait to get eaten by a meat-loving polar bear, when Kitty smiles her Kitty-smile.

"See, I told you you'd get used to being here."

Seriously? How can she not get my sarcasm?

CHAPTER 3

There's one good thing about being a waitress. I'm on opposite shifts with Kitty. There's still the problem of sharing a room, but Kitty just comes here to sleep and change her clothes. If she's not waitressing, she's checking out the tourist shops and drinking coffee in one of the hotel restaurants. She's always quick to make friends. Quick to lose them, too. If we're in the room at the same time, I grab a book and pretend I'm learning for school.

Which, by the way, isn't half as easy as I thought. First problem: I don't have Internet access. It's 2012, people, and I have to go to the library at the community complex to get Internet access? It sucks. Because that's exactly what I wanted to avoid. Being the new kid all over again. Luckily, I can pretend I'm just another tourist. For now, anyway. October and November are the busy seasons here, because of the bears hanging around town until the sea ice is thick enough that they can go out there, hunting seals and whatever stuff bears do. Then it slows down.

By then, Kitty might feel the urge to move again. Five years, seven months, and eleven days was her personal high. That's when we were still a complete family. Dad, Kitty, me, Grandma Millie, and Toby the dog. Three weeks, four days, and five hours her low. We have moved nine times since Dad left us. Which is an average of one year, one month, two weeks, and three-point-five days. How's that for statistics? So far, we've been here for nine days and eight hours. There's still a chance of setting the record for a new low.

"In for some more books? Emmylou, right?" The gray-haired librarian takes the books I hand her over the counter.

Great. So I've only been here for nine days, eight hours, and a couple of minutes and the librarian already knows my name. I don't know hers and I don't have any intention of learning it.

"I'm Lisa. Are you new in town?" she asks.

"Just passing through," I mumble as I wait for her to pass me back my library card.

"Yeah, that's what most people do. Just here to work during the Polar Bear season in the fall or the Beluga Whale season in the summer. Some work the Northern Lights tours in winter. Not many want to stay."

No, why would anyone, I think—but I keep it to myself. "So, you live here year round?" I ask instead.

"I've been here for twenty-two years now. I love it here. Mind you, it gets crazy in the bear season, but I've got my library to hide in." She hands me my card. I'm free to go, but something about Lisa makes me pause. The way she looks at me makes me think she's actually interested in me. I linger for a second.

"That's an interesting variety of books you picked. For school?" she asks.

"Sort of." And then I tell her that I'm homeschooling and that I have to send in my outline for my studies to the Ministry of Education, and that I don't really know what an outline is, and I'm not going to enrol in high school because we won't stay long. I bite my lip. I don't know why I told her all that.

There's an awkward silence and I quickly grab my books.

"Do you have your paperwork here? Would you like me to have a look at your outline?" Lisa asks.

I put my books down and fish in my back pack until I find the dog-eared copy I got from the Homeschooling Office of Manitoba's Education and Training Ministry. Lisa studies it for a few minutes.

"Okay, looks like you need to plan what you'll learn in Language Arts, Mathematics, Science, and Social Studies. What are your interests?"

My interests? What does that have to do with what I need to learn? Maybe this was a stupid idea. I bet it's half a century ago that Lisa was in Grade 10. She probably knows even less what I'm supposed to do. I eye the copy of my homeschooling plan she's holding in her hands. I need that back.

"Okay, let's forget about the outline for a while. Is this your first time in Churchill?" she asks.

"Yeah," I say, not sure what she's trying to get at.

"Okay, great. Where are you from?"

"Does it matter?" I ask a bit too sharply. I don't want to have to tell her that I've lived in nearly every province, in none of them twice.

"No, it doesn't," Lisa quickly says. "But if you compare where you came from with the geography and people and wildlife you see here, is there anything that's different? Anything that makes you curious?"

"Well, there's the polar bears, of course. I've never been to a place where a polar bear might be sitting on your front step when you come home from buying groceries."

"Good. That's a start. What do you know about the bears?"

"Uhm … there was one near town yesterday …"

"Probably more than one," Lisa adds. "What else?"

"They're endangered?" I'm not so sure about that one, but I remember Coca-Cola having all these ads to protect the polar bears, or something like that.

"You're not sure?" Lisa asks. "Maybe that's something you'd like to know about them? What else?"

"What I want to know or what I do know?"

"Both."

Come to think of it, there isn't really much I do know. They're a major tourist attraction in Churchill, but what about other places in the Arctic? Do they have so many bears there as well? Where are the polar bears before they come here, and where do they go later in the year?

"I guess there's a lot I don't know," I confess. "Would be neat to know how many there are and what they do during different times of the year, and why the sea-ice is so important to them, and what happens with climate change. I mean, how it influences the bears. And I guess the interaction with humans. Why do the bears have to go to jail? And what happens when they release them?"

"Good, Emmylou. Very good. Keep thinking." Lisa types something on her keyboard and scrolls down the screen. "That could all be under the topic of 'Dynamics of Ecosystems: Observe and document a range of organisms that illustrate the biodiversity within a local or regional ecosystem. Investigate how human activities affect an ecosystem.' It's all here in the Science Curriculum. You hit it bang on."

"I did?" I'm not sure if she's mocking me. The way she put it, I wouldn't even know how to start.

"Well, yes, dear. Once you start looking into the environment of a polar bear, you'll find a whole range of animals, plants, fungi ... on the land, in the ocean, in the air, even. A whole biological community of interacting organisms. And then you asked about climate change. You'll have to learn about Weather Dynamics; that's another one in the curriculum."

Wow. The way Lisa puts it, I could even get excited about science. "What about chemistry and periodic tables?" I ask, before I get too excited.

"You're interested in them?"

"No, totally not."

"Well then, let's focus on the Churchill ecosystem, polar bears, and climate change."

I smile. "Thanks. Do you have books on that?"

"I sure do. That would be a start. But you're right in Churchill, girl. Surely there are other ways than books to find your answers."

"How?"

"Well, you could check out the interpretive center. You'll also find the Hinterland Who's Who information sheets there."

I'd definitely prefer reading books in my P.J.'s to hunting down information around town, but I just nod.

"What about Social Studies? How am I supposed to learn about that?"

"Anything that interests you about the history or the people of the area?"

I immediately think of the boy on the train. I wonder if it's different growing up here. I feel the blood rush into my face when I think about his eyes in the reflection of the window.

"Ahm ... I was at Cape Merry the other day," I say quickly. "There are the ruins of a fort across the river from there. Why was it built and who lived there? Does it count?"

Lisa laughs. "I'm not your teacher, girl. Of course it counts. Anything you want to learn about counts."

"When I went to school, I was always questioning my teachers, why we had to learn this and why we had to learn that. And now that I don't have a teacher, I'm trying to guess what my teachers would have wanted me to learn. I guess that doesn't make any sense."

"Don't worry—you're a smart girl. You'll be amazed what you can learn on your own."

I can feel my palms getting sweaty. I'm afraid if I say any more, she'll find out that she's wrong about me. I'm not smart.

"I better go."

"I can look up some math programs for you, if you want. I'm here Tuesday to Thursday from …"

"Thanks," I call, already halfway through the door. I hate it when people think I'm smart. I don't know what makes them think that in the first place, but I know that now, I'll always be worried that Lisa will find out I'm not what she expects me to be. The more I worry, the less I make sense when I talk. I know it's stupid, but there's nothing I can do about it.

Big wet snowflakes greet me when I step out onto the street; I let them melt on my face. The sky is so gray that it feels like late afternoon, even though it's still early in the day. My shift won't start until 6 PM. I hug myself tight against the wet cold and walk down the street as fast as I can, but I can't stop the memory from catching up.

It was a snowy day like today. We had just moved—to Saskatoon, I think it was. I was waiting outside on the swings for Mom to come back from the parent-teacher interview in my new school, watching the snowflakes melt on my red stockings. I was cold, and I was glad when I finally saw Kitty rush out the school door.

"Why are you not participating in class? Why is your teacher asking questions about our home life? What's wrong with you, Emmylou?"

I didn't know, so I said nothing.

"Geez, Emmylou. You can't mess up in school. Next thing, social services will knock on our door … and that's the last thing we want. Or do you want them to come and take you away?"

I shook my head, suddenly scared.

"You're not stupid, so there's no reason for you to be failing painting rainbows or whatever it is you do in Grade 2."

I remember thinking that I'd already known how to paint rainbows since kindergarten, but I had the feeling that letting Kitty know about this fact wouldn't help my cause. So, instead, I played with a hole I had in my stocking until my finger fit through it. Strange what details can suddenly come up in your memory. I still know exactly what Kitty said.

"Emmylou, look at me. You're a smart girl. Of course you are. You're my daughter. Now say it."

"I'm your daughter?"

"Geez, Emmylou."

After that, Kitty was on edge, always asking what my teacher was saying to me, always telling me what to tell my teacher. But they were lies, and I was never good at lying. In the end, I felt like I was hiding, hiding who I was. Hiding that I wasn't the smart kid Kitty expected me to be.

Not long after, I woke up in the middle of the night. Kitty had pulled all my clothes out of my cupboard.

"Don't just sit there and watch. Help me pack!"

I try to shake off that memory. I haven't thought about it since ... since Grade 2, I guess. Back then, I was too young to understand, but even now, it doesn't make any sense. What did I do that was wrong?

I find myself walking toward the train station. The wind is driving the snow horizontally across the streets and into my eyes. I keep my head down, shielding my eyes with my mitts. I can barely see ahead. It doesn't matter; there's not much to see.

In the wind shadow of the train station, small trees huddle together, surrounded by a landscaped rock garden that doesn't look much different than the tundra, except here, it's confined by the paved parking lot. Icicles are hanging from the roof, giving the train station a ghostly appearance. The building is big for a town so small. A city building standing lonely at the edge of nowhere. When was it built? And why? For a second, I think of adding the questions to my social science outline. But then I think, who really wants to know about this forsaken place?

Then a thought enters my head and I immediately feel wide awake. What if I took the next train back to Winnipeg? And then hitchhiked to Calgary? In a few days, I could be with Maya. Her parents would understand, wouldn't they? They could let me stay with them till Maya and I are eighteen, and then we could share an apartment or something. If Kitty can just pack up and leave, why can't I?

I push against the heavy wooden door, leaning into it with my whole weight. To my surprise, it opens easily. I feel a draft of warm air as the cold outside sucks the warmth from the building. I quickly step in and close the door. Nobody's in the entrance hall, but I hear a muted voice talking somewhere in one of the back rooms. I check out the train schedule. There's only one destination. South. Next train leaves in two days. No train for two days! No wonder nobody's in the building.

I'm just about to leave when I notice the wall with flyers of all sorts. Hotels, tourist attractions, tours, but also the "Hinterland Who's Who" flyers Lisa had mentioned: Arctic foxes, beluga whales, bearded seals, walruses, wolves, polar bears … It's kind of hard to picture that they're all here, just outside of town—or even in town, as in the case of the *Ursus maritimus*. I pull out the flyer on polar bears and sit down on the long wooden bench across from the ticket counter. I shiver when I read that the great white bear can weigh up to 800 kilograms. Eight hundred. That's me times fifteen. You'd think he would be slow, weighing that much, but he can run as fast as forty kilometers an hour. No way any human could get away from a bear going that fast.

Before I even know it, I've read the whole pamphlet and then I'm on to the next, because on the polar bear one, it said that he can detect a seal breathing-hole covered by snow and ice from up to a kilometer away. That makes me curious about what a seal breathing-hole is, so I study up on bearded seals and harbor seals.

I pull my feet up on the bench, getting as comfy as I can on the hard wood. It's nice and warm in here, and even the glow of the ceiling lights has a warm feel to it. I try to imagine what it would be like to actually see those animals. I mean, I've seen them on TV and stuff, but I've never been to a place where I actually could see them in their natural habitat, in the wild. *Natural habitat!* I'm already talking as if I've written the flyers myself.

"Can I help you?" A guy in a Parks Canada uniform leans on the wooden counter. How long has he been watching me? Was I talking to myself? I quickly jump up. The guy is stroking his goatee while he's waiting for my response. It must be the first beard he's ever grown—or tried growing, I should add. It's patchy, revealing that he's not as grown up as he thinks. He looks ridiculous in his uniform—like a boy scout in an adult's uniform.

"Ahm … no thanks. Actually, I was just about to leave." I quickly gather up the flyers and sort them back into their slots on the shelf. One of the ceiling lights flickers and makes a low buzzing sound. Suddenly the train station doesn't feel so warm and cozy anymore, just a place where people move on from.

"You can keep the flyers," the Parks guy says.

I hesitate. I don't really need them if I'm leaving in two days. I glance over at the clerk, worried he can tell what I'm thinking. I quickly stuff a couple of flyers into my pocket.

"Did you see our interpretive center yet?"

"Hm?"

"Here—I'll switch the light on for you."

He seems keen. Too keen. Before I can find an excuse, he's already waiting for me at the entrance to the one-room interpretive center. *Our Land, Our Stories* is written in big gold letters above the door in English, French, and a language made of weird symbols.

ᓂᑕᐣᑭ·ᐁᓯ/ᓂ∩ᐸᒡ·ᐃᓯ·ᐃᓂᐅ·ᐊ

"That's syllabics," the Parks guy explains.

I nod as if I'd known that all along. "Which language?"

"Good question. Cree maybe? I'm Lars, the interpretive guide here. I'll show you through."

Reluctantly, I follow him.

"Wapusk National Park and the Hudson Bay Coastal Lowlands are one of the world's largest known polar bear maternity denning areas," Lars explains in a voice that tells me he's probably good at boring kids to sleep. "Here we have a life-size polar bear maternity den," he continues, leaning his arms onto the glass wall that keeps visitors from stepping too close to a diorama. He pauses, can't resist playing with his goatee. All I can see is a heap of fake snow and some of those spindly spruce trees—fake as well. I step closer and look inside the den entrance. A polar bear is curled up inside, a tiny cub huddled by her side. Both dead, yet frozen in time as if still alive. Immediately, the picture of my grandma is in my head.

I never wanted to look into the coffin, but Kitty made me. "This is your only chance to say goodbye, Emmylou. You'll regret it later, trust me, puppy." Kitty taking me to her mother's coffin and me quickly closing my eyes. But then I looked. Just once, real quick. And I saw her. Grandma Millie—she was there, but also not. Her hair looked nice like it always did. I could even smell the hairspray that held her white curls together. But her skin looked gray and waxy like a plastic doll. Not real at all.

Grandma Millie always made me feel special. Like I was smart and beautiful. With her, I always felt safe. Until I saw her for the very last time. I was so scared, and she couldn't make that feeling go away. I had just turned five. I remember that because I still have the stuffie my Grandma gave me for my fifth birthday. Silly—a black and white puppy dog.

Not very long after, we moved. Without Dad.

★

"The park covers 11,475 square kilometers ..."

I hear the Park Ranger's voice far away, almost as if I was just waking up. Goodbye, I say in my inside-of-my-head voice to the cub, who will never feel its mother's warmth again.

I squeeze between Lars and the tepee in the center of the room and move toward the exit. I feel a bit bad about leaving the guy who was going to give me a private tour but, then again, I never asked him to. I glance at a diorama of a man clad in fur clothing, standing next to a life-size caribou. I have less trouble looking at the fur on the man than the caribou itself. I wonder if that's the clothes they still wear today further north, but I don't feel like stopping to find out. I've had enough of dead things for today.

As I step outside the train station, a gust of cold air sweeps away the suffocating stuffiness I felt in that building.

★

"Where were you?!" Kitty is staring at me across the room, like she'd find the answer written somewhere on my forehead. What did I do now? I stand on the threshold to our room, resisting the urge to shut the door and leave. There's nowhere I can go.

"Studying." The familiar feeling that it doesn't matter what I say is creeping up on me.

"Studying?" she asks, clamping her hands onto her hips.

"For the homeschooling thing." I say, wishing she would give me a clue what she wants to hear.

"Where?" she asks sharply.

"The library."

"Don't lie."

"What?"

"I phoned there. They said you left two hours ago."

"I went to the interpretive center after."

"So why didn't you tell me?"

"I just did."

"Before you left! And don't you sigh at me."

"I didn't sigh." I just took a deep breath, hoping to avoid the unavoidable, but it's too late. My words are now coming out faster than I can think. "Can't I just go for a walk without telling you where I'm going? It's not even 5 PM, Kitty."

"Do you think a polar bear looks at his watch before he eats you?"

"You could have thought about that before we moved here," I reply.

"I knew it." She sounds almost triumphant. Like I had just proved her point. Only I don't get what her point is.

"You knew what?" I ask.

"You're angry."

"*I'm* not angry. *You* are. I walk into this room after I spend a miserable day in this polar-bear-crazy town you dragged me to and, before I can say 'hello,' you're already yelling at me."

"Who is yelling? Listen to your voice. I get it. You're mad. Fine. But don't take it out on me."

"I'm not mad," I say, but it's not true anymore. I feel it coming, the anger taking charge of my voice. "You're driving me crazy. At least in Calgary I had Maya, but you couldn't stand that, right? That I had a friend. With a normal family. You … you just pack up on a whim and then we're off to God-knows-where.

Without a warning. Without asking me. But you don't care."

"*I* didn't want to move, either. And I'm tired of you nagging at me for trying to do the thing that's best for us."

"For us or for you?"

"Just take a knife and stab it into the wound. Geez, Emmylou, you know very well how much I care about you."

"If you cared so much, then why are we here?"

"You just won't let it go, will you?"

"Why is it so hard to tell me?"

"I did tell you, Emmylou. And I'll say it again: it wasn't a good place for us to be. Couldn't you tell that? All the negativity and then the lies that Dennis told about me and how everyone looked at us, and that job at that bar ..."

"So your boyfriend was an asshole and your job sucked—I get that. That still doesn't explain why we had to leave Calgary, or Saskatoon, or Nanaimo, for that matter, and why ..."

"Just forget about it then."

"No, Mom, if you don't tell me ..."

"What? Are you threatening me now? What are you gonna do? Phone your dad? He doesn't give a shit about you and you know that."

Phone my dad? Where did that come from? I haven't seen him since I was five.

Kitty sighs and plunks on her bed.

"I was worried about you, okay?"

"And that's why you yelled at me?"

"No. I mean ... I don't know. I'm sorry, okay?"

"Okay," I say, but it's not okay. Nobody just packs up and leaves because their boyfriend turned out to love football games and beer better than never-ending arguments nobody can win.

CHAPTER 4

I haven't told Maya that I'm coming, but last night I made up my mind. Kitty treated me all day as if nothing ever happened yesterday, like it all was fine between us. It's not. I know it's just a matter of time before things build up again. Only this time, I won't be around when it comes to that.

The train is leaving at 7:30 PM tonight. I count the tips I saved, which isn't much, because most people don't tip for spilled coffee and food that has already been on someone else's table. So I take Kitty's tips as well. She's made more than three times as much as me. I stuff extra clothes in my backpack, my phone, toothbrush, and my diary.

I look around our room. There isn't much personal stuff staying behind. A few books, clothes, one of Maya's drawings of us eating ice cream. She's licking my cone and me hers, smiling Manga cartoon faces with big shiny eyes. Hidden behind the plastic frame with Maya's drawing is a small porcelain figurine.

It's Paddington Bear, standing with his suitcase in hand and looking up with pitiful black eyes, peeking out from under a big red hat. A sign dangles on his blue raincoat, handwritten in imitation of a child's scribble. *Please look after this bear.*

I let my fingers glide over the smooth, cool porcelain and then I toss it in the garbage. I don't know why I even kept it that long. I found it in our garbage bin the day after my seventh birthday. It was wrapped in silky tissue paper inside a little gift box. I was waiting for the school bus, my pockets stuffed with birthday candy. I ran to the garbage container to throw my wrappers in, and that's when I fished it out from amongst the cake-smeared paper plates. I wondered how it got there, but when I opened it up, I knew: my dad had hidden it there for me to find. I carried it around with me for the longest time and, even when I got older, I still hung onto the bear—and the childish belief it actually did come from my dad. Fact is, I've never gotten anything from my dad since he left.

When I can't fit any more in my pack, my eyes fall on Silly, the black and white puppy dog from Grandma Millie. Her button-eyes look accusingly at me as if she knows already what's coming. I bury my nose deep into Silly's black-and-white fake fur. Sometimes I think it still smells of her. Grandma, I mean.

"Sorry, Silly. You'll have to stay or Kitty will know right away I'm gone." I put her quickly on my pillow where she always sits, grab my pack, and leave. Before I close the door, I glance one more time at my bed. Silly's head leans crookedly to the right, turning away from me.

My eyes fall onto Kitty's bed, the bed sheets crumpled, one pillow on the floor, like she's been fighting demons at night. I feel a lump in my throat.

"Fight what you have to fight; just don't drag me into it," I say to the empty bed and close the door behind me.

Once I'm outside, it takes my eyes a few seconds to adjust to the bright sunlight. The snow is white and smooth as a blank sheet of paper. For the first time in days, there's not a cloud in the sky. The sky is so blue I can't resist the urge to stretch out my hand, trying to touch it—of course that's stupid. I quickly glance behind me. Nobody seems to have noticed except a couple of tourists who are looking up, toward where I was stretching my arms, cameras at the ready. I grin. Who cares if anyone thinks I'm crazy? I'm leaving.

Nobody is at the ticket counter yet. I still have four hours before the train leaves. The Parks guy is doing a tour of the interpretive center, but he hasn't seen me yet. I stuff my backpack under the wooden bench and leave the building.

I'm unsure where to go, when I hear dogs barking somewhere by the river. I cross the train tracks and follow the sound. A gravel road all covered in snow leads to a bunch of shacks. The one on my right is weathered and silver-gray, but the door and windows were painted not too long ago in bright yellow and red. The building on my left has all sorts of things nailed to the outside: antlers, an old rusty saw, a NWT license plate in the form of a polar bear, an old wooden crutch.

The next shack boasts an outdoor couch without cushions; a little dog with shaggy fur is curled up on it, its nose tucked under its tail. A few shacks down the road I see an old school bus sitting crookedly on three tires. There is a stovepipe coming out of its roof.

At first I think the buildings are just storage sheds of some sort, but then I see that there's smoke coming out of some chimneys, and some even have satellite dishes on their roofs. I kind of like this place. It's as if old things that nobody has a use for anymore find a new life here. Something that looks like an old mailbox serves now as a birdhouse, looking out on the river below.

Two dogs stand on top of an old crate and bark toward

the river. When I walk by, one of them jumps off the roof of the makeshift doghouse and runs toward me. I take a step back from the reach of his chain. What are they barking at? The river pushes ice floes with its slushy current toward the sea. But that's not what the dogs are barking at. I walk around a rusty old tank before I can see what the dogs are looking at. A dog team! An old man is sitting on the sled and a younger one is putting harnesses on big furry dogs. He hooks them to long lines spread out like a fan on the snow-covered ground. I run to get a closer look.

And then I stop so quickly I nearly stumble over my own legs. It's the boy from the train. The one whose reflection I saw in the window, and the old man who picked him up from the train station. The boy notices me and raises his hand in greeting. The old man turns and, when he spots me, he motions me to come with a gesture of his arm. I walk a bit closer. Closer, he motions. When I'm just about touching the sled, he says something to the boy and points at a dog that's running from dog to dog, licking their faces.

"He want you to stand on Qaqavii's line. So he can't run around," the boy explains.

"Me?" I ask, even though it's obvious I'm the only person here. "I don't know anything about sled dogs. Won't they bite me?"

"Only if you bite first." The boy smiles at me. It sounds

beautiful, the way he talks. He speaks slowly, carefully finding each word. His voice is deep and calm. I blush.

I approach the dogs. There are eight of them in harness. Two more lines are strung out for the last two dogs.

The one the boy calls Qaqavii runs toward me and flops on his back, exposing his furry belly to me. The dog reaches out with his paw as if to tell me to come and pet him. I carefully let him sniff my hand and he licks it. The dog wags his shaggy tail. There's something puppyish about him. His movements are full of enthusiasm, yet slightly uncoordinated. He's got standing-up ears that wiggle as he tilts his head and looks at me. His nose is white and so are two dots above his eyes. The rest of his fur is mottled, a little bit of everything: gray, brown, tan. His coat is so thick I can't tell how big he actually is. All I know is that he's the smallest of the bunch. He's not as pretty as the white dog in front of the team, or the reddish-white one with the long fur around his face that almost looks like a wolf, but he's for sure the cutest. It almost looks like he's smiling at me. I smile back.

"Qaqavii! Tighten up!" The boy calls and drags the dog by his collar until the line is stretched out again. "Stand here. Like this." He steps on the long line right where the harness is attached and Qaqavii's bum is pulled down. I put my foot where the boy showed me and, for a second, we stand so close that his smell drifts over to me. It's a weird mix of the fruity scent of shampoo and the musky animal odor of his fur parka. A bit like wet dog, only sweeter.

I glance at him as he sprints up to the dog yard. His snow pants are made of heavy brown cotton—at least I think they were brown at one time. They're so dirty that it's hard to tell. He's wearing insulated rubber boots, no mitts, and a blue and white toque with a fluffy pompom dancing around his face. But the coolest thing is his parka. It's made out of caribou fur, just like the one I'd seen in the diorama at the train station. Someone spent time making a pattern out of light- and dark-colored furs and it fits perfectly—as if made just for him.

I stand on Qaqavii's line while he tries to lick my leg and wriggle free at the same time. I laugh, but the old man's voice quietens me. I don't know what he says. The sounds are deep and guttural. Qaqavii must understand, because he hunkers down—for about thirty seconds; then his attention is captured by the black and white dog that the boy leads by his collar from the dog yard. The dog tries his best to wriggle free, pawing my leg as if he's asking me to let him go. I stifle a laugh.

"Whoo," says the old man. He sounds annoyed.

The boy harnesses the black and white dog and, with a flick of his fingers, he attaches him to the line. How is he doing that?

I realize there is a piece of bone or antler or something attached to the harness, which is slid through a loop on the line. How neat! I take my mitt off and let the antler piece glide through my fingers. I am surprised how smooth it feels. It's shaped like a half-moon and, once slipped through the loop, it won't come undone on its own.

"That toggle is old. Older than my grandfather. Is made from ivory." The boy smiles at me.

"Ivory?" I ask. The picture of elephant tusks comes up in my head. How did the ivory get here? Isn't it illegal?

"From walrus. Waaaay up north." He points across the river.

"Oh. Cool," I say and quickly turn away. I don't want him to see my face turning red. Walrus tusks. Of course. Why didn't I think of that?

I bend over to pet Qaqavii and notice that his harness is homemade, too. A light-colored leather, cut into strips and sewn together with rough thread. I wonder what it's made of and who made it, but I'm too worried I'll embarrass myself again, so I don't ask.

"From the bearded seal," the boy says, like he's read my mind. "My grandfather taught me how to make dog harness."

"You made it? That's cool," I say.

"I hunted the seal, too," he says and turns to get the last dog.

I don't know what to say or even think. I can't picture myself killing an animal and I'm pretty sure it's wrong, but then again, it doesn't feel right to think that, because he didn't do it just for fun. He made a harness for his dogs or his grandfather's dogs and maybe they even ate the seal meat. What's the difference between that and eating beef from the grocery store that someone else killed? I'm trying to reason with myself, but it's not working. I look at the boy differently now. He's not just a boy. He's a hunter. One who has a different understanding of life and death.

I watch him as he walks down from the dog yard with a big white dog that looks exactly like the one who's waiting patiently in his harness, a little ahead of the other dogs. The dog looks strong; but the boy picks the dog up by his collar and walks him on two legs as if he's done it a million times.

He looks young and grown-up at the same time. There's something about him that connects him to a world much older—and yet he's just a teenager like me.

The wind is biting cold, but neither the boy nor his grandfather seems to mind. My cheeks start to hurt and I rub them with my mitts. I'm not dressed warmly enough and I have no idea what I'm doing here. I should feel completely out of place but, oddly enough, I don't. Maybe it's because they don't really care who I am. They just needed someone to stand on an unruly dog's line. Could have been anybody. I like that. That I could be just anybody.

★

The boy and the old man exchange a few words in a language I don't understand. The boy nods and turns to me.

"He wants you to come. You sit here." He points to a spot at the front of the long narrow sled. I walk over and sit next to the old man on the fur that covers the wooden crosspieces. It all happens so fast, I don't even have time to question if I should go with two strangers—never mind not knowing where we're going. The strange thing is, there's nothing strange about it—it just feels natural.

The sled is made of wood. It looks like a ladder, but the only thing that's holding the runners and crosspieces together is yellow rope tied neatly around each piece. There's plenty of room for all of us, but no handlebar to hold onto like you see in pictures of racing sleds. The boy sits down behind me.

The old man passes me a rope that's tied to the sled. He pretends to lose his balance while hanging onto the rope. I get it. I hold tight onto the rope, so I won't fall off when the sled starts moving. The old man points to my mitts and talks to the boy.

"My grandpa wants you to borrow these." The boy passes me his mitts.

"What about your hands?"

"Inuit don't get cold," he says. And then he adds with a grin, "I take yours."

We swap mitts and I feel the warmth from his hands when I slip them on. The silver-gray fur on the mitts is really short. On the palm side there's no hair at all, just black thin leather, and yet the mitts stay warm, like they're creating their own heat.

"They're warm," I say. "Thank you."

"Sealskin. My grandma made them. You stay here long? Maybe she make one for you."

I don't reply. My train leaves in a few hours.

The old man motions me to pull my hood up over my head, and then he makes a strange guttural sound, and the dogs leap to their feet and throw themselves into their harnesses. The sled jerks and I nearly lose my grip on the rope. We're moving. Fast. The dogs are pulling us as if we weren't even there. That's so cool. The dogs' stubby legs move so swiftly it's nearly impossible to tell which leg belongs to which dog. Their curly tails wave in the air, bouncing up and down with every step. Their heads are lowered, as if they're focusing all their energy on where they want to go. It almost feels like flying—if it wasn't for the rocks we're hitting every now and then, jerking the sled and nearly throwing me off.

I can hear the dogs' rhythmic panting and the sound the runners make as they crunch the snow. It seems so effortless, the way we glide over the snow, the way the old man talks quietly to the dogs—if he talks at all.

There's a thin layer of hanging ice clinging to the rocks along the shore of the river, and further out, the open water between ice floes looks dark and forbidding. The dogs are running straight for it. I feel panic. How do you stop a dog team? Do they know not to go where it isn't safe?

"La laa," says the old man, and the dogs veer off to the left—away from the river. It's neat how they move all at the same time. All except one. The young dog. Qaqavii. He continues running straight, bouncing up and down and looking back. The sled skids sideways and the force of nine dogs pulling to the left jerks Qaqavii's line and wipes him off his feet. He tumbles through the snow in an involuntary somersault.

"Yaai," the old man says, and the dogs slow down long enough for the struggling dog to get back on his feet. Poor guy. He looks like he's trying hard to catch up to the other dogs, but somehow he ends up next to the sled, close enough for the old man to reach out to him and give him a nudge with his boot.

Qaqavii hunkers down and scurries as fast as he can to catch up to the other dogs. I feel a sting in my chest. The old man didn't hurt the dog, but when I see how he hunkers down, I feel like someone had given me the boot. I feel so sorry for the young dog, who is still more of a puppy than an adult, that my throat becomes scratchy. I wish I could hug him and hold him tight. But I can't get to him.

The dogs are running flat out. We follow the train tracks out into the open space between the river and the town.

"Is this tundra?" I ask and then bite my tongue. What a stupid question. Probably every child who grew up here would know that.

"Ii," the boy turns to me. "You say tundra. We just call it land. Nuna." He turns to watch the dogs and I let my eyes drift over this treeless land that's stretching out in front of us.

The wind has blown away the snow from small ponds, leaving a polished surface of gray-blue ice. On the open stretches, the wind has even blown the snow away from the land, exposing a yellowish brown vegetation crouching low to the ground. Wherever there are rocks, the snow is deep, forming beautiful drifts with sharp ridges. From down here, they look like miniature mountains.

The train tracks are leading away from the town. There are

trees here and there and the snow is deeper. It feels warmer where the trees protect us from the cold wind.

The dogs are amazing to watch; their backs arch with every leap forward, but the sled runs even and smooth. There are ten altogether, but my eyes are glued to Qaqavii. Most of the time, he pulls his share and he doesn't stand out from the other dogs. But once in a while, he sidles up to the dog next to him and licks his snout like a puppy urging his mother to give him food. The older dog growls and then snaps at Qaqavii and he hunkers down, not quite understanding what he did wrong, causing him to fall behind. When his line goes slack the old man reels him in and gives him a smack with his mitt. Holding tension on the line, he releases him again. Before the puzzled dog knows it, he's at the end of his line, keeping it tight now—at least for a little while.

I catch Qaqavii's head tilting sideways. He's looking at the dog next to him. I know what's coming next. He won't be able to help himself; he'll lick the other dog's face.

"Qaqavii! No!" I call and then cover my mouth quickly. I don't mean to interfere, but I don't want the young dog to get another swat with the mitt. To my surprise, Qaqavii stops bouncing and runs straight forward.

"Qimmiujatuluatuq, tainna," the old man says, and I can

tell by the way he looks at me that he approves. I smile, and from now on I call Qaqavii's name in a stern voice every time he starts looking at his neighbor.

My cheeks are getting cold and I rub them with the back of the mitts. How far are we going? Where to?

"I have to be back before 7:30," I say.

"We turn back soon. This is first time this year the dogs go running. And Qaqavii, he is young. We don't go far," the boy says.

The old man gives a command, and the dogs turn away from the tracks and into a treeless clearing. I have a million questions racing through my head. About the dogs. The old man. The boy. But the terrain is so bumpy that all I can do is focus on holding on to the rope and making sure I don't fall off.

"In summer is hard to walk here. You have to jump from hummock to hummock, so you don't get wet feet," the boy explains. English must be his second language and yet he knows words that I don't. Like hummock. I figure it must be all the bumps. The snow has drifted off the tops and I can see the thick, frozen moss exposed to the elements.

And then I suddenly only see sky. One runner rides up on a hummock and the other one stays low. I scream, but the sled is surprisingly flexible, and we ride over the bumps while I'm hanging on as well as I can, regaining my balance and then bracing myself for the next encounter with another hummock.

"Look. Wolf tracks," the boy says.

I look to where he's pointing, but I don't see any tracks. Just snow. We hit a bump and I nearly lose my balance. After that, I don't dare look anywhere but ahead at the next hummock and rocks.

"La laa," the old man calls. The dogs turn in a wide circle, and then we're back on the trail next to the train tracks. Then he makes a low guttural sound that you could almost mistake as a sound from the dogs themselves. "Wooh!" The dogs stop and gulp down big mouthfuls of the crusty snow. The red dog rolls in the snow, his four feet kicking in the air. The rest of them lie down. Except Qaqavii. He runs back to the sled. The old man says something to the boy, and the boy jumps off the sled and drags the unruly young one back to the end of his line. He swats him with his mitt.

"Wooh." Qaqavii hunkers down and the boy returns.

"How come all the other dogs understand the commands, but not Qaqavii?" I ask.

"Is his first time running. He learn from the other dogs. Qakuq, he is issuraqtujuq —the lead dog. He is very smart. Know exactly what we say." The boy points to the big white dog at the very front of the team.

"Taqluk, the one with the black patches, he is next to the leader—tuklia, we say. Qaqavii, we call him kinguliqpaaq. He the last dog. His trace is shortest."

I hadn't even noticed that the lines are all different lengths, much less that it all has a purpose. That it's all planned out carefully, where each dog goes.

"How do you pick your lead dog?" I ask.

"I told you. He the smartest." He says it like it's the most logical thing in the world, but I still don't get it. How do you know which dog is the smartest? It's not like you can ask them to fill out an IQ test.

When the last dog is done eating snow, the old man gives a command and the dogs jump to their feet. The dogs hit the end of their lines so fast that it feels like the sled is catapulted forward. Losing my balance, I try to grab onto the runners, but touch the snow instead. My mitt gets pulled off my hand and I fall backwards, bumping into the boy. He's grinning so wide I can see he's missing two teeth. He pushes me up and, when I regain my balance, I try to see if I can spot my mitt.

"I lost ..." I was going to say "mitt" but, before I end my sentence, Barnabas dangles the mitt in front of my face. He starts giggling and then—to my total surprise—the old man throws himself backward, dangling his feet in the air in mock imitation of my mishap. He laughs like it's the funniest thing. I don't think it's funny at all. I think of jumping off the sled and walking back to the train station, but the sled is going too fast.

"It's not ..." I was going to say funny, but then Qaqavii, who has been bouncing along and looking at the commotion behind him, trips over the rope that's tied between the front of the runners and is flung into the air. He lets out a surprised yip and lands on the old man's lap. Dog and man stare at each other as if each is asking: "Where did you come from?" It's so funny that I burst out laughing. And then the three of us are laughing. I laugh so hard, it feels like my chest is expanding, or like I had more room to breathe. I don't know how to explain it. All I know is that I don't want to stop laughing. Ever.

Suddenly, an image is in my head. Grandma Millie, Kitty–and Dad is there, too. The four of us laughing at something I said. I don't remember what. I just remember the feeling, us all together as if nothing could ever tear us apart. And then my body starts heaving and I have to bite my lip real hard to stop the tears from coming. Qaqavii whines and wiggles his way from the old man to me. He licks my nose and I bury my face in his thick, oily fur.

I hear the old man talk as if far away and then the boy's voice.

"Don't worry. Is okay."

And for a moment, I believe that it's going to be okay. That I'm going to be okay.

★

The sun is setting as we run back along the river. The dogs seem more relaxed now, pulling steady, but slower. The old man and the boy talk quietly to each other, sometimes explaining things that are new to me. A strange feeling comes over me that I can't quite place. I'm still nervous and excited, but there's something else—it's as if I don't have to worry about what I'm doing, like I'm taken care of.

"Wooh!" The old man calls and the dogs stop in the dog yard. The boy unharnesses the dogs in the fading light. I stand next to the sled, unsure of what to do. It's not far to the train station. I probably have at least another hour.

The old man is rolling up the fur blanket. Actually, it's not really a blanket, just fur skins thrown on top of each other. He ties a blue rope around each skin, using a knot that's fast and efficient, and that I have no clue how to do. I'm of no help. Maybe I should leave.

"You wanna take harnesses off? Look." The boy slips first one paw and then the other through the harness loops and then slides the last loop off the dog's head. He's done in a few seconds. The dog closest to me has mean-looking scars on his face, so I walk over to Qaqavii. He rolls over for a belly rub as soon as I lean over him. I grab one of his paws and try to wriggle it through the harness, but there's no way I can get it through the loop without bending his leg in ways it isn't supposed to bend. I pull the harness closer to his head and try again. He licks my hand and then jumps to his feet. He runs around me so quickly that I'm tangled in his line before I can step aside. I glance at the boy. He has unharnessed and walked another dog to the dog yard, while all I've done is tie myself in a knot with Qaqavii. For a second, I'm worried they'll laugh at me again, but then I think, if it wasn't so embarrassing for me, it's actually quite funny. I grin at the boy and shrug my shoulders.

"Qallunaaq!" he says.

I have no idea what it means but I don't ask. Somehow I don't think I'd like the answer.

"Let me do Qaqavii, you take Qakuq. He is an old dog. He show you."

How's the dog going to show me? I want to ask, but the boy is not paying any attention to me. He's undoing Qaqavii's toggle and I'm free of his trace. I walk over to the white scar-faced dog and let him sniff my hand. The dog shows no interest in me. But when I touch his harness, he lifts his right paw, and all I have to do is guide it through the harness. Then he lifts his left one.

"Good boy!" I say and try to pull the harness over his head. It's so tight it won't come loose. Qakuq pulls backward and twists and turns his head until the harness slips over his big furry head. That was easy!

"Sapkutailili qimmiq!" The old man points to the dog.

"Don't let him go!" the boy yells.

Too late. Qakuq runs full blast down the riverbank toward the gray and gloomy towering buildings of the port. Shall I run after him? There's no way I can catch up to him.

"I'm so sorry," I say.

"Qakuq," the old man calls and, for a second, the dog slows down and looks back. He bounces for a few steps as if he's trying to make up his mind, and then he runs off full tilt. A white dot, quickly disappearing.

"Is he … is he going to come back?" That's so typical of me. Sometimes I just don't get things until it's too late, and then it doesn't matter how good my intentions were … all that matters is that I messed up. I wish I had never come on the dog sled ride with them.

"He come back when he get hungry," the boy says and shrugs his shoulders.

Isn't he mad? What about his grandfather? Is he mad? I glance at him, but he's rolling up the traces as if nothing happened. Kitty would totally lose it but, then again, Kitty is Kitty.

"How do I say 'I'm sorry' in your language?"

"In Inuktitut? Ugguaqpunga"

I turn to his grandfather. "Ugguaqpunga. For letting the dog loose, I mean."

"Aajuqnaqmat," he replies.

I turn to the boy.

"It can't be helped," he translates.

I'm so mad at myself for letting the dog go and, at the same time, so worried something bad might happen to him. Like getting hit by a car or eaten by a polar bear. But they're right. It can't be helped. Neither my anger nor my worry will bring the dog back. And yet ... I know I won't sleep tonight if I don't know if the dog is safe.

"Come," the boy waves at me. "You want to help feed dogs?"

I follow them to one of the bigger shacks. The old man hangs the dog traces and harnesses on a nail by the door. He talks briefly to his grandson before he steps inside. The boy nods and walks around the building. He opens an old freezer. It's full of frozen fish and ... "What's that?" I ask, pointing to a frozen lump about the size of my upper body.

"Seal," he says under his breath as he struggles to lift it out of the freezer. He grins at me apologetically. "It's a big one."

"That's for dog food?" I ask, hoping desperately he's not going to offer me a chunk.

"Best dog food ever. Makes their fur thick and oily. Wanna try?"

I kick myself for asking that stupid question. Now I don't know if he's teasing me or being serious. Either way, the answer is the same. "No, thanks."

The boy grabs the ax that's leaning against the freezer and starts chopping pieces off the seal. As if on command, the dogs start a chorus of howling and barking.

"They know is supper time," the boy says and, again, I'm not sure if he's kidding or if the dogs really know that he's chopping meat for them.

A frozen chunk hits my arm and I step back.

"Here, you can pick up the pieces." The boy hands me an empty canvas sack, but I have a hard time finding the meat in the quickly approaching dark.

"Wait here," he says and walks around the house.

I hear the door creak and then it's silent. I'm alone in the dark. A dead seal my only company. Waiting for a boy with an ax, who's talking to a man whose language I do not understand. I feel like a stranger. I mean, I'm used to being a stranger, with all the moving from place to place. But this is different. Here I *am* a stranger. Our worlds are so different that everything needs explaining. I wonder if they feel like strangers in my company as well, but then I think, there's nothing I know that they don't know.

I don't really want to pick up chunks of dead seal, even if it's the best dog food ever and, for a second, I think of just walking away. The lights of the train station beckon, warm and welcoming, from across the tracks. The world I know, just footsteps away.

"Here. Take this." The boy passes me a headlamp and I slip it over my toque. A circle of white light surrounds me but, at the same time, the night beyond the reach of the lamp suddenly feels darker. Why did I not walk away? Or tell the boy now that I have to go?

I pick up the meat and drop it into the canvas sack. It's not the first time the bag has been used for that. I can tell it was white at one time, but now it has mostly the color of dried blood, dark red and black.

Stop being so ... grossed out, I tell myself. Just because the chicken I eat comes wrapped in plastic doesn't mean it's not a dead animal.

When the sack is bulging with meat chunks, the boy puts the ax away and we walk over to the dogs. As soon as they see us, they run in tight circles at the end of their chains' reach, bouncing with excitement. Like a happy dance. The boy throws a chunk to each dog and the dogs in turn eagerly devour their chunks, holding the meat in their front paws while they rip off pieces, exposing their big white teeth.

"Qakuq," the boy calls into the night, but there's no sight of him. "We wait for a bit," he says and sits on a doghouse.

I climb on Qaqavii's house. He gobbles down his food as fast as he can, while wagging his tail. When he's done, he jumps next to me. I scratch him behind the ears and he leans into me. When I stop, he nudges me with his nose until I start petting him again.

"Switch off your head lamp," the boy says. "Then you can see better."

I do as he says and, to my surprise, the night does not appear so black anymore. I can see dark shapes against the white snow. Rocks by the river. And all the dogs and their houses. There isn't even a moon yet—or is there? I look up and I see the most amazing night sky I have ever seen. The stars are so bright and there are so many. Some seem close, others far, far away. And there's a bright streak of stars. It looks like a path up into the sky. The Milky Way? I've never seen it before—or maybe I just never noticed it. I don't know which.

The boy lies on his back and I do the same. There's not

enough room for Qaqavii and he jumps off. I hear his chain rattle as he crawls into his house. And then it's silent.

"What's your name?" the boy asks into the dark.

"Emmylou," I say.

"Emmalu?"

Emmalu. I like how it sounds. I nod. "And yours?"

"Barnabas, but at home everyone call me Barney."

"Barnabas? Is that from the Bible?"

"That is only my English name. I have an Inuktitut name, too. Qaniutuq, named after the old man's aunt. The old man, he is my irniksaq, my nephew, but qallunaat are always confused, so I say he's my grandfather here in Churchill. At home, everyone knows I'm his aunt."

"You're named after his aunt? I thought …" He is a boy, isn't he? I roll over and prop myself up on my elbows, trying to make out his features in the dark. His cheeks are round, but his face is more angular than a girl's face. The black hair that's sticking out under his toque is short, but that doesn't mean anything, I guess. There's no roundness to his body, but then again, he is wearing winter clothes. How can he be the old man's aunt?

"See. I told you," he says.

"Told me what?"

"You are confused. Like all qallunaat."

"What are qallunaat?"

"A qallunaq is a white person. Like you."

I feel a sting. It's like there's now a wall between us, as if we're sorted: Inuit here, white people there. Except I don't feel "white"—or maybe I do and just don't understand what it's supposed to mean. I feel all sorts of things: That I don't really belong anywhere, always just passing through. I feel out of place when my friends talk about things that matter. Like who said what to who on Facebook. I just don't know how to be interested in those things. I wonder if he's on Facebook, Qa … Qaniusomething … I can't even say his name. It feels like the wall just got an inch or two higher. I guess, he's right—I *am* a qallunaq. I don't belong here.

CHAPTER 5

"A ticket to Winnipeg, please." I rummage in my backpack for my purse. The train station is filling up quickly and people are standing in line. The clerk types something on his keyboard. Please, please let there be an open seat!

"One way?" he asks and continues typing like he already knows the answer. I guess not too many people buy return tickets from this station.

"Yes, please."

"Sleeper or Economy?"

"Economy." I know it's a two-day train ride cramped on a train seat, but I can't afford a berth.

"Escape Fare?" he asks in a matter-of-fact way.

"What?" I feel my palms getting sweaty. Does he know? Has Kitty told him not to sell tickets to me?

"Non-refundable. Or would you like Economy Plus? Completely flexible."

"Oh. Ahm ... Escape Fare, please. It's for the train tonight."
And there's no way I'm gonna change my mind in the next
half hour before the train leaves. Escape Fare. If only he knew.
I smile.

"That's $208.95 with the taxes."

My smile disappears. Ouch. I have only $280 and a bit of
change. I won't have much left when I get to Winnipeg, and
then I still have to get to Calgary. I still haven't told Maya. I was
worried she'd tell her parents and then they'd contact Kitty.

I count out the money while the clerk prints out my ticket.

"The train is ready for boarding. Just pick a seat," he says as
he pushes the ticket over the counter. "Next, please."

When I hold the ticket in my hands, I realize it's real now.
I'm leaving. Leaving this weird isolated town that's overrun
by crowds of tourists and polar bears. No more waitressing,
no more fights with Kitty. She always *says* she wants the best
for me, it's just ... I don't see it. Like last night, when we were
fighting and she said that I mean so much to her. I ... I heard it,
but couldn't *feel* it. Somehow she always gets it wrong—or I get
it wrong, and then we argue. I don't know. I just can't breathe
when I'm close to her. And yet, I already miss her. Somehow I
missed her all my life—or maybe not her. Maybe I just missed
having a mom who behaves like a real mom.

I walk out onto the platform. A gust of ice-cold wind funnels along the building and blows right through my toque. My earlobes start to prickle. I feel like I've walked into a freezer, and it's only the end of October. I wonder what this place is like in the depth of winter, but I'm relieved I don't have to find out.

I walk through the first two train cars. Strangers are showing strangers pictures on their cell phones. Reliving their polar bear adventures. Outdoing each other in their stories—but I bet they're all the same. Went out on a Tundra Crawler adventure, saw a bear, took a picture, went home. I'm not good at that kind of thing. Enjoying what people are supposed to enjoy, I mean.

"Cheer up, Moody Broody." That's what Grandma Millie always used to say, but the words sound hollow when I say them. When I reach the third car, I'm lucky. There's just an older gentleman reading a newspaper and nobody else. I sit down by the window facing the train station. I crane my neck, trying to make out the Sleepy Bear Lodge amongst the lights of the town. I imagine all the people crowding into the restaurants, laughing and having a good time before rushing on to buy souvenirs from one of the galleries. Conversation starters for later, look-where-I-have-beens. I feel my throat tightening. I hate myself for feeling resentful because, deep down, I wish I could be just like them—able to laugh and kid around in a conversation, happy and excited at the sight of a polar bear from a Tundra Crawler window.

I turn away from the train window to look out the other side toward the river. All I see is my own reflection in the dark window. I switch seats and shield my eyes from the light inside the train. It's darker here on this side of the train tracks. No street lights and just the occasional light shining out of a window here and there. Which one is Barnabas's house?

I wish I hadn't lost the dog, because each time I want to remember the dog sled ride, the image is wiped out by seeing Qakuq run away, and I feel stupid all over again.

Here's the thing. It's not that I'm never excited about anything. Just excited about the wrong things, I guess. Because I did enjoy the moment when all the dogs pulled together, and what excited me even more was just being around the old man and Barnabas. Especially at the beginning when we didn't even talk.

How screwed up is that? How am I ever supposed to fit in if I like to be around people but don't want to talk? At least it's different with Maya. With Maya, I don't have to worry what I say or think. Plus she does most of the talking, anyway. And she's so funny that it's hard not to laugh, even if I would never do or say what she says. Maya will be disappointed if I don't have a polar bear picture to show off. I wonder what she's doing right now.

The PA crackles. "Ladies and gentlemen, thank you for choosing VIA Rail. The dining car is directly behind the engine car and we will be serving light meals and beverages for your convenience. The train will leave on time in twenty minutes." The thought of sitting alone at a table surrounded by merry tourists depresses me. Maybe I'll just get a couple of chocolate bars.

I press my face against the cold window, trying to count how many train cars to the dining car. There's something running along the train tracks, fading in and out as the train windows illuminate its white fur.

It's a dog!

I jump up from my seat. He's close to my window now. It's Barnabas's dog! I grab my backpack and run to the door. Darn! The door opens to the wrong side of the train. I jump off the train and run down the platform until I reach the end of the train and then across the tracks and back up the other side.

Where is he? I see movement to my right, just a little ways away from the tracks.

"Qakuq," I call and then think, that's stupid. Why would he come to me? Food, I need food. I drop my backpack and rummage around. Maybe there's an old forgotten cereal bar or something in my pack. It's too dark to see anything, so I just fish for things inside the pack. My socks, phone, something hard and bigger—my diary. I feel something brush my arm. Qakuq! I grab his collar before I can even think what I'm doing. The dog lunges backward and we both fall into the snow. He fights to pull his head out of the collar, but I'm not letting go. Not this time. Except ... what if he tries to bite me? This is the stupidest thing I have ever done. Battling with a sled dog whose scars tell me that he's definitely got more experience in that field than me. I could just let him go and run to the train. But I don't. Instead, I talk quietly and pet him with my free hand. Eventually he stops bucking and lies down.

"Let's go home," I say and stand up, dragging my backpack with one hand and the dog with the other. He doesn't move. I pull on his collar, trying to lift him to his feet, but he's like a dead weight.

"It's okay." I try again. "Come here." I put my backpack on awkwardly, always one hand on his collar. Then I kneel in front of him and try to coax him to come to me. He doesn't move. I have to think of the Little Prince and the fox, and how the fox demanded that the Little Prince tame him and how it took, like, forever. I don't have time for that. I have a train to catch and, besides, it's dark and cold and my hand is going numb.

"We gotta go!" I say, and this time I get up and pull hard, and when he budges, I pull even harder and start walking. He pulls forward so suddenly that I'm wiped off my feet. Boy, that dog is strong. He drags me through the snow. I'm about to let go when he stops. I scramble to my feet.

"Let's try again," I say as soon as I catch my breath. I tug on his collar and then brace for him to bolt. We start an awkward and uncoordinated dance, both of us pulling in opposite directions and both of us afraid to step on the other's toes. And then I remember how Barnabas lifted the dogs up by their collars when he walked them to the sled. I lift Qakuq until only his back feet touch the ground, and then I start walking. The dog hobbles along, our dance more coordinated now. He doesn't have a choice. I feel bad about that, but then I realize he's way more relaxed now. Like he's accepted me as a leader and he's happy to follow.

I'm glad the moon is up now and shining bright; it's not hard to follow the road. Our shadows follow us silently, disappearing when we step into the shadows of the houses and reappearing in the spaces in-between. I'm moving as fast as I can. Even though the cold wind hasn't stopped blowing, I'm breaking into a sweat. There's the house with the couch on the porch. That was right next to Barnabas's house, wasn't it? The dogs by the river bark excitedly when they sense or see us. Actually, it's not really a bark. More like a howl or ... I don't know. Almost sounds like they're trying to talk.

I recognize the ax leaning against the house. This must be it. I let Qakuq down on all four feet, so we can both catch our breath, and knock on the door. I hear shuffling inside and then the door opens. Barnabas's face appears, looking worried. But when he sees me, he smiles.

"We thought it was the police. Only police knock on the door. Police and qallunaat." He smiles his teeth-missing smile at me. "You found Qakuq."

He turns into the house and talks in Inuktitut. I only understand Emmalu. The door swings open and Qakuq suddenly bursts forward. I stumble forward and let go of the dog. The old man is sitting on the floor next to pieces of cardboard, eating his supper. Qakuq dashes for the meat, but the old man is quick to throw his slippers at the dog.

"Annit."

Qakuq cowers down and the old man gestures at the dog and the door, while talking to Barnabas. Then he motions me to come in.

Barnabas grabs the dog's collar and drags him to the door.

"My grandpa wants you to sit," he says as he leaves with Qakuq.

I turn toward the old man. Only now I realize there's another person in the room. An old lady is sitting in the only bed in the cabin. Her hair looks tangled as if she's been in bed for a long time. Her blanket is pulled up over her legs and a piece of cardboard with meat is lying on her covers.

"Hi, I'm Emmylou," I say to her.

"Elisapii," she puts her hand on her chest. "Ipilii," she says and points at the old man.

"Ipilii?" I try to get the pronunciation right. I-PEA-LEE.

"Ii." She smiles a toothless smile, lifts up a piece of meat and raises it toward me. She wants me to eat?

I haven't eaten since I left early in the afternoon. My stomach is grumbling, but I'm not sure if it's from being hungry or from the thought of eating what looks very much like the meat we fed to the dogs.

The old man motions me to sit down on the floor. I hesitate. Would I make it to the train station if I ran now? I glance at the old couple, their eyes shining at me in the light of a gas lantern. There isn't much inside this cabin. No table, no chairs. Just a bed and an old couch. Pieces of an old pallet are scattered on the floor, ready to feed a rusty woodstove that looks like it's built out of an old fuel drum. On the wall by the door, clothes are hanging on bent nails, and a few dishes are on the only shelf.

My throat chokes up. These people who have so little want to share it with me. I can't just walk away.

I slip off my backpack and sit on the floor. The old man smiles. I hear the train whistle and then the ground shakes as the train rattles by.

I bite my lip. Escape Fare. I can't return the ticket.

★

The door bursts open and Barnabas comes in. He smiles when he sees me sitting on the floor.

"You like Inuit food?" he asks. It sounds like a trick question and I don't know the answer.

"I … I haven't tried," I mumble. "And … ahm … I'm not hungry," I add quickly.

"Try some maktaaq." He grabs a big strip of meat, takes one end in his mouth and pulls out his knife from his hip belt. He cuts the meat awfully close to his lips and then grins at me. "Is good," he says as he passes the meat to me.

I can't get rid of the feeling he's enjoying the situation. As if he already knows my reaction. All eyes are on me now. I reach for the meat. Not to impress Barnabas, but because I don't want to offend the old people. I try cutting a piece off while it's lying on the cardboard, but it's surprisingly slippery and tough. Do I have to put it in my mouth first so I can pull and cut at the same time? I get a sick feeling coming up from my stomach with the thought of putting that meat in my mouth, but if they're eating it, it shouldn't hurt me, right? I put the meat in my mouth and am surprised that it's actually rather tasteless. When I grab for the knife, the old woman waves her hands at me as if to say no.

"Tamna qallunaq! Apguijutilugu maktaarmik." She sounds like she's scolding her grandson and cuts up pieces of her own meat with a half-moon-shaped knife. I've seen that kind of knife before. Maybe a miniature version as a necklace in one of the galleries in town. A typical Inuit knife, but I don't remember what it's called. The old woman rips off a piece of cardboard and passes it to me with neatly cut little squares on it.

"Maktaaq," she explains. "Beluga." She pulls at the skin on her arm and then points to the little squares.

"That's … whale skin?" Images of the white whales frolicking in the green waters of the river mouth pop up in my head. They look like dolphins, only bigger and whiter. There're photos and postcards and artwork of them all over town. They're nearly as famous as the polar bears in Churchill, except they're only here in summer. I can't eat them! But then I think, that must have been the food for the people of this area for a long, long time, before the Europeans came here. I don't know when that was, but I wonder if the old couple still lived that way? Surviving with the food that they could hunt and gather. How could that be wrong?

I put a piece of beluga whale skin in my mouth. It's like trying to bite through chewing gum. I can't get it into smaller pieces. I shove it with my tongue to the back of my mouth and do my best to smile.

"How do you say 'Thank you' in Inuktitut?"

"Matna," Barnabas replies.

"Matna," I repeat.

"Eat," the old lady says, pretending to put meat in her mouth.

I stuff a few more pieces into the back of my mouth.

"Good," I say and it's not even a real lie. It doesn't taste fishy or anything, so it's a lot better than I expected.

Barnabas laughs. "You have to swallow," he says.

"Hm?" I try, but it doesn't want to go down.

He passes me a glass of water and I finally wash it all down.

"More?" He asks.

"No, thanks." I say, shaking my head. Everyone laughs. But in a good kind of way.

It feels like the ice has been broken. Nobody pays attention to whether I'm eating or not and I'm glad for that. I feel a lot less hungry now, which is amazing, considering I barely ate three little cubes.

They ask me where I'm from and I'm okay with the question, now that they already know me a little bit. I tell them I lived in Calgary last, but that I was born in Nanaimo, BC. I'm not sure how to answer the question about how long I'll be staying. It's gonna take at least a couple of weeks collecting tips to buy another train ticket. I evade the question by saying my mom works at the Sleepy Bear Lodge.

I find out that Barnabas is from Arviat in Nunavut, the next town north of Churchill, if you go straight up the coast of Hudson Bay—which you can only do by skidoo in winter or boat in summer, because there's no road. Or you could fly, which is really expensive.

Barnabas goes to school in Churchill, but only because he came down to look after his grandfather, while his grandfather, in turn, is looking after his wife Elisapii, who needs to have some special treatment in the hospital, which they can't give her at the health center in Arviat. I didn't quite get it, but it sounded like Elisapii's family wanted her to be here. So Barnabas, who is also the old man's aunt, because of the name spirit that is now living in Barnabas from the old man's dead aunt, was sent down by his parents to look after his grandfather/nephew—I probably still didn't get that right, but it doesn't sound so crazy anymore.

I picture my grandma's name spirit still hovering above us,

waiting for her name to find a new home, and I decide right there, if I ever should have children—which I already decided I will never have—but if I do, then I will name the girl Millie, and if it's a boy, I will name him Millie as well, but I'll call him Milo, so he won't get teased in school.

The longer we sit and talk, the more glad I am I missed my train. When Elisapii sees me shifting uncomfortably on the floor, she motions me to come and sit on her big bed with her. Barnabas stretches out on the floor and the old man leans against the sofa—still sitting on the floor. The lantern hisses and shines a circle of light around us. It's kind of cozy. Like a sleepover party, except only Elisapii is in her nighty.

I wish I could stay here and talk all night, but it's getting late and Kitty will be worried. I feel bad that I didn't even think of Kitty until now, but now that I have, I can't get her out of my head. She'll be so mad. So what. Let her be mad. I was going to be on a train, anyway. But I can't relax. It's like Kitty's suddenly in the room here with me. Or maybe not her, just her anger. I slide off the bed and hold out my hand to Elisapii.

"I have to go," I say. "Nice meeting you."

She holds my hand tight like my grandma used to do and pats it while talking in Inuktitut for a long time. I don't know what she says, but I nod and say, "Matna."

Old Ipilii says something and Barnabas translates. "You can come back. We go train dogs after school."

My heart starts beating really fast, and I have to take a deep breath so I don't sound too excited. "Okay," I say. "What time?"

"After school," he says, as if he has to explain everything twice to me, but he still doesn't tell me a time.

"See you then," I say, not wanting to ask again. I grab my backpack. Barnabas opens the door for me.

"What did your grandma say?" I ask as I step into the cold darkness.

"Nothing, goodbye only," he mumbles.

That was a long monologue for a "goodbye only."

"Bye," I say and feel my cheeks turn red. I wonder if he remembers me from the train, and I wonder why he was on the train, but I'm too embarrassed to ask.

CHAPTER 6

"Ouch!" I rub my shin and try to feel what I hit. It's the corner of Kitty's bed.

"Emmylou?" Kitty's night lamp switches on. I squeeze my eyes until they adjust to the light.

"Thank goodness!" Kitty jumps out of her bed, fully dressed. For a second I think she's coming to give me a hug, but halfway there she stops.

"Where on earth have you been? You know you were supposed to have the 6 to 10 shift?"

"Oh, shit! I forgot. Sorry." It's the truth. I did forget, because I didn't even think I would be here anymore, but I hardly can tell her that as an excuse.

"You forgot?"

"I … I walked down to the river and there was this boy with his granddad and they have sled dogs. They wanted me to help, and then we went on a dog team ride and there was this dog,

Qaqavii—he likes me—but then I lost their dog—not Qaqavii, one of the other ones. So … so I stayed. I found the dog and I brought it back and now I'm here."

Kitty doesn't say a thing. But I know she's mad.

"Mom?" I want to tell her I'm kind of glad I missed my train. And that I'm sorry for making her worry. And that it was so cool to go out with the dogs and to see Old Ipilii and Barnabas together, and that she would like Elisapii because she's a bit like Grandma Millie, even though they're so different. But silence hangs between us that feels colder than the icy wind down by the river.

Kitty picks up the phone and dials a number.

"Yes, this is Kitty Leroux. I called earlier to report my daughter missing … Yes, you were right; she just came home … No, no, everything is fine. She was hiding from a polar bear—that's why she couldn't call me … Where? Hold on." Kitty presses the phone to her chest, and glares at me.

"What?" I ask.

Kitty puts the phone back on her ear. "She can't remember. We're new in town … Thanks. Bye."

"You called the police? Because I was late? Geez, Kitty. Why did you lie to them?"

"What was I supposed to say? That you went on a fun little

adventure with some boy and didn't think of calling your mother?"

"It's not some boy. His grandfather was there, too."

"And for that you needed two hundred dollars?"

"What?" Shit.

"Did you think I wouldn't notice? What did you do with it?"

"I …" Think, Emmylou. Fast. "I lost it." Which is kind of true. On a train ticket with no refund.

"Don't lie!"

"I'm not lying," I say, but it doesn't feel right. "I bought a train ticket."

"I saw your clothes missing." Kitty wraps her arms around her as if she's trying to hug herself. She's shaking and I don't think it's from the cold. "Where's your ticket?"

"Gone."

"Just give it to me."

"It's true. I missed … I didn't take the train. It's non-refundable … the ticket, I mean." I pass her the ticket.

Kitty wipes her temple as if she has a sudden headache.

"Promise you're never, ever going to do that to me again."

Silence.

"Promise," she repeats. This time more urgently.

I bite my lip. I can't make a promise I cannot keep. So I say nothing.

"Why are you doing this to me, Emmylou?" There it is—the blame, the anger. It's the same thing over and over again.

"Why do *I* do this to you? Who's the one always running off?"

"But I'd never leave you," she says. For the blink of a second, I feel there's something other than anger, but then I'm not sure if I just think that because I want it to be there. And suddenly I'm upset and angry with myself, because I'm looking for something that so obviously doesn't exist between us.

"No, you just leave your crappy life behind, and don't give a shit about mine," I yell at her.

"When are you going to grow up and behave like an adult? I'm done with this topic," Kitty yells back. And just like that, we're back in our all too familiar pattern. I flop down onto my bed and pull my blanket over my head. The truth is, I'm done with it, too. I'm tired of arguing. Tired of hurting.

"Geez, Emmylou, go and have a shower at least! I bet those dogs were full of fleas."

I bang the bathroom door shut and let the hot water scorch my face. How can you be so close to someone and yet feel so lonely?

"Morning, Emmylou!" Kitty pulls my blankets away. "It's daylight in the swamp!"

"It's still dark out!" I grope for the blanket and pull it back over my head.

"Yeah, well, that's what life is like in the great white north. Dark when you get up, dark when you go to bed. Come on, let's have breakfast together."

How come she's in such a good mood all of a sudden? Did she forget the argument we had last night?

"I have a surprise."

I groan. With Kitty, surprises are not always a good thing.

When I was maybe eight or ten, Kitty took me to an amusement park. I can't remember where that was or where we lived, but I remember the giant rollercoaster. Skyrider, that's what it was called. I didn't want to go, but Kitty insisted it would be fun.

By the time the ride was over, my knuckles had lost all color and I was pressing my lips together, trying desperately not to let the vomit come out. Most of all, I remember being strapped in next to Kitty, my eyes squeezed shut, only knowing by Kitty's laughs and screams if we were going up or down. I still feel that way.

"Aimee is filling in for me after lunch. And it's your day off. So we can do something together."

"Aimee?"

"The French girl."

"Marie?"

"That's what I said," Kitty says, her voice regaining a bit of its usual edge.

"You said—" I quickly bite my tongue. I suddenly feel like we're walking on a tightrope, balancing words on either end of our poles. One wrong word and we'll both tumble down. "So ... what's your surprise?" I peek out from under my blanket.

"Let's do something fun together. Forget about all the arguing. Start new." Kitty unfolds a sheet of paper with a handwritten note. "I talked to Marie and these are the things she recommends. We can go to the Eskimo Museum, although museums are usually not much fun; or we can go to the Arctic Trading Post and I'll buy you something nice, maybe jewelry or a nice sweater; or we can go on a Tundra Crawler Tour, but Marie thinks we might need to book in advance, so we would have to check that; or ..." and Kitty pauses and smiles at me "... we can go on a dog sled ride."

Honestly? What choice do I have? Kitty hates museums, I hate jewelry, and we're too late for the polar bear tour, so that leaves us with a dog sled ride, which I had already planned anyway. Only without Kitty.

★

Dogs are barking and jumping at the end of their chains. It's total chaos. Kitty and I are squeezed with four other tourists in what looks like a converted golf cart. Two helpers are rushing to hook up dogs to the cart, while a third tries to stop the dogs from jumping over their lines. Another thirty or so dogs go haywire, running around in circles on their chains.

"Welcome," a guy yells over the noise. He's wearing—guess what?—yes, a red down parka. Worse yet, on his head is a fur cap with the tail of the dead animal still attached.

"I'm Peter Patterson." He introduces himself, pausing as if waiting for the guests to recognize his name. "I'm the owner of Aurora Dog Sled Tours and your tour guide today. And these dogs here," he swoops his arms over the dog yard, "are the stellar athletes trained to compete in one of the toughest races in Canada—the Arctic Quest—which leaves every year from right here in Churchill." The barking gets so loud that I cover my ears until the last dog is hooked up.

"Hike, hike, hike!" Peter Patterson yells as soon as the team is ready. We shoot out of the dog yard and the barking of the dogs left behind turns into a woeful howl. Then it's quiet. Other than the constant "click, click" sound of cameras and the musher—Peter Patterson—telling us about his Arctic Quest adventures.

"The race runs two hundred and fifty miles along the unforgiving coast of Hudson Bay to Arviat, a small Inuit community in Nunavut."

Arviat! That's where Barnabas is from. It makes me wonder how his grandfather's dogs came to Churchill. Did they run them here? Two hundred and fifty miles? How is that possible?

"The race attracts some of North America's top mushers, but not all will finish. I have been in eight races and finished three times. Last time I came in second, but this year I have a winning team."

"Are any of these dogs going to race?" The tourist in the first row leans closer to Peter Patterson, like he's hoping some of his fame will rub off on him.

"Yes, the gray and white leader there in the front. She's been in four races. The two wheel dogs here in the back are my power horses. They've been in the last three races. And that black one behind the leader, he's my up-and-coming star." He points to a skinny-looking dog with floppy ears and not much fur. I want to ask if the dog doesn't get cold but, before I muster the courage, Peter Patterson is already talking on.

"In the first year, we faced such a bad blizzard that a musher's tent was blown across the tundra—with the musher in it—and a year later I nearly died of hypothermia when the teams were surprised by a rainstorm, followed by a sudden temperature drop to minus twenty-eight—not including the wind chill. This race is a true test for man and beast. Man against nature."

Minus twenty-eight? The big round thermometer at the lodge showed minus twenty-four today. We're all still alive.

I can't help but think about the old man and Barnabas, how comfortable they were out on the trail and with the dogs. Do they know about the race? Would they call it: "Man against nature"?

"Haw!" the musher yells. The trail makes a left turn and the dogs don't really have a choice to go anywhere else, but the tourists ooh and ah when the dogs turn left. Ahead of us is the dog yard, and the next group of tourists is already waiting.

The dogs in the yard start barking and the dogs on the cart pick up speed. More oohing and aahing. Don't they see it's not how it's supposed to be? We're not even on a sled. I bite my lip and try to concentrate on the dogs instead. Like Old Ipilii's dogs, they lean into their harnesses, focused on only one thing: moving forward. These dogs run in pairs, though. Two side by side connected to one single line in the centre, not fanned out like Ipilii's dogs. I wonder why, but before I can ask, a woman with long blonde hair and too much makeup speaks.

"Did any woman ever compete in the race?"

"That's not a world for women out there. There are bears and wolves, and handling a team of ten to twelve dogs is not a piece of cake," Peter Patterson says as he jumps off the cart to pose with his dogs for pictures. It bugs me, the way he talks. As if a woman in the race would diminish his accomplishment.

"Excuse me!" Someone taps me on the shoulder.

I turn around.

"Can you move a bit, so I can get a better shot of the dogs?" A middle-aged man with a frosty moustache and red cheeks waves his camera in my face.

I squeeze closer to Kitty, so Icicle Moustache can snap his selfie. Kitty puts her arm around me.

"Great, isn't it? I'm glad they didn't make us ride on a sled. This is way more comfortable, don't you think?" Kitty turns to the woman behind her. "Could you take a picture of us? This was my daughter's idea—to go on a dog sled ride. Do you have kids?"

The woman shakes her head a polite no.

"You don't know what you're missing," Kitty says, passing her the camera.

I think about all our fights and arguments and I wonder, if this woman had a daughter, whether her daughter would be counting the days to leave her mother—and suddenly I'm sad, because I think how horrible it must be to have a daughter that wants to get away from you as far and as fast as possible.

"Smile," the woman says and Kitty squeezes me tighter.

I try my best to smile, but I'm afraid it's not good enough.

CHAPTER 7

"Emmalu, you back." Barnabas beams at me as if I'd shown up the next day, as I had promised I would. "I'm going out. You coming?"

I nod and watch Barnabas sort the dogs' harnesses, laying out one for each dog.

It's over two weeks since I first (and last) met him. I'd missed the first date, because I went with Kitty on the dog "sled" ride, and then I spent some time in the library, figuring out my outline and sending it off. Lisa found me a math program I can use, but it's a lot harder than I thought, to figure it all out on your own, and Kitty isn't really a great help. Besides, all her math skills fit on the notepad she uses for waitressing. Luckily, the progress report isn't due until January, so I've still got half of November and all of December to figure it out.

I walked down to the river a few times but I was never lucky. Once, all the dogs were gone, and I didn't hang around to wait for them to come back. The other times, the dogs were there, but neither Barnabas nor Old Ipilii were outside and I didn't dare to knock on the door.

Each time I came down to the river, it looked different. The first time I was there, the tide must have been going out. Chunks of ice were going by fast, crashing into each other and spinning on their way to the ocean. They looked like pancakes, only much bigger and made of ice. There were lots of them, bobbing in the current, and just as many stranded ones along the shore. Where the river meets the land at high tide, frozen puddles had formed. I jumped from puddle to puddle, crunching the ice under my feet until all that remained were broken shards. I used to do that when I was little—jump on frozen puddles. Except, back then, things didn't break so easily.

The next time I came, the puddles were hidden under fresh snow and the river lay still. The pancakes had grown in size and numbers, small ones squeezed among bigger ones like they were neatly arranged in a giant jigsaw puzzle. In between the ice floes, the water wasn't really water anymore, but not ice yet, either.

Today, the river is wide open again; ice floes are piled up against the shore, and a cold wind blows from the river. I try to listen to the river's sounds, but all I hear is the young dog whining for attention. Barnabas leads one of the two big white dogs to the sled—is it Qakuq?— and hooks him to the longest line.

The dog sits patiently, waiting for the rest of the team. Barnabas hands me a harness. "For Qaqavii. You remember him?"

I smile. "Of course."

Qaqavii jumps up on me as soon as I'm within reach. I wrestle the harness over his big round head.

"You want me to hook him up?" I ask.

"Ii," Barnabas says and I guess it means yes.

Qaqavii and I walk over to the sled and, although it's been a while, I remember that his is the shortest line. I fiddle the toggle through the loop at the end of his harness and stay with him.

"No, sit!" I say and put my hand in front of his nose when he tries to jump up. I don't want to get him into trouble. He doesn't get it the first time, so I step on his line like Barnabas showed me. Qaqavii has no choice but to plant his bum in the snow. After a while, he stops wiggling and sits, trying hard to contain his impatience.

Barnabas hooks up the red dog with the long fur, the wolfish-looking one. "This is Aupaluk."

"Aupaluk?"

"Ii. Means red one. Come." He waves at me as he walks back to the dog yard.

"This is Pamiuluk's harness." He points at a dog with a stumpy tail and passes me her harness.

"What happened to her tail?" I ask as I slip the harness over her head.

"Her mother bit it off. It was her first time with puppies. Maybe she thought it was the … what do you call this thing?" He points to his belly button.

"Umbilical cord?"

"Ii," he says, like it's the most normal thing in the world that a mother's best intentions end up in the mutilation of her puppy. Pamiuluk doesn't seem to mind, though. She howls just as excitedly as everyone else. I pet her behind the ears and she leans into me, looking up with dark brown eyes that are warm and trusting.

"You're beautiful," I whisper and Pamiuluk wags her stumpy tail.

Barnabas tells me every dog's name but, by the time all ten dogs are hooked up, I can only remember half. A big male, whose neck hair always stands up when another dog comes close, has the funniest name—Shark-Tail. Barnabas's little sister meant to say his fur stands up like the feathers of the Sharp-Tailed Grouse, but she was only three and called it Shark-Tailed Grouse. So the name stuck. She also named the smallest female in the team—Princess—and tied a pink ribbon on her collar. So she's easy to remember. Princess's littermate is Grumpy, the big rough-looking white male, who likes to growl a lot. The other names are all in Inuktitut and I have a hard time remembering those—except Qaqavii, of course.

"Ready?" Barnabas asks and sits on the far left of the qamutik, leaving lots of room for me to sit next to him.

"Where's your grandpa?" I ask.

"In Winnipeg. With my grandmother. For tests."

I can't tell from his voice if he's worried or not. It can't be helped, I think, and don't press any further.

"Ha-ii," Barnabas calls and the dogs jump to their feet. Qaqavii looks confused for a second, but when the dogs start pulling, he, too, lunges forward. We run toward the river. Like on my first run, we make a sharp turn to the left. The dogs are running so fast that the sled swings sideways. Too late, I try to hang onto the crosspieces. Barnabas grabs my sleeve at the last second, saving me from falling off.

"You changed your mind?"

"About what?" I ask.

"About coming. Look like you were in a hurry to leave."

I try to punch him with my elbow but he ducks away and grins. Not knowing what to reply, I turn my attention to the dogs. Qaqavii looks a lot more focused. You can still easily tell him apart from the other dogs. He is bouncier and has to move his stubby legs a lot faster to keep up, but his line doesn't go slack as often anymore.

The trail feels a lot smoother now with the extra snow. It's quieter without the runners scraping over exposed rocks. The pulling must be easier, too—we're going a lot faster. Because of the snow or because it's just the two of us? I like going fast, but I miss Old Ipilii. It was easier with him being there. I didn't have to think about what to say to Barnabas. Barnabas is quiet now, too. He doesn't even talk to the dogs. They're following their tracks from the previous runs. Their paws tap over the snow, fast and surefooted, flinging up snow as they run. Actually, no, not snow. Tiny ice balls form under their feet and, when they let go, they fly fast as bullets, hitting me in the face. The longer I watch the dogs, the less I feel the need to talk. I listen to their quiet panting, the tapping of their feet, and the swoosh of the runners gliding over the snow. In no time, we leave the wide open land behind and trees begin to dot the landscape. Snow clings to the stunted spruce trees, which makes them bend low to the ground under the heavy weight. When we reach the clearing, Barnabas calls the dogs to turn.

"That's as far as we can go," Barnabas says.

"How come? The dogs are tired?"

"No, they want to go far. But the trail get too narrow over here. Not good for fan hitch."

"What do you mean?"

"The dogs get all tangled in the trees."

"Why don't you run them side by side like …"

"Like quallunaat? Too dangerous when we go north. If their lead dog falls through the ice, all the other dogs follow. If my lead dog falls through the ice, the other dogs spread out and go where is safe. They have long lines, too, so they can swim and nobody drowns. Haala!"

The dogs turn. Qaqavii's the last one to notice, but when he does, he sprints to the right, quickly catching up to the team, all the while keeping his line tight.

"How come you're not going over there if the dogs want to go further?" I point to the open area across the train tracks.

"We don't go there."

"Why? What's there?"

"Ghosts."

"Ghosts?"

"Is old Dene Village. Is haunted."

"There's a village there?" I crane my neck but I see no buildings.

"Not anymore. But the ghosts, they still there." And then he doesn't say any more, and I'm getting a feeling so dark, so real, even though we're talking about something that doesn't exist, that I'm not sure I even want to know more. I change the subject.

"When you moved to Churchill, how did you get your grandpa's dogs here?"

"He ran them," Barnabas says, as if it's no big deal.

"How long did it take?"

"Three days, but he travel all day, only rest at night. He was lucky. No blizzard."

"Three days. That's crazy long. How far is it?"

"About two hundred and twenty or two hundred and fifty miles—depends on where you go."

"Where did he sleep?" I ask.

"First night, he go all the way to Nunalla. There is an old trading post—you know the Hudson Bay Company? But nobody uses it anymore. His dogs, they can sleep out of the wind close to the building."

"And Ipilii? Are there, like, beds and everything still in the trading post?"

"No, Old Ipilii, he builds a small snow house—iglu we call it. Is lots warmer than a building without heat."

"Really?" I say and then feel stupid. Of course it's real. Except I didn't know people still make igloos. "Where is Nunalla?"

"About halfway between here and Arviat, by the Manitoba / Nunavut border."

"He ran over a hundred miles in a day?"

"Long day but it was late in spring. Dogs are strong then and daylight hours long."

"And then?"

"Then he camp one more night by North Knife River, not far across the river from here. I take you there when we can go north. He camp there, waiting for the tide to be right to cross the river," Barnabas continues. "His dogs are tired now and we never cross the river at night. Too dangerous if you can't see bad ice, and bears are out hunting. Except for that big race. People travel at night then. Everyone try to be so fast, people take risks."

"What race? The Arctic Quest?"

"Ii."

"You race?"

Barnabas nods. "My grandpa, he has fast dogs. The first year of the race, he was first to Arviat. He just go, never stopped at a checkpoint. Him and his partner, they only speak Inuktitut and the race marshal, he never told them they had to go sign in and out of each checkpoint. There is one by North Knife River and Nunalla, too. One more at Big River.

"At the first river crossing, it was no good where the

qallunaat trail went, so my grandfather and his partner went wa-a-ay out on the sea ice and go without a trail. And still they faster than anyone else. Nobody's there when they get to Arviat. They bring their dogs home and feed them and then go back to the finish line. When they get there, they are disqualified."

"Disqualified?"

"Ii," Barnabas says. "Because of race rules. You have to sign in at the checkpoints. Next time, I went with him. That time we go to every checkpoint and we finish third place."

"You each run a team? I mean, did you each have a dog team?" It's easy to slip into Barnabas's sentence structure. I kind of like how he talks.

"No, always two partners on one sled. For safety. We race together since I am twelve years old. This will be my fifth time."

I silently do the math in my head. Five years ago he was twelve. So he's seventeen now. And I'll be sixteen soon. I feel myself blush.

"Are you going to race this year?" I ask, looking the other way.

"If the dogs are good. And my grandma ..." he doesn't finish his sentence. I nod.

"When is the race?"

"First weekend in April."

Too bad that it's in April. Who knows where I'll be by then.

CHAPTER 8

Barnabas and Old Ipilii are taking the dogs for a run three or four times a week now. If I don't have to work, I'm in the dog yard just before school's out. Old Ipilii lets me harness all the dogs, and when Barnabas comes home, we're ready to go.

It's November 23 today. My birthday. But I keep it to myself. I never liked the attention you get on your birthday. I didn't choose to be born that day or any day—period.

"I be right there," Barnabas calls as he runs into the house. A minute later, he's back, chewing on a piece of caribou jerky.

"Want a piece?" He holds out a leathery strip of dark brown jerky.

"I'll save it for later, once we get going," I say and stuff it in my pocket. I've come to like the taste of it. It's dry and rather tasteless at first, but after chewing it for a while, it releases its flavor—slightly salty, but also pungent and wild.

Barnabas sits on the sled behind Old Ipilii and me. The

dogs jump to their feet; their ears prick up, their bodies shivering with excitement. When Barnabas pulls the hook, the three of us call "ha-ii," but the dogs are already pulling.

We don't talk much. There isn't much to say. Barnabas would rather not talk about school and I would rather not talk about Kitty. He knows that I'm here with my mom, but he doesn't know about our constant moving, and that I almost left—and I like to keep it that way.

I've got a new work schedule from my boss, but I know it was Kitty who arranged it. I'm working on all those evenings when the train is scheduled to leave.

Kitty isn't happy about me going running with the dogs. I should do something with my "peers" she says—so I hang out with Marie once or twice a week to get Kitty off my back. I listen to Marie talk about all the cool places she's been, and all the cool guys she's met, and I have nothing to say. I once tried telling her about running the dogs, and she told me how she'd worked for two weeks as a handler for a dog musher in the Yukon and knew all about it. Shoveling poop isn't exactly like running dogs, I thought, and didn't bother her with my stories after that. But I don't mind listening to

Marie. She's a good storyteller and it keeps the truce between Kitty and me.

Luckily, Kitty never asks about my schoolwork, not directly, anyway, but she lets me know that if I want to go to university, I'd better be good enough for a scholarship—which I am not even sure you can get when you're homeschooled. Never mind the fact that I'm not exactly scholarship material. I don't know if I even want to go to university. So what's the sense of trying?

The dogs are strong and fast now, but even though they run the loop in shorter and shorter times, we're losing the race with the daylight by a few minutes more every day.

I love to watch the sun set over the river. The river seems frozen nearly all the way across. The high tide has washed the snow away, turning the ice into a mirror for the sky. Just before sunset, the ice on the river glows as if lit by a fire inside, blurring what is water and what is sky. Sometimes the sliver of a moon is already on the eastern horizon, slowly emerging from the red sky that's turning deep purple, before losing its color to the approaching night. Today, it's a full moon and, for a few minutes, sun and moon both cast their light on us.

"We have two shadows," I say, watching twenty faint

shadows following the dogs along either side of the trail. And then, slowly, ten of them fade away, while the other ten become stronger, more distinct. With the fading sunlight, the dogs lose their color, appearing more and more like shadows themselves. Almost like ghosts.

Suddenly I think of the old Dene Village. I looked at maps of Churchill, but neither the one in the train station, nor the ones in the tourist flyers had Dene Village marked on them. Is it just a legend?

As soon as the sun disappears, it feels colder. The moon is so bright, we don't need a headlamp tonight. Back at the dog yard, Old Ipilii leaves us to look after the dogs. He looks stiff lately, pressing his hand on his right hip as he walks.

Barnabas and I feed the dogs. I've come to love the sound of the dogs' teeth ripping the frozen flesh. Qaqavii always shakes his piece first, like a wolf breaking the neck of its prey.

"It's dead, Qaqavii, believe me," I say but, as usual, he doesn't. He approaches it carefully, then pounces on it and quickly shakes it. He drops it, watches it, and then—finally reassured it will not bite him—he tears into the seal meat.

I can see Barnabas's silhouette in the moonlight and, although I can't see his face, I feel he's watching me.

"You good with the dogs," he says. "They like you."

"I like them, too," I say, glad for the darkness, as I can feel my face turn red.

"They ready to go farther, as soon as the ice on the river is safe."

"When will that be?"

"When the river is frozen," he says. "Any day now, if it stays cold like this. You wanna come check it out?"

I follow him to the river. Barnabas walks onto the ice.

"Hey, it's wide open over there!" The moonlight is reflected in the water halfway across the river.

"Is good here." He walks a step further.

I carefully set one foot on the ice. Then another. Suddenly, there's a noise, like a whip being cracked. I jump back to shore, my heart pounding, even though the water can't be deep where I was. The ice booms, a deep rumbling sound at first, then higher frequencies like voices—only not from humans—a song from beneath the ice. Barnabas spreads out his arms but doesn't move.

"What is that?"

"Is the sound of the river making ice." Barnabas slides back to the shore and picks up a rock. He throws it far out onto the river. The rock glides along the surface with a deep rumbling sound, while the river responds with a much higher frequency, like it's playing a glass harp.

I carefully step onto the ice and sit down, pressing my ear closer to the otherworldly music.

"It's my birthday today," I say when the river falls silent again, surprising myself by my own confession.

"Hope you had a good birthday, Emmalu."

I nod, even though he can't see me in the dark. I did have a good birthday.

I used to get upset with my dad on my birthdays, upset at him for not sending me a present. I don't even know why now. I mean, why it always came up on my birthday. I already knew he wasn't thinking of me. But today was different. I ... I didn't expect anything from him—or anyone. I had a good day going out with the dogs, and watching the sun set, and listening to the river music. That's pretty special, isn't it?

"How old are you?" Barnabas asks.

"Sixteen."

"Really?"

"What did you think?"

"Younger."

Ouch. He thinks I'm still a kid. Now that I think about it, I do feel younger around him. As if I'm his little sister and he looks out for me—the big brother I never had.

My bum is getting wet from sitting on the ice and I stand

up. I don't want to leave but I'm getting too chilled. The cold is creeping up my lousy winter jacket and the wind is blowing through my zipper. It doesn't matter how many sweaters I wear underneath, I still feel cold. Worse is my face. My jacket doesn't have a fur trim around it, and the wind burns my cheeks. I constantly have to rub warmth into them with my cold hands.

I think about the parka Kitty and I saw at the Trading Post. It was handmade somewhere up north, the lady in the store had said. It was dark blue with red and yellow trim along the bottom, and had the same slip-over anorak style as Barnabas's caribou parka—without zippers that let the wind through. The hood fit perfectly. It was pretty expensive, but I told Kitty that if she wanted me to stay, I'd need good clothing—plus my birthday was coming up pretty quick. Did she get it for me? She was at work when I got up this morning, but her shift should be over soon.

"I better get going," I say.

Barnabas stands and turns to me. My skin suddenly feels all tingly. And although I like the feeling, I get so nervous that I step away.

"Maybe next weekend, I take you across the river if ice is good."

"I'd like that," I say, feeling the heat rise into my cheeks.

"You look cold." Kitty is balancing a tray with hot coffee, tea, and blueberry pie in her left hand, while with her right, she reaches out to feel my cheek.

"I'm okay."

"You've been out with that boy again?"

"And his grandpa and the dogs," I say, not sure what she's getting at.

"I talked to Peter Patterson. You can help him out with his dogs; then I don't have to worry about you going down there."

"Down where?"

"You know what I mean. The Flats."

"The Flats?"

"That shantytown you always go to. Where the squatters live and the drunks and the people not from here."

"The people not from here? What the heck are you talking about?"

"Why do you always have to make a fight out of everything? I just arranged with Peter Patterson that you can help him with his dogs, so you don't have to hang out with those people."

"Why don't you hang out with Peter Peterson and his stupid dogs? You don't even know 'those people.'" My yelling attracts the attention of a tour group a couple of tables away.

"Hold on a sec." Kitty delivers the orders with a smile, turns on her heels, and, with a scowl and a look, points toward the kitchen. I push the door open. The brightness in the kitchen and the stainless steel counters always take me by surprise. It's so sterile and uncozy, so different from the rest of the lodge that I never know which one is the real world—the kitchen, with the glaring fluorescent lights and the clanging and banging of pots and pans, or the dining room, with subdued lights and conversation and laughter from tourists waiting to be served.

"Two Arctic Char and a medium-rare steak," the chef calls when he sees Kitty—over the noise of the range hood above the stainless steel gas stove.

"Just a minute," Kitty yells back and then turns to me. "I know exactly what kind of people they are. People in town are talking, and I've seen that falling-down shack and the dogs on chains, and the boy with his filthy clothes and ..."

"You followed me?"

"I'm your mother, Emmylou. I'm worried. It's not a good place to be for a fifteen-year old girl."

"Sixteen."

"Sixteen? What's the date today? Oh, shit."

No parka for me or any kind of present, I guess.

"Well, fifteen or sixteen, it's no different, I don't think you should go there. You know what I mean."

"No, I don't," I say and stomp out of the kitchen.

Back in my room, I clutch Silly to my chest and bury my nose in her fake fur. Stupid! Stupid! Stupid! I thought it was a good day. How could she forget my birthday? I feel the tears burning on my cheek and wipe them away with Silly. Grandma Millie would never have forgotten it, and Grandma Millie wouldn't call Barnabas and Elisapii and Old Ipilii "those people."

CHAPTER 9

"Emmylou, wake up. I need you to fill in for me for an hour, okay?"

"Now? You said you'd do the morning shift." I blink into the lights, but it's impossible to keep my eyes open.

"I'll be right back."

"Where you going?"

"I need to get something—a surprise." She smiles at me.

I sit up. "I hope it's blue, starts with a 'P,' and is made to slip over my head."

"You'll see."

"Mom, I'm serious. And if it's too much, I can pay half."

"Just wait." Kitty smiles.

It's busy in the restaurant this morning, but breakfast is easy. It's a buffet and all I have to do is clean plates off tables and refill coffee. I think about going out with Barnabas this weekend, picturing myself in my new parka—warm and grown-up looking.

"Morning, Emmylou. What makes you smile so bright this morning?" Marie is shoveling down scrambled eggs and toast. She's helping out as tour guide today and goes out with the boss to hunt down bears for trigger-happy tourists—camera triggers, that is.

"More coffee?" I ask, trying to hide my smile.

"No, thanks. I gotta run. I 'ave to clean out the bus still and the tour starts in fifteen minutes. It's crazy what you find on the bus after the tourist leave. Yesterday, someone left a straw hat. Like that's gonna do you any good in Churchill," Marie says with a smile. "You 'ave to come one day, see the bears."

I shrug my shoulders. It's not that I don't want to see the bears, it's just I don't want to be with straw-hatted tourists, chasing bears with big giant monster truck buses, or whatever those Tundra Crawlers are. And certainly, I don't want to see one just walking around by myself. So chances are good that I'll be the only person in this town who won't see a bear.

"Have fun," I say as I take her ketchup-smeared plate.

"You, too," she smiles.

It's hard not to like her. She always sees the bright side of things. As if nothing really bothers her—not even cleaning up garbage after tourists. How does she do that?

The tourists clear out of the dining room to go about their daily adventures. I wipe the tables and eat a couple of pancakes in the kitchen while the chef is out smoking. When I come back into the dining room, Kitty is sitting at a table, her cheeks red and her eyes shining bright. There are two plastic shopping bags on the bench next to her, one of them big enough to hold my parka.

"Happy birthday, sweet sixteen," she beams at me. "Sorry, I didn't wrap it. Here." She puts the big plastic bag on the table. I reach for it. "No, wait. Sit down. I'll get you a hot chocolate." She squeezes out of the bench.

"Without cream, please," I call after her. I watch her swing the kitchen door open, and then I slowly turn the big bag until I can peek inside. And then I wish I hadn't. It's not the dark blue anorak; it's something baby blue. I push the bag back into its original position.

"Happy birthday to you, happy birthday, dear Emmylou …" Kitty is carefully carrying a tray with two hot chocolates and a plate with a banana chocolate muffin, a burning sparkler stuck in the middle of it. She sets the muffin in front of me, continuing to sing, while I watch the sparkler burning down until it bends from the heat and sheds black ashes over my birthday muffin.

"Emmylou, what's wrong?" Kitty passes me a paper napkin.

"I don't know," I say, wiping my eyes and trying hard to

contain a sniffle. What *is* wrong with me? When did I stop liking baby blue and sparklers on my birthday cake? And when did things start to get so complicated with Kitty?

"Is it because I forgot your birthday?"

I shake my head.

"Here, look what I found for you." She pushes the shopping bag closer.

I bite my lip and shake my head again. I don't want to know what's inside. Don't want to see the disappointment on Kitty's face when she sees mine.

"So what's this all about now? You don't want your birthday present? Did I do something to you?"

"No! I …" I don't know what to say, so I take the bag and pull the baby blue jacket out. It's not a pullover anorak. It doesn't even have a zipper to keep the wind out. Just big purple, ridiculous-looking buttons.

"Try it on. I think this looks a lot sharper, not like that baggy thing you tried on last time."

"It's baby-blue and purple, Kitty."

"But those are your colors. Make your skin tone come out real nice."

"It's not practical."

"Practical for what?"

"It's too tight and it's going to look dirty right away, and it doesn't have a hood. It won't work for running dogs."

"Then don't use it for that."

"What am I supposed to use it for then?"

"Go out, make some friends."

"I have friends."

"I mean real friends."

"Real friends?"

"Teenagers like you."

"Like me?"

"Emmylou, you have to get out. Go hang out at the bakery, watch a movie at the town complex."

"I *am* getting out if you haven't noticed."

"And I don't understand why you keep going back there. Are you … they're not asking you for money, are they?"

"What?"

"For booze or whatever."

Really? "That's … racist, Kitty."

"Of course you have to find some way to turn this against me. There's nothing racist about what I just said. I don't have anything, personally, against Eskimos or Inuit or whatever they're called now, but look where these people live. What am I supposed to think?"

I have a sick feeling in my stomach. How can Kitty—or anybody—think that about Barnabas's family? They are the most generous people I know, even if they don't have much to give—or maybe it's *because* they don't have much to give. It makes me realize how little I have to give them in return, and yet nobody questions me.

CHAPTER 10

I don't feel like reading in my room and Barnabas is at school. So I put on my new ugly parka and walk east, down Button Street, and then on toward the ocean. I can already see the rise of land, where the rock is exposed, even now in winter. I love walking on the rocks, the dark, cold smoothness. They feel old, those rocks, like they've been here a long, long time and will be here forever—but they also feel vulnerable in their nakedness. It's almost as if earth itself revealed her bare bones, no hiding under the plants and soil.

I climb onto the rise and see the wide expanse of the bay stretch out in front of me. White at first, where the ice has formed along the shore, and then a gray-blue, like the color of the sky where the ocean isn't frozen yet. The wind is blowing snow along the shore, a constant movement against the stillness of the rock.

It's biting cold up here. I huddle down behind a big

boulder, but then I'm worried I won't see if a bear comes by, and I suddenly get a strange feeling that someone is watching me. My heart pounds like crazy and I turn around in a 360-degree circle twice. No polar bear in sight, just an old woman walking toward the Churchill Cemetery. I can't resist the urge to follow her, be close to another human being.

It's a big cemetery for a town so small; more dead people here than living. Some graves are old, real old, and I wonder if the explorers and fur traders and all those people that the tourist flyers mentioned are buried here, and if anyone still visits their graves.

The old woman stops at what looks like a monument of some sort: a weathered cross on a plywood box with black plaques attached. She kneels in the snow, her hand tracing the name on one of the plaques. Deep creases wrinkle her face, almost as if sorrow and grief were carved into her skin. She hasn't seen me and I quickly walk deeper into the cemetery, because I don't want to disturb her.

I wander among the people long gone and read the names and dates on the graves. Some graves have fancy headstones or white picket fences around them; others just have a white wooden cross, no name attached. I turn to leave, when I notice the woman at the monument is gone.

I walk to where she had sat and study the names of people and the dates of their births and deaths that are written on the plaques. They all died between the mid-fifties and seventies, some of them still children, toddlers, and babies, too.

A chill runs down my spine and it feels like the air is suddenly heavier, more dense ... as if something was there, something I can't see. I leave the cemetery in a hurry. Once outside the gate, I look back, past the graves to the south, to what Barnabas called the old Dene Village, and then glance at the monument. Are those the ghosts Barnabas had talked about? How can I find out?

★

"Emmylou, how are you? I'd wondered if you were still in town." Lisa smiles at me as I return the books I had borrowed last month. "Do you want to return them all or renew?"

"Um ..." I've only glanced through them, read a bit here and there. I sigh. I guess I'll eventually have to do the assignments I gave myself. "I'll keep the ones about the polar bears if that's okay."

"No problem. How's home school?"

Not exactly what I want to talk about.

"Okay, I guess. I ... um ... I heard someone talk about Dene

Village and …" How am I going to ask her about the ghosts without sounding totally stupid?

"And …?"

"And do you know anything about it?"

"Not as much as I should, to be honest. It's the dark part of our history that people would rather forget."

"So it's true then that there are …?" I bite my tongue.

"That there are what?"

"Ghosts?" I say.

"If you mean the people are still haunted by what happened, yes, there are certainly ghosts."

I think about the old woman with the haunted look on her face. What did she see?

"What happened there?" I ask.

"Dene Village was a shantytown that the government put up for the Dene people. By the time I moved to Churchill, the Dene had already moved back to the land, so I never saw Dene Village or the place they lived before—Camp 10, I think they called it—up by the cemetery."

"Why didn't they live where everyone else lived?"

"There were no houses for them when they came."

"Why did they come, then?"

"It wasn't exactly their choice. Hold on." She types something into her library search site. "Hm … that's strange. It's not in our collection. Someone must have borrowed it and not returned it."

"What?"

"The book *Night Spirits*. It's about the relocation of the Sayisi Dene. I'll order it in for you."

"Relocation? What does that mean?"

Lisa smiles; it's a sad smile. "I think you'll find your answers in the book. It's best to read it in their own words."

"Okay," I say. "I'll come back for the book, then."

I turn to go, but then the image of the old lady at the cemetery comes up again.

"One more question: Dene Village doesn't exist anymore, right? Did they all leave?"

"Most of them live at Tadoule Lake now. Only a few stayed in Churchill."

But their ghosts are still here, I think. As I walk down onto the street, I look at the people more closely, trying to figure out who they are. That guy in the old army parka that just drove by on his skidoo, the one with the dark skin and high cheekbones; is he Dene? What's his story? How do all the stories fit together? And how do I fit in?

CHAPTER 11

"Easy," Barnabas calls, but the dogs don't listen. Every single dog is loping as fast as it can. Qaqavii and Princess are letting out sharp short barks, not being able to contain their excitement. Grumpy is snapping into the air and Qakuq pulls so hard that he's running sideways. It's their first time crossing the river this winter.

The last few runs they pulled with little enthusiasm around the same loop they'd run day after day. Now they can't wait to see what's ahead of them, like me. I'm sitting in the front, Barnabas behind me. Old Ipilii stayed home. They both walked across the river early this morning. The ice is early this year, the old man had said. Last weekend it already looked frozen, but Old Ipilii did not let us go until now. It's been cold the last few nights and it's even colder today. The dogs' faces are frosty and steam escapes their mouths in tiny clouds.

We bounce over snow-covered piles of ice along the shore,

and then through a maze of rocks. Barnabas is trying to steer us clear of the obstacles by dragging his feet on either side of the sled. He's doing well until there's a rock right ahead of us. The team splits, half the fan runs left, the other right. I brace myself for the crash, but Barnabas jumps off, pulls the sled over and throws himself back, all within a few seconds.

"How'd you do that?" I ask.

"I dunno. Just did it without thinking, or we would have smashed into that rock."

"Do you want to sit in the front again?"

"No, next time you jump, okay?" He smiles. I know he's teasing me, but I sure wish I could do what he just did. Luckily, there's no immediate need to repeat his acrobatic act. The ice is smooth now, really smooth, with little snow. The sled skids sideways, jerking us and the dogs. Nevertheless, the dogs pick up speed, their paws flinging small ice balls into my face.

Ahead of us, the ice becomes jagged again. From down here where I'm sitting, it looks like a rugged mountain range, a mysterious kingdom impossible to describe. The dogs wind through the jumbled ice sculpted by the river, the sled's runners scraping noisily over the ice. Suddenly, the sled tips up. For a second, I only see blue sky, and then the sled comes crashing down. We're back on shore on the other side of the river. The dogs pick up on a skidoo trail and we climb up onto the land. There's more snow here, so the sled runs more quietly now.

I move my cramped legs. Only now do I realize how cold I am. I pull my toque further over my ears and rearrange my two scarves, trying to keep the wind from blowing through my jacket. I'm wearing the new one, and I'm happy to discover dark marks on the baby-blue fabric, where Qaqavii rubbed with his greasy fur against me. Maybe one day my jacket will look like Barnabas's pants, impossible to tell what color they once were, each stain a story.

After a short rise, the land dips down again. It feels a bit like being in a valley. There are big boulders along the trail, and small spruce trees grow where the land provides protection from the harsh wind.

"Does this place have a name?" I mutter through the scarf covering my mouth.

"Seahorse Gully," Barnabas says. "That's where the Tuniit lived."

"The Tuniit?" I ask.

"Qallunaat call them the Dorset people. Way before Inuit. I don't know much, only that the Tuniit lived in stone houses. They were giants, but friendly."

Friendly giants? A fairy tale?

"What happened to them?"

"I don't know."

I never thought much about who lived in the Arctic until the talk with Lisa the other day. I thought it was always Inuit, but now there are the Tuniit and the Dene, and maybe even others that I don't know anything about, even though it's part of my country.

"Does Old Ipilii know, or Elisapii?" I ask.

"Our legends tell stories but nobody really knows. Not even qallunaat scientists. Qaqavii, tighten up!" Barnabas's attention turns to the dogs. "You ask too many questions—don't forget to watch your dog."

I like how Barnabas calls Qaqavii "my" dog. I watch him run and he's less and less bouncy, but it's still easy to pick him out in the team. He gets distracted easily, stumbles over his own legs when he's not paying attention, and just can't help himself from being a puppy.

Barnabas stops the team. Qaqavii runs to where the snow has drifted deep around a big boulder. He stuffs his head under the snow and sneezes. He tries to catch his breath, but sucks in more snow and has to sneeze again. He shakes his head as if he wants to shake the sneeze out of his nose, but it doesn't work. He sneezes again and again. Barnabas and I burst out laughing.

"You're such a puppy," I tell him and ruffle him behind the ears. Qaqavii sneezes into my face.

"Let's go or we won't get to Button Bay and back before dark," Barnabas calls.

I settle next to him on the sled.

"Can we go see the giant's stone houses?" I ask.

"There's not much left. Just stones where the walls used to be, but it's all under the snow. All the interesting things they found are long gone. They all in museums."

"What things?"

"Tools. Like harpoon heads. Also knives and scrapers. And burins."

"Burins?"

"Made from flint. Like a chisel. Maybe used for carving."

"Carving what?"

"Wood, bone, ivory. Go look in the museum."

"In Churchill?"

"Yes, go past the Northern Store toward the bay."

"What's it called?"

"Used to be Eskimo Museum, but now is Itsanitaq Museum."

"Itsanitaq?"

"Ii. Things from the past. Lots of things—like carvings and tools and stories. You see for yourself."

"I will," I say, but I'd rather not think about Churchill right now.

The gully is leading us uphill through a boulder garden. The trees are thinning out. Their trunks are almost branchless on one side, spindly twigs on the other side. They're all leaning to one side like they're caught in the never-ending struggle against the north wind. The dogs are slowing down, and Barnabas jumps off the qamutik and urges them on.

"Do you want me to jump off, too?" I ask.

"No, is okay. They have to learn to pull some weight."

The dogs strain in their harnesses and then stop, just as we're reaching the top of the gully.

"How far are we going?" To my left, the land stretches as far as I can see. To my right, the trail turns toward the bay.

"Just across Button Bay down there and then up on shore again." Barnabas points north, but I can't tell which is bay and which is land. All the way to the horizon, it's flat, empty. I turn my face away from the biting wind and the overwhelming space ahead. Once again, I feel as if someone is watching me. Out of the corner of my eye, I see someone standing on the other side of the gully. I turn around to get a better look, but all I see now is a rock glowing in the late afternoon sun.

And then the strangest thing happens: I can see myself and

Barnabas and all the dogs as if from above, like I was the rock looking down, and then I see shadows—no … not shadows—actually, I don't really see anything; it's more a feeling. It feels like we're not alone, like there's a presence, but I can't make any sense of it. I hear children laugh, but when I try to focus on the sound, I realize it's the dogs whining. Without a command, they suddenly rise to their feet and strain in their lines. The trail leads downhill and the dogs gather speed. For a short second, it feels like we're flying, and then we're out on the sea ice. The jumble ice is bigger here, sheets of ice towering tall above us, as if frozen in time by a force bigger than I can understand.

"Wooh!" Barnabas calls but the dogs don't listen. There's no sign of tiredness. The dogs are straining in their harnesses and pulling hard, their noses close to the ground.

"Oh, oh," Barnabas says, "we better head back." He sounds nervous.

"What? Why?" I ask. "Isn't the ice safe?"

"Look," he says and points in the snow.

I don't see anything. Just snow and ice and dog tracks.

"Nanuq. Polar bear."

"Where?" I scream, and before I realize what's happening, I'm hanging onto Barnabas's arm.

"I don't know," he says. "That's why we should go back. The dogs, they are chasing. See all the tracks?"

I let go of his arm and strain my eyes. Now I see it. Imprinted in the snow, there are round tracks, bigger than my outstretched hand, and oval ones bigger than a human foot.

"What are we waiting for? Go back!" I yell.

Barnabas smiles. "Not so easy. My grandpa, he used dogs to hunt bear. They go crazy when they smell bear. They don't listen to me," Barnabas says. He drags his snow hook. It slows the dogs, but they won't stop.

"Left! La laa! Left, left!" Barnabas calls but the dogs don't turn. I frantically look around, seeing bears lurking behind jumble ice, but when I blink, they're gone.

"I try stop the dogs and you jump off and chase them left, okay?"

"Wait!" I yell. "How?"

"You just jump off and chase them left. Like this." He stretches his arms out and makes a shooing movement as if he's trying to herd a bunch of runaway chickens.

"Wooh!" Barnabas yells at the dogs. The snow hook scrapes noisily over the ice but the dogs keep moving.

"Jump off!"

"Now? We're going too fast!"

Then, suddenly, the hook catches in a crack in the ice. The sled comes to such a sudden stop I'm catapulted off the sled. Startled by my involuntary flight exercise, the dogs turn away from me—and turn left!

The sled swings around and we're back on our old tracks. The dogs put their noses down and start chasing the scent the other way with the same enthusiasm. I scramble to my feet and run behind the team. Qaqavii bounces next to me, his line slack on the ground.

"Jump!" Barnabas calls.

I throw myself forward and grab the last crosspiece with my right hand. Snow is blasting in my face and crawling up my sleeve. My arm feels like it's being pulled out of its socket, but the thought of being left for bear food gives me a strength I didn't know I had. I hang on until Barnabas manages to stop the dogs. In less than a second, I'm on the sled.

"Not bad for a qallunaaq," he teases.

I bite my lip hard to stop the tears from welling up and rub my shoulder.

"You okay?" he asks.

I nod.

"There he is!" Barnabas sits backwards on the sled, pointing out into the bay.

I see movement in the jumble ice. Something not quite as white as the ice, a yellow shape, with a black nose pointing in our direction. Slowly, he rises, until he stands on his hind legs. Oh, my God. He's got blood all over him. This is not the cute, fluffy tourist attraction I've seen in pictures. This is a skilled hunter, a killer at the top of the food chain.

"What's he doing?" I whisper, my heart pounding like crazy.

"He can't see us but he caught our scent. He's trying to figure out what we are."

"Is he … he can't catch up to us, can he?"

I watch the distance between us and the bear increase, and then I remember that he can run at a speed of forty kilometers an hour. We're not even going half that speed.

"Barnabas! What's he doing now?"

I watch as the bear goes down on all four paws again.

"See all the blood on his nose and paws? He's got a seal or something. He won't bother us. She, I mean."

"She?"

"Look!"

I sit on my knees and then I see them, two cubs coming out from hiding behind their mother's back. I watch them until they blend in with the jumble ice. My heart still pounds like crazy, but my head feels light and my skin feels all tingly, in a good way. It's strange—I've never been so close to actually being eaten, and yet I have never felt so alive.

The dogs follow their tracks back over the peninsula and through Seahorse Gully. I'm surprised when I realize we're back home. The town's noises seem far away. My mind is still out on Button Bay, seeing the cubs wrestle over a chunk of seal, watched over by a mama bear that would do anything to protect her cubs.

CHAPTER 12

Big white flakes are falling like feathers out of a dark purple sky. I watch out our attic window as the snow settles onto the windowpane. The wind picks up and the snowflakes turn into a curtain of white, turning the red industrial building across the street into muted grays.

We won't be running dogs today. Not just because of the weather, but also because it's Tuesday. It's too dark now to run dogs after school, so Barnabas skips school on Wednesdays and we run dogs on Wednesday, Saturday, and Sunday. His teacher wasn't impressed, but his granddad told Barnabas to tell his teacher that he's teaching Barnabas Inuit knowledge and that's more important than school.

I don't really feel like hanging out in my room, so I decide to check out the museum.

A man is shoveling the stairs leading up to the entrance of a building with gray-blue siding and white window frames. *Itsanitaq Museum,* a small sign says in plain letters. In the front yard is one of those big stone sculptures that look like a person, like the one that is on the Nunavut flag. There are lots of them here in Churchill, made of gigantic rocks stacked on top of each other. There are also small ones in the souvenir shops, where they're made of glass or soapstone. It's a real touristy thing, but I wonder what the meaning behind them is. I have to ask Barnabas about it.

"Hi," I say to the man, who's wearing a dark blue parka not unlike the one I wanted so badly. A golden cross around his neck swings back and forth as his shovel scrapes noisily over concrete steps. I run up the stairs.

"Hello," I hear as I'm already pushing the glass door open. I glance back. The man leans on his shovel, the step he just cleared already reclaimed by drifting snow.

I shake the snow off my parka and enter the museum. The first thing I see is a stuffed polar bear in a glass case. Behind it another glass case. This one with a prehistoric-looking animal—a muskox. I've never seen one before, but I don't like his dead glass eyes and the fading fur. I have the urge to leave, but then my eyes fall on the carvings on the shelves along the walls. Hundreds of them. Maybe even thousands.

There are carvings from caribou antlers, walrus tusks, and whalebone. They are perfect little scenes of people hunting seals on the ice with tiny harpoons lifted high; dog teams chasing polar bears over tongue-like snowdrifts; women collecting eggs in little baskets while ivory geese flap their wings in protest; men wearing fancy parkas, carved from soapstone, dancing to the unhearable beat of the drum in their hands; and ivory children playing in front of ivory igloos.

All of a sudden I have the same feeling I had in Seahorse Gully. As if someone is watching me. I turn around, but the only people here are tourists in the gift shop. Nobody is paying attention to me.

I'm about to turn to the next showcase when I see it. A small sculpture, shaped like a bird, his head tilted toward me, his face more human than bird. There are signs carved into the bird, lines that are crossing each other. It looks older than the other carvings. The whole sculpture is only a couple of inches tall, but there is something powerful, something ancient that I don't understand. I feel cold, then hot. I want to touch the little bird, set him free from his glass prison but, at the same time, I'm scared of what might happen if I do.

I turn away from the carvings, and two life-sized kayaks catch my eye. They're made from driftwood, bones, and sealskin. Harpoons and paddles are strapped to the deck as if someone was just getting ready to go out on a hunt. I resist the urge to let my hand glide across the tightly stretched skin. It looks so fragile, and it's hard to imagine that people used to hunt seals and walruses in these kayaks. Maybe even Old Ipilii hunted in one of these. Or if not him, then his dad.

Behind the kayaks is a showcase with clothing. There is a parka that looks like the one Barnabas wears. It feels weird to see it behind glass. I wonder who it belonged to and what that person would think about seeing it in a museum. I feel like I'm watching someone through a keyhole—like I'm not supposed to be here. And yet I can't turn away.

I check out the carvings on the wall far away from the little bird sculpture and discover a really cool one. A bunch of people are standing on a caribou antler. One of them is looking up at a large creature suspended on a stick above the people. It has a human head and hands, but the arms look more like flippers, and where there should have been legs, there's a fish tail or maybe a seal's tail. The creature floats in the air like it's flying or maybe swimming in the ocean—or maybe both at the same time. "*Name Spirit*" reads the small card next to the carving. Is this how Barnabas got his name from the old man's aunt? I look at all the little antler people and wonder who will be the bearer of that big spirit hovering above them.

"We're closing in five minutes."

I jump at the voice from behind me. The fluorescent light on the ceiling is unnaturally bright, the sound of shuffling feet on linoleum floor unnaturally loud.

"Oh," I say, "I was just leaving anyway."

"Fascinating, isn't it?"

The woman talking to me is an older lady with unruly dark hair, combed back in a not very successful attempt to tame it.

"These were all acquired by early missionaries of our diocese," she explains.

"They were?" I ask. Stupid question. She just said so. It's just … when I hear of missionaries, I think of residential schools and all the bad things that happened there. I wonder where all the carvings came from. Were they taken away? Stolen?

"Every piece that's here has its own story. Actually three stories: there's the story of the carving, the story of the artist who made the carving, and there's the story of how it got here."

"How … how did they get here?"

"Many of the earlier carvings were sent by priests to Brother Volant, who lovingly placed them in a display case," she says while searching the glass case with her eyes.

"Ah, here it is. See?" She points to a delicately carved ivory sled; caribou skins and a tiny snow knife are tied to it with thread made of some animal part—even the soapstone dogs wear miniature harnesses.

"This one was a gift to Brother Volant. It's from the Pond Inlet area. He loved to visit Inuit in their camps. The further north the better. Mostly, he traveled in winter by dog team, and that's how he came to know many artists."

"He traveled by dog team? Really?" Duh! Of course. They only had dog teams for transportation in winter. But I look at the pieces differently now. They're not only a representation of life in the past, they are *from* the life in the past. Maybe that's what's so beautiful and at the same time so unnerving about them. Maybe they can transport us back there. Into the past. But what *is* their story?

"You say it was … a gift? Who gave it to him?"

"He stayed two weeks with a family near the northernmost mission. He accompanied them while they were hunting seals and visiting relatives, all the time learning Inuktitut and recording their way of life. When he was called back to Churchill, he was given the dog team by the father of the family, because the journey between the camps was sometimes more important to Brother Volant than reaching the destination.

"Without his vision, the museum wouldn't exist today." The way she says it, it's like it's the most normal thing in the world, that a Brother from Europe sets out in the middle of the winter and travels thousands of miles by dog team, stays with an Inuit family, learns their language, and then comes all the way back.

"So he learned Inuktitut and bought all these carvings in two weeks?"

"No, no," she laughs. "He lived with Inuit for nineteen years. And the carvings come from many different Catholic priests who started collecting back in the nineteen thirties. Brother Volant had the vision of the museum, and he was the curator once it was established. And I carry on his legacy. I'm Rosemary, by the way."

"Emmylou," I mumble, not sure if she really wants to know.

"The carvings are a testimonial to Inuit culture, their traditions, their stories, their way of life. Brother Volant realized how important it was to preserve that rich culture for future generations."

"How did he end up in Churchill?"

"Come to the front with me. I'll give you a book."

I follow Rosemary to the gift shop and she takes a book from the shelf: *Carved from the Land: The Eskimo Museum Collection.*

"I have a meeting I have to go to, but here's a chapter about the Brother and the museum." She flips the book open and points to a picture of a young man dressed in caribou clothing, wearing a huge cross around his neck, complete with Jesus nailed to the cross. He looks comfortable in his beautiful caribou parka, but he also looks serious, as if he's worried about something. I wonder what he was thinking when the picture was taken.

"Bring it back some time." Rosemary escorts me out the door and locks up behind me. I clutch the book under my arm to protect it as well as I can from the swirling snow.

A snowdrift has formed against the lodge's doorstep. I reach down to sweep it away with my mitt but, when I open the door, snow finds its way in anyway. The dimly lit entrance hall feels cozy on a day like today. I brush the snowflakes off my new book and shake the snow off my jacket. I don't feel like going to my room, so I go to the restaurant and order a hot chocolate. My favorite table is empty and I squeeze into the booth in the back corner of the restaurant.

Kitty and Marie are joking with the guests as they deliver their orders. They seem to be everywhere at the same time, smiling, chatting, praising their guests' good menu choices, balancing empty plates and full beer glasses. Marie is only three years older than me, but I don't think I'll ever be such a good waitress. She makes it look so natural.

I lean my head against the window, but I can't make out any

other buildings. Just the snow, falling more and more heavily as the sky darkens.

"Here you go, Emmylou." Kitty sets the hot chocolate in front of me with an extra bowl of whipped cream. I don't like how the cream makes a scummy layer on the hot chocolate, but I smile anyway. I know whipped cream is her favorite.

"Thanks, Kitty," I say.

"I'll be right back—just have to get that order for table six."

I leaf through the book. An ivory carving of a man on a qamutik, running his dogs toward a half-built igloo, catches my eye. There's an airplane behind him but he can't see it. The family building the igloo is looking up at the little plane like they're seeing it for the first time. The carving is from 1955. *Sighting of His First Airplane*, it's called. There is something about that man standing tall in the middle of his igloo, his dogs huddled behind the igloo walls ... I don't know what it is, but it's like the tiny plane changed the perfect little scene underneath its wings. What did the man in the carving think? I wonder if he ever finished building the igloo for his family.

Kitty plunks down next to me. "It's slow today, like everyone's hibernating in their room."

I grab my hot chocolate with both hands, feeling the warmth seep through the mug.

"What are you reading?" Kitty leans over and reads out loud. "Ilitqusituqait Uqausillu Asiutaililuguit ... How do you pronounce that?" Kitty shakes her head and then reads the English subtitle: *"The old ways and language and not losing them ...* Why are you reading this? For school?"

"No ... I mean ... maybe there's something I can use for school. I don't know yet. The museum lady lent it to me," I say.

Kitty flips through the pages but doesn't stop to read anything.

"It's kind of sad," I say.

"What? The book? Why do you read it if it makes you sad?"

"It's not just the book ... it's the whole thing."

"What thing?"

I don't really know why I'm sad. It started in the museum while I was looking at those carvings. "What happened to the people, I guess. Not just the people, but also the land, the way it all changed."

"What happened is in the past. What's the sense of dwelling on that? Shouldn't you read something more ... useful for your homeschooling? Where are your math and science books? If this isn't working out, you can always go back to school. I can talk to the principal right now if you want."

"No! I'm working on it."

"Well, I'm still responsible for you and, right now, all I'm seeing is that you're filling your head with all sorts of nonsense instead of school work."

"What are you talking about?" And then I quickly add, "Never mind," because I already know what this is about. Going out with the dogs, hanging out with "that boy"—as if Barnabas carries some contagious disease.

"Never mind, never mind. You're just like your dad. Always dismissing what I have to say."

"What?" My dad? What's he got to do with it?

And then I remember something. Kitty and Dad arguing: "Never mind, just let it be." My dad. Who was he talking to? Me? Kitty? Why were they always yelling at each other?

"What was he like? Dad, I mean. I don't remember much."

"That's probably for the best."

"Why did he leave?"

"He didn't leave. We did."

"You told me ..."

"Yeah, well, you were five, Emmylou."

"I'm sixteen now."

"And I'm at work."

"You always have excuses.

"He doesn't give a shit about me or you, so why would you even bother?"

"Because ..." I say, but I don't have an answer. Because I want him to care about me, but at the same time, *I* don't want to care about *him*, because he's done nothing to deserve it.

"Okay, if you must know: he thinks he's the only one who's got the world figured out, and everyone who doesn't think like him is stupid. He's manipulative, controlling, and everything is just about him. Happy now?"

"Wow. And I'm just like him?"

"No, that's not what I said. Geez, Emmylou, don't always twist my words around. Can't we just talk like friends?"

You never listen, I want to say but I don't, because it wouldn't change a thing. I'd rather go and talk to Elisapii who doesn't speak English, or Lisa who is a stranger in a library, than try to have a conversation with Kitty.

"I'm going to see Barnabas."

"In this storm? You wouldn't even see a polar bear if it was sniffing your nose. You stay put. I'll bring you another hot chocolate."

I don't have the energy to put up a fight, nor do I really feel like going out in that storm. Kitty brings me another hot chocolate and a second bowl of cream. Both stay untouched. I'm just about to open my book when I overhear people at the next table talking.

"... thirty-three million dollars. What are they going to do with it?" a booming male voice asks. "Buy more booze?"

Uncomfortable laughter.

"No, seriously," the same voice continues, "the government built them houses and made sure they weren't starving, and what did them Indians do? Too lazy to work and spent all their government money on booze and beat their wives—that's what they did, I tell ya."

"Dennis ..." A woman's voice.

"Don't 'Dennis' me. I'm not ashamed of speaking the truth. It's my tax dollars that's gonna pay for it if it comes to that settlement, right, Hank?"

"I don't know, Dennis. I don't really know the whole story." Another male voice, then Dennis again.

"But I do. I lived here long enough to see it all. Squatters, that's what they were. And the government built them houses up by the cemetery and that wasn't good enough, so they built Dene Village, and were they happy? No, sir. They walked back into the forest where they came from and, thirty years later, they still want more money from the government and an apology. For what? For giving them free houses?"

I take my book and squeeze out from my booth. The woman who I think is his wife smiles apologetically at me, but I just throw her a dirty look.

Just then Kitty approaches the table and sets a golden beer with perfect white foam in front of the Dennis guy. "Enjoy," Kitty replies and nudges me with her elbow, while throwing me a dirty look. "The customer is king." She pats the guy on the shoulder, but I know the message is for me.

Back in my room, I flip through my new book but can't get back into it. I wish I could have said something to that guy, but I don't really know what he was talking about. A settlement for what happened to the Dene here in Churchill? What he said wasn't right, I know that, but I don't know how things were, so there was nothing I could say. Or was there?

Why would Kitty throw *me* a dirty look? Why do we always end up arguing about something? It's like going down a train track and you blink, and suddenly you're on a totally different track and, no matter what, it always ends with the train derailing. Like in the restaurant. We were talking about living in the Arctic a long time ago, and suddenly it's about my dad. Where's the thread here? I guess the only thing those two subjects have in common is that they both happened in the past. So both things shouldn't really matter today then, should they?

CHAPTER 13

The gas lantern shines a circle of light around the three of us huddled around the book. Barnabas and I sit on either side of Old Ipilii, who carefully turns the pages. Elisapii is sitting in the shadows in her usual spot on the bed.

"Tuktu," Old Ipilii says, tapping with his finger on a photograph of a stone caribou. His eyebrows wrinkle in worry while he rubs his belly. His hands gesture as he talks, reenacting the story for me.

"No tuktu," he says. It's the first time he's trying to talk to me without using Barnabas as translator.

The old man cradles an imaginary baby, imitating its cry, and I understand he is in his camp, the family out of food. He points at his rifle by the door, then holds his hands in front of his eyes adjusting imaginary binoculars. His shoulders slump. The hunters find no game? Old Ipilii motions up and down with his hand as if holding a stick or something.

"Iqaluk," he says, his hand flexing back and forth, moving like a fish in water. "Tukisiviit?" he asks.

I shrug my shoulders. I don't know what he's saying. He talks quickly in Inuktitut and Barnabas translates now. "The women, they try to catch fish, but is winter and the ice is thick. Fish in winter is starvation food, not much fat, but they try everything."

The old man nods and continues his story. Suddenly his eyes go big and the smile in his face makes his wrinkles look like rays of sunlight around his watery eyes.

"Takvatuqamiaq tuktutaqalilauqtuq nanimiaq." He holds his hands in front of the lantern and casts a shadow of a caribou onto the wall. One caribou after another runs along the wall and the old man lifts an imaginary rifle and begins shooting. He pauses and talks to Barnabas in a quiet voice.

Barnabas translates for me. "'Caribou are like ghosts,' my grandfather says, 'they come from nowhere, fill up the land, and disappear again.' That is an old saying, he says, old as the land that gave birth to the caribou."

Old Ipilii tells us stories, casting shadows on the wall. I find out that he was born in a tent in summer. His family camped near a Hudson's Bay Company post, way up north near a place called Iqaluit. He remembers a Brother but his name wasn't Volant. He was like a child, he says. Always watching, always learning. He was a good one, he says, as if there were other not so good ones—but I don't ask.

Old Ipilii tells us stories from way back when he was a little boy. He talks a lot about going hunting with his dad by dog team and setting fox traps, so they had furs to trade for flour and tea and rifles. He lived in an igloo for six winters, and then they moved to town, but they still built igloos when they went out hunting with the dogs.

I wish I could see what it looked like way back then. There were children and dogs everywhere; men went hunting, women gathered eggs and berries, and made clothing and looked after the children. At night, they huddled together in their tents or their igloos, warming the air with their breath.

When the gas lantern begins to flicker, the old woman sends Barnabas outside. I hear him rummaging in the freezer and he brings an ice cream pail to his grandmother. It's not ice cream, though.

"Seal blubber. The old way to make light," Barnabas explains.

His grandmother scrapes the oily blubber into a half-moon-shaped bowl that looks like it's made out of the same stone as the soapstone carvings. Barnabas passes her a pouch and she takes out fluffy white balls that look like cotton balls.

"What's that?" I ask.

"Arctic cotton. From the plant in summer, but you can use store-bought cotton, too," Barnabas explains, while Elisapii pulls the cotton apart, rubs seal oil on it and arranges it carefully along the edge of the soapstone lamp, using a stick that looks like it's specially made for it. She lights her wick and, after some fussing, little flames shine bright and warm, just in time before the gas lantern lets out its last hiss.

She tends to the wick and then finishes her sewing project—a pair of mitts, just like the ones Barnabas lends me when we go running dogs. She chews the leather of the finished mitts.

"Qaigit!" She waves me over and I sit on the bed next to her, careful not to tip the stone lamp. The old woman takes my hand and slips the mitt over it. She smiles her toothless smile when she sees how well it fits.

"You." She points at me.

"For me? Really? Thank you!" I want to hug her, but I am worried about spilling the oil lamp and setting the bed on fire.

"Pualuk," she says and points at the mitts.

"Pualuk?" I ask. "That means mitts?"

"Ii." She nods.

"Matna," I say. The only Inuktitut word I know. I stroke my new mitts while I try to imagine what life was like when the two old people were young.

"Did your grandpa have his own dog team when he was a boy?" I ask.

Barnabas shifts uncomfortably on the floor. Old Ipilii nods at Barnabas, waiting for his translation. Barnabas talks hesitantly, looking down at his feet. Old Ipilii's expression changes, the friendliness gone, his eyes distant and cool.

"My grandpa, he only went out with his dad for the first seven winters." Neither of them says any more. The silence becomes uncomfortable. The seal oil lamp begins to flicker and darkness surrounds me.

The night is clear and the cold has a mean bite to it. I'm glad for my new mitts. I don't like to walk in the dark. My thoughts get carried away and I see bears lurking in the shadows wherever I look. But when the old man told Barnabas to bring me home, I refused. I don't want to be a scared qallunaaq.

It's only a short walk across the train tracks and then I'm on the main street. Everyone leaves their doors unlocked, so if I see a bear, I just have to run to the nearest house. Besides, most of the bears have left town now. The sea ice is strong enough for them to go north along the bay. With the bears gone, the tourists have left. It's a lot quieter now. I only have to work the occasional shift and the people in Churchill seem to hibernate or migrate south. Just a few businesses are open daily now.

Before I cross the tracks, I look back to Barnabas's house. I see a dim light shining warmly through the dark. I imagine them getting ready for bed, all three crawling under the covers of that big bed that takes up nearly half the space of their cabin. I imagine them all cozy and snug, telling stories in the dark until they fall asleep. And then I imagine myself with Grandma Millie under one blanket and I feel warm and fuzzy inside. But then I try to picture Kitty there as well, and Dad—he would be there, too. But it feels strange—not cozy at all.

CHAPTER 14

"I've got something for you." Kitty puts a package of small pills onto the book pile on my bedside table. "Just in case."

I glance at the pills. Are those what I think they are? My stomach tightens. She has never even asked how I feel about Barnabas, or how he feels about me. So what is this? Because he's a boy and I'm a girl? Because I turned sixteen last month?

"Thanks, but no thanks." I say.

"If you won't stay away from that boy, you take those."

"Mom, it's not like that." A sick feeling rises in my stomach.

"He's a boy, Emmylou—all boys are like that."

I really feel sick now. It's not that I never kissed a boy before. Actually, just once, to be honest. His breath smelled like baloney sandwich and I remember the wet feeling in my mouth. I didn't get why all the girls in my class got so excited about this, but when he told me he was gonna show me something cool, I followed him. We went into an old run-down strip mall. The escalator wasn't working and we walked up the spiky metal stairs. There were no shops upstairs, just storefronts with broken glass. It smelled like pee and I had the feeling that I didn't really want to see what he had to show me. When he pulled me close and when his cold and clammy hands felt their way under my sweater, I pushed him away. "Keep your sticky fingers to yourself," I'd said and walked away, but I was still shaking when I got home.

Barnabas is not like that, or is he? Is that why he takes me out with the dogs? To have … no, he would have tried already, wouldn't he? Or maybe it's me? Maybe I should be interested in him more that way? Sexually, I mean. Maybe it's another thing that's not normal about me. Maybe I should … I can't even finish my own thought. It feels so wrong. All I want is to hang out and spend time with him and the dogs and his grandparents and … I don't know … listen to him talk, be quiet together, and enjoy going north with the dogs, each time a bit further, each time knowing it's just us and the dogs, and that's all we need in that moment. Is this not good enough? Should I take those pills? And then the sick feeling gets stronger and I shove those pills back at Kitty.

"I have no intention of taking my clothes off at minus-forty while bouncing along on a dog sled," I say, but it doesn't feel like me. The whole thing just feels wrong.

"Don't be smart. I want you to be back before dark from now on."

"Kitty! It gets dark at 4:30! That's just totally backward. I'm sixteen!"

"Exactly. I don't want you to make the same mistake I did."

I feel my stomach tighten as if someone had just kicked me. Mistake? That's what I am?

I grab my jacket and mitts and run down the stairs without another word. I always used to have an answer when fighting with Kitty, something smart to say, but what is there left to say if your mom just told you you're one big mistake?

CHAPTER 15

I'm late and the dogs are already hooked up. Old Ipilii is sitting on the qamutik, sipping steaming tea from a thermos. Nobody has seen me yet in the shadowy light of early dawn. The dogs are curled up, their noses tucked under their tails. Princess and Grumpy cuddle close to each other; Qakuq is sitting up, watching over the team. The dogs know we're going for a run, but they're not as crazy excited anymore. They've settled into a pleasant routine, waiting, relaxed until it's time to go. Even Qaqavii keeps his nose tucked under his tail. He doesn't look so puppyish anymore. The muscles around his shoulders are tight and bulging. He's strong and easily keeps up to the adult dogs.

Qaqavii is the first one to see me. He lifts his head and thumps his tail in the snow. The old man and Barnabas turn to see what he's looking at.

"Emmalu, I was wondering if you come. Cold, eh?"

Barnabas smiles at me. As always, I can see the gaps of his missing teeth. I love his smile, but today I can't look at him.

"You okay?"

"I'm fine," I say, but it's not how I feel. I've been looking forward to the weekend for so long. It's getting dark so early now, and it's so cold at night that we didn't train last Wednesday because of the weather. I miss him when I don't see him. And sometimes I do wonder what it would be like to kiss him, but I'm too scared of wrecking our friendship. What if he didn't like me that way and he wouldn't want to take me out again—or worse, what if he did like me and, for him, that means it leads to the other thing?

"My grandmother says to give you this," he says and passes me a furry bundle. "Is too cold today for quallunaat clothes."

I unfold Elisapii's bundle. There are two parkas: an inner caribou anorak and a windproof fabric shell with fur trim around the hood. I take my jacket off and slip Elisapii's clothes on. The fur is warm against my cheek, as if the dead animal still shares her warmth with me.

"What's the fur?" I ask.

"Wolf," Barnabas says.

I stroke the long coarse hair. A picture of a wolf comes up in my head and I feel the silly need to thank her.

"Ha-ii!" Old Ipilii calls and the dogs perk up their ears. Qakuq stands up, his line tight. And then everyone is standing, looking at us to make sure they heard right.

"Ha-ii," Barnabas repeats and the dogs lunge into their lines.

We bounce over the rough ice by the riverbank, and then the dogs follow their trail across the river, through the maze of jumbled ice and then up the peninsula on the other side. To my right are the ruins of Prince of Wales Fort. The cannons are still intact and, although I know they haven't been used for centuries, I feel uneasy every time we pass. The Hudson's Bay Company built the fort to fight off the French—or was it the other way round? All I remember is that when the other traders did come, they surrendered the fort right away, because there weren't enough people there to fight, which is a good thing, I guess. What I don't get is why they were preparing for war in the first place. I mean, they were all strangers in a country far away from their homes, so how could they fight over something that didn't belong to either of them? The more I learn about the history, the less I understand. To be honest, I don't even want to learn any more about the traders and explorers. What I do want to know is what was life like before they came?

It's only when we leave the fort behind and I see the wide expanse of Button Bay below us that my mind turns to the dogs and the land that stretches before us. The sun is rising across Button Bay, a small orange circle on the faraway horizon. The dogs' breath rises into the air like golden steam, but there's no warmth to the rays. We reach the spot where we saw the bears. There's no sign of either bear or dead seal.

The dogs are strong now and want to go further and further. Just like me, they seem to want to know what's behind the next rise. Old Ipilii drew me a map from memory of Hudson Bay between Churchill and Arviat, and Barnabas wrote all the river names along it. The Churchill River is the biggest river that flows into the bay. Sometimes it's impossible to get across. Where there's a trail one day, there's deep water the next day. It's got something to do with the tides or the cycle of the moon, but also with a dam they built further upriver. I'm not sure, but Old Ipilii knows.

Today, we're going across North Knife River, and maybe even as far as the Seal River. That's about thirty miles. Then we'll camp out for a few hours and run back. I'm glad for Elisapii's clothes. It's amazing how light the anorak is—"amauti," Barnabas calls it—and how warm. Its hood is big and more like a pouch. That's what all the women carry their babies in—or nieces and nephews and grandchildren. I'd love to see that.

In Arviat, you see it every day, Barnabas says. He talks lots about home now. About his little sisters and the baby twins. He calls them "big boy" and "bigger boy," because only his mother knows which one is which. He talks about his cousin, who is also his hunting partner when the caribou are passing by on their way south from their summer pastures way up north.

Next week, Barnabas and his grandparents will go home for Christmas. They'll only stay a few days because of Elisapii needing her treatment. Barnabas wanted to take the dogs, but Old Ipilii decided they should all fly with Elisapii. So I'm looking after the dogs. I'm really nervous, but also really proud that they trust me. I can even take them out running, they say, but I'm not sure I'll do that.

"Haala!" Old Ipilii calls and the dogs turn away from the boulder-strewn shore toward the bay. We run toward a huge pressure ridge, sheets of ice nearly two feet thick that are towering high above the frozen sea. It's impossible to imagine what forces lifted the ice and pushed it about, then left it turned up for the wind and drifting snow to shape into jumbled ice sculptures. Where the wind has polished the pushed-up ice, I can see seaweed frozen into the clear ice and I'm reminded that below me is an ocean still moving—rising and falling with the moon's pull.

"Haala!" There's an opening in the pressure ridge, just big enough for the team to slip to the other side, but the dogs don't see it. Old Ipilii grabs his whip and lets it crack on the left side of the team, herding the dogs right until Qakuq sees the gap. The fan moves close together and then Qakuq jumps. The other dogs follow his lead and, before I understand what's happening, our sled runs toward open water.

"Whoa!" I scream. Qakuq looks back, hesitating.

"Ha-ii! Ha-ii!" Barnabas and Old Ipilii yell and the dogs lunge into their lines, leaping across the open water. I see bottomless ocean as our sled bridges the gap.

"You nearly made us fall in the water," Barnabas says. "You can't stop when we cross a lead."

"Sorry," I say, still shaking. "That's why the sled is so long. It's like a bridge!" I say.

"More like a teeter-totter if you stop at the edge," Barnabas replies and grins at me. Not funny.

"Why is there open water?"

"From pressure of ice expanding and pulling apart. It will freeze soon again. But further out, away from the shore-fast ice, there's always cracks. Kind of dangerous out there, if you don't know what you are doing. Especially in spring, if you are near the floe-edge, is easy to get set adrift on an ice floe."

"Why do we go here, then?"

"Less rough, no?

Barnabas is right. It's smoother now, ahead of us just a

white expanse of flat, snow-covered ice. I listen to the rhythmic panting of the dogs and the tap-tap-tap of their feet. I take a deep breath and feel myself relax again.

The air tastes fresh and slightly seaweedy. It's cold enough to hurt my lungs, but it also feels good, like it's clearing out all the stale air that has been sitting inside me for too long. The sky always seems bigger out here, or maybe I feel smaller—either way, it all seems to fall into place, like this is the way it's meant to be.

"Qaqavii! Smarten up!" Barnabas's voice wakes me from my daydreaming. The sled suddenly skids sideways and then comes to a halt. The dogs are on slippery ice, crouching low. Qaqavii's legs are splayed out and he's shaking. Barnabas jumps off the sled and pulls Qaqavii up on his feet and gives him a slap with his mitt, but Old Ipilii doesn't seem to agree. After a short conversation, Barnabas unties the canvas bag with the Coleman stove and gets out the teapot. I get off the sled, but as soon as I step on the ice, I slip and hit the ground hard. I land next to Qaqavii, whose eyes are bulging out. He pants nervously. I rub my hip. That's going to be a bad bruise.

"Are we on the river?" It looks no different than the bay except the ice is slippery here, like a skating rink. Why are we camping here?

"Yes, we at North Knife River, first checkpoint in the race."

"We could go back there, where there was still snow." I slide on my bum back to the qamutik and carefully pull myself up.

Barnabas shakes his head. "Qaqavii, he never been on slippery ice like that. My grandfather wants him to learn."

Learn how? I want to ask, but I know better by now. Old Ipilii doesn't explain things much; you learn by watching. He chips river ice with his ax, puts it into the teakettle, and lights the stove. He doesn't so much as glance at Qaqavii who lies down, still shaking, still panting.

"Can I go to him?"

"Ataatatsiaq, Emmalu aktuqtulluaqpauk Qaqavii?"

"Nauk."

Barnabas shakes his head no.

"He's scared of the slippery ice," I protest, but Old Ipilii and Barnabas have their backs to me, sheltering the Coleman stove from the wind. I feel left out. There are days when Old Ipilii seems keen to show me things, but then there are times when he gets short with me and I can't figure out what I've done wrong. Sometimes I think it's something that happened a long time ago—like that night when I asked if he had his own dog team when he was a boy. But what does that have to do with me? I wasn't even born when he was a boy.

I sneak over to Qaqavii and he rolls over, so I can rub his belly.

"Hey, boy, it's okay. Just ice, see. If you're careful you can stand up." I try to roll him over and lift him onto his feet, but Qaqavii cowers, making himself heavier than he is.

"Come on, buddy." I try again and lift him off the ground, but he stiffens and refuses to put his feet on the ice.

"Emmalu, come have tea."

I shuffle over to them, inch by inch, and take the cup that Barnabas is holding out to me. It feels good to hang onto that old rusty tin cup. I can feel the heat through my new sealskin mitts. It's so cold outside that the steam of my cup rises into the air like smoke from a chimney. Old Ipilii's mitts are lying on the qamutik. Does he ever feel cold? I wonder whether you just don't feel the cold the same way, if you once lived in an igloo with only a seal-oil lamp to keep you warm.

"My grandfather tells me about one of the last times he went out with his dad. They had three young dogs in the team. All scared of the ice. But his dad wants them to be good dogs no matter what, so they take them to where the ice is very slippery, like here. Then they have tea and wait. The three young dogs, they don't move. My grandpa was impatient like you, so he starts walking around, looking for ptarmigans. He finds one and tries to shoot it with his slingshot, but he misses and the ptarmigan flies up to where the dogs are lying. When the dogs see the ptarmigan, they forget to be scared of the ice, and all three hunt after the ptarmigan. After that, they were good."

"You're teaching Qaqavii not to be scared of the ice," I say.

"Looks like you need some practice, too." Barnabas grins.

I reach over to give him a punch, but Barnabas runs away, taunting me with his big smile. I glance at Old Ipilii. He grins like a boy and nods in Barnabas's direction.

Go play, he seems to say. I chase after Barnabas. Don't think about it being slippery, I tell myself. To my surprise, I keep my balance. To Barnabas's surprise, too. I run into him at full speed. We tumble over and slide on the ice like curling rocks. And then we laugh so hard that I don't notice Qaqavii joining us until I feel his slobbery tongue licking my ear. I try to push him off, but Barnabas holds my arms down and I can't defend myself from Qaqavii's face wash. I scream and Barnabas lets go of me.

"You sound like my little sister," he teases me.

"I bet she hates her big brother," I tease back.

We both smile and I feel my face flush, so I quickly change the subject.

"The story your grandpa told us ... you said it was one of the last times he went out with his dad with the dogs. What happened after?"

"What happened was not good."

And then he says no more. I think about the book I was supposed to pick up from the library. *Night Spirits*. I get the eerie feeling that Dene Village isn't the only place with ghosts.

CHAPTER 16

The Northern Lights are dancing bright tonight, changing colors from green to red to white. I'm lying on my back on Qaqavii's dog house. It's Christmas, and Barnabas and his grandparents are in Arviat. Kitty knows I'm with the dogs. She gets that I need to come here and feed them, but I didn't tell her that it actually doesn't take that long to throw them each a chunk of meat.

I watch as an arc of faintly flickering green becomes more and more intense in color, spiraling across the sky until the edges turn a bright red.

"These are our ancestors playing soccer in the sky with a big walrus skull," Barnabas had told me. I'm not sure if he was pulling my leg, but the longer I look at the Aurora, the more I like the idea of the dead being up there in the sky, watching us and lighting up the sky with their play.

"Hello, Grandma Millie," I say into the night and then feel stupid because Grandma Millie wouldn't play soccer with a walrus skull. Or would she? I wonder if all our ancestors are in the same sky. If not, what would happen—let's say—if Barnabas and I were to die? He would go to his ancestors in the sky and I—where would I go?

I suddenly feel sad without knowing why. I climb off the doghouse.

"Hey, Qaqavii, where will you go when you die?" I ask.

Qaqavii wags his tail and licks my face as if he's never thought of the question. Most of the time, I try not to think about dying, but sometimes I can't help it. If one day we all have to die, then why does it matter what we do while we're alive?

I recall the night when I was going to run away and how Qakuq had made me miss my train, and I wonder if this was all just a coincidence—or maybe meant to be.

Only two months ago, I couldn't wait to get out of here, and now it makes me sad to think of leaving. Of not being with the dogs, not running north under the endless sky, not sitting with Elisapii and feeling the warmth of her bony hand resting on mine, not listening to Old Ipilii's low and guttural voice telling us stories, and Barnabas's smile with his missing teeth as he translates and teases me.

Qaqavii whines and paws my parka.

"I will miss you, too. Most of all." I play with his ears,

while he rests his paw on my knee. It's like all my life the list of people and things I miss just gets longer. Most of all, I miss my grandma, Dad and Mom, and me being a real family—a family like Barnabas's family, with a mom who wants him and grandparents who are alive.

I remember a Christmas at Grandma Millie's—probably the last one. She'd put a curtain up between the kitchen and the living room and I wasn't allowed to peek through, so I wouldn't disturb Santa bringing the presents. I did peek and I saw Grandma Millie under the tree. She insisted she was just making sure Santa had a cookie and a glass of milk, but I was sure I'd caught her peeking. In the end, Santa did deliver lots of presents, and Grandma Millie played piano and sang carols until I fell asleep on my dad's lap, Silly in one arm and my new doll in the other.

Late at night, I was woken up by noises. Something hitting the wall, yelling, glass breaking. When I went to see what was happening, Dad brought me back to bed, telling me I'd just had a bad dream. I still remember his smell, a mix of peppermint and rotten onion. For some reason I always thought that's what bears smelled like. What if he was a bear, a predator lying in wait for its prey? Like Santa Claus was Grandma Millie and the happy memories nothing but an illusion?

Qaqavii nudges me and then lifts his nose toward the sky. A quiet, mournful howl escapes. The other dogs pick it up and soon they all howl, sad and beautiful, and a bit off key.

Above us, the Northern Lights' spiral unwinds, forming a river in the sky, tumbling north toward Seahorse Gully. The lights near us fade, becoming brighter on the other side of the river. I suddenly have the urge to follow them. What if I took the dogs for a run? My heart starts pounding like crazy.

I run to the house to pick up the harnesses before I can change my mind. I drag the qamutik down to the river. It's hard to move, like the cold has turned the snow into sandpaper.

I harness the two big white dogs, Qakuq and Grumpy, first, because that's what Barnabas always does. I take one at a time and clip them to their lines. They sit nearly motionless, but when I shine the light of my headlamp on them, I can see that Qakuq is trembling. Is he excited—or nervous like me?

When I hook up Aupaluk, his trace tangles around the other lines that I laid out so carefully. I untangle them and take half the lines off. Better not to take all ten dogs—I'd rather go slow. Pamiuluk is so excited that she keeps running around and around on her chain. She won't stop and I don't know how to catch her, so I go over to old Taqluk instead. He lies in his house as if he hasn't even noticed the commotion around him, but when I step into his circle, harness in hand, he darts out of his house and runs to the end of his chain, where he waits patiently for me to slip the harness over his head.

"Good boy, yes, you are," I say and he rubs his head against my legs until I give him a scratch behind the ears. When we walk to the sled, I don't even have to lift him off his feet. He just walks next to me as if he's done this a million times—which he has, I guess.

I need one more. Qaqavii is jumping at the end of his chain. He propels his whole body into the air as high as he can, lunging forward at the same time until he reaches the end of the chain, which stops him for a second in mid-air before he falls back to the ground. Then he does it all over again. Maybe I should take one of the more experienced dogs? Princess is small and easy to handle.

"You stay home, okay? Maybe next time," I tell Qaqavii as I walk by his circle.

Qaqavii's howl is so heartbreaking that I change my mind.

As soon as he's hooked up with the other four dogs, he runs to Aupaluk and licks his face. Aupaluk snaps at him.

"Quit it! Both of you!"

Qaqavii crouches down.

"That's better. You're a big dog now, remember? No more licking faces, okay?"

I pull the snow hook. "Let's go."

The four adult dogs take off at full speed. Qaqavii doesn't move.

"Qaqavii! Ha-ii!" I try in Inuktitut.

He scurries to his feet, catching up and regaining his confidence in the run.

In the light of the headlamp, I clearly see the dogs closest to the sled, but Qakuq and Grumpy fade out into the shadows. Darkness is hiding whatever dangers might be close.

I remember Barnabas telling me to shut my light off so I could see the stars better. I switch my headlamp off. The dogs turn into shadows dark as the night. I resist the urge to switch the light back on.

I'm so scared that I almost feel sick. Scared of doing something wrong with the dogs, but even more scared of the darkness, of the things I can't see. Didn't Barnabas say they never run at night? I shudder at the thought of running into a polar bear.

And yet, there's another feeling that's even stronger. As if my fear has woken it up, the feeling of wanting to live. It's like nothing else matters—trying to figure out how to fit in, to find out what I want, what Kitty wants, what the homeschooling office wants, what Barnabas and his grandfather think of me, what the librarian thinks of me, what I think of me. All that doesn't matter. What matters are those five dogs ahead of me and that we stay together. That's all.

We run into the night; Seahorse Gully is ahead, the town behind—and I'm in between.

Despite the dark, I can make out all the dogs, their backs arched, their paws moving swiftly. I can even see bits and pieces of the jumble ice close by so I can brace myself for the jerks.

There is no moon. The only light comes from the Aurora dancing high above. The dogs strain their lines as they pull me uphill into the Gully.

"Keep going! Pick it up," I jump off the sled and run next to them. With my weight gone the dogs pass me quickly, and then the qamutik is ahead of me. I sprint as fast as I can and throw myself forward grabbing onto the last crosspiece before it's out of reach. The team comes to a sudden halt.

I lie panting in the snow behind the sled.

"Whoa," I gasp. "Ha … ha … have … a break." I'm not sure if the dogs need one, but I sure do. I pull myself onto the sled and then roll over onto my back so I can look at the sky. The Northern Lights are faint, but the stars are shining bright. I try to find the Big Dipper, the only constellation I know. There are so many stars that I get confused.

Old Ipilii said that his dad taught him how to navigate by the stars, and even tell time during the darkest time of the year, when the sun would only linger near the horizon for a few short hours. There are two stars that always shine brightest just before twilight, so hunters could get ready in the dark, taking advantage of the little light they had during their hunt.

A tiny flame shoots across the sky. A shooting star! Make a wish! I try to think of what to wish for, but I all I want right now is to just lie here.

A low growl suddenly pulls me out of my sleep. I sit up. My teeth are chattering. I'm cold. Really cold. Did I fall asleep while I was gazing at the stars? The snow has an eerie green tinge to it. The Northern Lights are right above us, dancing fast, changing colors, spiraling around me until I feel dizzy.

And then I hear a crackling sound like a radio trying to pick up a signal. And then a whistle—like the sound of the wind only more human. Taqluk growls louder, low and guttural. The Northern Lights answer with a laugh. Distant, barely hearable, but undeniably there. People laughing. Lots of them. A beckoning sound that makes the hair on my neck stand up. There are voices, murmuring, hissing, mocking. And then I hear dogs howling, but they are not mine. The lights are so close I swear I could touch them, flickering angrily. What is happening? I suddenly long to be back inside, where it's warm and light and noisy. And it's like the dogs read my mind. They suddenly bolt past me, swinging the sled around.

We run back across the river and, when I dare turning around, the Northern Lights have faded into a green haze hovering above Seahorse Gully.

CHAPTER 17

Kitty hasn't seen me yet. She's flopped on a wooden bench next to the kitchen door. Her face is illuminated—red, green, red—in rhythm with the blinking lights from the fake Christmas tree. Christmas carols are blaring from loudspeakers in competition with the tourists yelling merrily over each other's voices.

"Mom!" I wave to her, but my voice is swallowed by the flurry of background noise. Kitty's black dress has slipped, exposing her boney shoulder. She has stripped her dress shoes off, her left big toe red and swollen.

"Hey, Mom!"

Kitty straightens her dress and makes room for me to sit next to her.

"Emmylou, you're back. Are you okay? You were gone for an awful long time. Did you feed the dogs? Gosh, you feel cold." Kitty presses her warm hand against my cheek. I wish she would put the other one against my other cheek, warm me up from outside in. I lean against her shoulder and close my eyes against the blinking party lights.

"Grandma Millie always had real candles on her tree, didn't she?" I ask.

"I don't ... yes, I think so. You remember that?"

"I remember the matchbox with the really long matches. And I was allowed to light the bottom ones, the ones I could reach."

Kitty lays her arm around me. "I miss her."

"Grandma Millie?" I look at Kitty, surprised. She never really talks about her. Or Dad. Or her feelings, period.

"I don't miss the fights, but she was a place where I could always go to. She was home, in a way."

"And now we're homeless." Both of us.

"I wouldn't go that far. Plus, you got me," Kitty says.

I feel it's wiser not to respond. Too easy to escalate into an argument, and that's the last thing I want.

Suddenly Kitty laughs out loud. "Do you remember Toby peeing on the Christmas tree?"

"What? No!"

"He had his favorite tree in Grandma's yard that he peed

on, but one day she cut it down for her Christmas tree, so I guess Toby figured we'd given him an indoor toilet for Christmas." Kitty laughs and her laughter is contagious.

"Funny you don't remember that. You and Toby were always so close."

"I remember Toby but not after Dad left."

"No. Toby went with him."

"How come he took the dog but not me?" As soon as I ask the question, I know how stupid it is.

"I wouldn't let him—that's why."

Kitty slips her feet back into her shoes, and I know that this conversation is over.

"Mom. Did he do anything … to you? Or us?"

"We split, Emmylou. And it wasn't pretty, but that's all there is."

"Why did he never phone me or send me a Christmas gift?"

Kitty shifts her weight, as if the bench had suddenly become unbearably uncomfortable.

"I better help Marie—it's been a busy night." Kitty stands up and walks away, but then she stops and turns. "How long do you have to feed their dogs?"

"Why?"

"Geez, Emmylou, can't I ask you a question?"

With Kitty, it's never just a question.

"Until they're back," I say sharply.

"Don't be smart."

"They said sometime later this week."

Kitty nods and turns her back to me.

"What if I don't want to leave?" I call before she's out of reach.

"What did you say?"

"I don't want to leave," I repeat.

"Who said we were going to leave?"

"We always leave. I didn't want to leave Maya and now I don't want to leave ..." Leave what? With Maya, that's easy. She was my friend. But it's not the same with Barnabas. I mean, he's my friend, too, but it's different. There's more than that. I mean, not like the girlfriend/boyfriend thing, although sometimes I wonder ... no, I don't, not really. What I mean is, with Maya, it was about having fun and doing girl things.

I want to keep going north with the dogs, further and further into that barren land. Every time I go, it feels less barren. Like Seahorse Gully. At first it was like any other place out there, but then Barnabas told me about the Tuniit, and then I thought about them every time we went by, wondering if I could find the stone circles come summer and the snow is all gone.

MIRIAM KÖRNER

And now the Northern Lights, coming so close and whispering to me. I'm not sure if I'll ever tell anyone about that, because maybe it was just my imagination, but I know I will remember it from now on, every time I pass by the top of the hill.

I want to tell Kitty about what it felt like, taking the dogs for a run all by myself, but I don't know how to explain it so she would understand. If I think about it now, it's not such a big deal anymore, because what happened, what really happened, was only on the inside, invisible. No, not invisible, because I can just about see it.

CHAPTER 18

With Barnabas and his grandparents still in Arviat, I'm spending more time in the library. Lisa is visiting family in Winnipeg, and that's just as well. I'm behind in all my assignments and I know she'd give me a hard time—in a good way, but still, it doesn't alter the fact that my progress report is due, though there's no progress to show.

I got sidetracked, reading the book Lisa had ordered for me about the story of the Sayisi Dene relocations and, since then, I have a real hard time writing about the history of Cape Merry and the fort and all that. All I see now is the beach down by the Cape where the Dene people were dropped off after they'd been taken away from their homeland. Two hundred and fifty people were just left there on the beach, with winter on the doorstep and nowhere to go.

And all because some government officials visited Duck Lake, and the Dene had just had their fall caribou hunt, and they

MIRIAM KÖRNER

left the dead caribou on the shore to freeze for winter, when they would need them—like they had always done. Except this time, some lady took a picture of it, and Natural Resources thought they'd found the reason for the caribou decline—which in the end wasn't really a decline, just the natural cycle of the caribou. The thing I don't get is, if you look real close at the picture, there aren't that many fresh carcasses, really. There's a lot of old antlers and bones and rocks you could mistake for dead caribou, but surely the government would see that, wouldn't it?

But they loaded all the people and their dogs into a plane and flew them to Churchill, and now the people were nearly starving and freezing to death, because they had to leave their log cabins and tents and dog sleds and everything behind. Besides, they were inland people and didn't really know how to hunt animals of the sea. They sent them to North Knife River by boat, but there wasn't enough food or shelter, so they had no choice but to walk back to Churchill.

And then finally, the government built them houses, and you'd think that would be a relief, but the houses were just shacks and hard to keep warm, and they were built next to the cemetery, even though the Dene would never live in the same place people buried the dead if they had a choice. I mean, if they had a choice, they wouldn't have lived in Churchill at all, because it wasn't their home and there was nothing for them to do.

All along, people were dying, and then things went from bad to worse because the adults started drinking, and then bad things happened to the children—the girls, especially, and the women, too—and then I put the book away because I couldn't bear all the sadness and despair.

But I can't stop thinking about it, so I go back to the cemetery, looking for where Camp 10 used to be. There's nothing there, nothing visible, but the whole time I walk between the ocean and the cemetery, the hair on my neck is standing up. I look for the old woman, but the cemetery is deserted. An icy wind is blowing and snowdrifts are forming around the gravestones and crosses.

I go back to the monument. The faded petals of a plastic flower stick out of the snow. I unbury it and place it on top, but the wind wants to grab it and hurl it away, so I have no choice but to bury it again.

My eyes drift over the names on the plaques. And then my heart starts beating like crazy. I know that name and that one, too. From the book, *Night Spirits*. And suddenly I feel really sick, almost throwing-up sick, because it's not just some book about history, it's real and it's here, and I wonder if the old woman is that little girl in the book who found her mother frozen to death, or the one whose family died in a house fire. And I wonder, what would I say to her if I saw her again? I feel my palms getting sweaty at the thought of it and I quickly walk away.

★

"Emmylou, how many times do I have to ask you to switch off that darn light?"

"Hm?" I use my finger as a bookmark and look at Kitty. "Were you talking to me?"

Kitty sighs, loud and theatrically, but it doesn't get a rise out me. I'm at the part in the book where they finally moved the Sayisi Dene away from Camp 10 by the cemetery and into new houses at Dene Village, and for a split second, I have the hope that things are turning out to be okay in the end. But they don't. The alcohol and violence and despair moves with them—now just out of sight of the townspeople. I think of the guy at the restaurant a while back, the one who said such bad things about the people. I wish I knew then what I know now and I would have told him …

"Emmylou! Don't make me ask you again! I have to work tomorrow morning, and you know very well I can't sleep with lights on. Put that book away."

I switch the light off and cuddle into my warm blankets,

but I can't help thinking about the girls hiding under the houses to get away from the drunk adults in their homes and the men preying on them. And then I hear voices outside my window, men's voices, loud, obnoxious, slurry. Then the sound of glass breaking and laughter.

My heart starts beating like crazy and my breathing is going too fast. *You're safe, Emmylou—don't be ridiculous,* I tell myself. I listen for footsteps in the hallway, and when I hear squeaking on the stairs—the top one, it's always the top one—I press my hand over my mouth to stifle a scream. I resist the urge to switch the light on, and instead feel my way over to Kitty's bed in the dark. I carefully lift her blanket and crawl under the covers with her. I'm lying stiffly on the edge, hoping not to fall out.

"Emmylou?" Kitty whispers and then skootches over, making room for me, and then we both lie in the dark, listening to each other's breathing. I cuddle against her shoulder, grateful that I have warm blankets and a mother who doesn't drink, and a place where I'm safe at night. I can't imagine what it would be like to be taken from the place where you belong. I try to picture the children at Duck Lake before the plane came and picked them up, but my mind draws a blank.

I never had a place where I belonged.

CHAPTER 19

It's mid-January. Barnabas and his grandparents should have been back two weeks ago. I don't know what's keeping them. Barnabas left a message for me at the Sleepy Bear Lodge, letting me know they'll be back later, but he didn't say why or when. I've run the dogs three more times since that Christmas night. To keep them in shape, but also because I love being out there with them.

The freezer with the dog food is just about empty now. It's hard to get the last seal meat out. It's frozen to the bottom of the freezer, and I have to lean over and carefully bang the meat loose with the blunt side of the ax. Yesterday, I went to the Northern Store to buy commercial dog food. It's $68.95 per bag and that was the cheapest. I could only afford to buy one bag, so Kitty chipped in and bought a second bag. Of course, it came with a condition attached.

"If I'm feeding my money to the dogs, at least I want to see them," she said.

So today, Kitty and I both walk down to the dog yard. It's minus thirty-seven. Too cold to be comfortable, even in Elisapii's anorak. I pull my hood tighter around my face against the wind and against Kitty's running commentary.

"Really, Emmylou, I don't get what draws you to this place. I know we didn't always have the fanciest of apartments, but we managed. So what kind of people live here? They don't want to work, or what? Look at this crap lying around. Who needs a car with three tires? Can't they fix it or get rid of it? What do people do all day here?"

I walk faster, pretending I can't hear her. But I do, and all the cool stuff that's lying around waiting for someone to do something useful with it suddenly doesn't look so cool anymore. The tires, stacked three high, that in summer must be planters for tomatoes, look like old ugly tires now; brown, dead plants are still tied to the wire support. The fire pit surrounded by a circle of three-legged chairs, milk crates, and even a couch, looks uninviting, as if those seats were not meant for me. And now I'm mad. Mad that she can do that to me, change the way I see things.

"I don't know what kind of people live here," I snap at her. "Most of them I just see passing by in their trucks, except Barnabas's family. And if they'd had a choice, they'd rather not be here, because they have a home in Arviat and their family is there. But they don't have a hospital that can provide Elisapii with what she needs to live. If she could, she'd rather be home, eating country food, and not having to deal with people like you looking down on them."

"That last bit was uncalled for. I didn't know why they were here and you never told me, so ..."

"... so you just make up your own story?"

"Of course not. I just see what's right in front of my eyes and that's pretty obvious."

"What's obvious?"

"Clearly you don't know their whole story. This is Canada, Emmylou, and you can't tell me that people that need medical care have to live in a shack. There's something wrong with that picture."

There *is* something wrong with that picture, but not with Barnabas's family—that much I know for sure.

We're close to the dog yard now, and I'm waiting to hear the sound of chains rattling as the dogs crawl out of their houses to welcome me. But it's quiet. The dogs are curled up in the back of their houses.

"Hey, doggies!" I call. Qaqavii scuttles out of his house and throws his paws on my chest. I hug him and ruffle his fur. Then the other dogs come out, slower than usual, their eyebrows and whiskers frosty. Qakuq yawns and Princess stretches. Pamiuluk wags her stumpy tail and Aupaluk rubs his frosty face with his paw.

"Don't they ever let them inside? Not even in this cold?"

"Look at their coats," I say, tousling Qaqavii's fur with my mitts. His guard hair is long and coarse, and underneath is the fine downy hair of his under coat. But now I'm not so sure anymore. They were kind of hesitant to come out of their houses, weren't they? Qaqavii leans into me and I give him a good rub, until dog hair is clinging all over my mitts and pants.

"Are you cold?" I ask. Qaqavii wags his tail, but I'm not sure if that's a yes or no. I wish Old Ipilii was here. He'd know. He'd tell me that that's how they used to live, ever since he can remember.

How does Kitty always manage to do that? Make me question everything I do? I always feel like I fail some sort of test, except she never tells me the question.

"They're fine," I say through gritted teeth. Qaqavii rolls over in the snow, exposing his soft belly. "What? You want a belly rub now?" He looks so cute, looking at me with his big brown eyes, stretching a paw out for more belly rubs. I feel my anger at Kitty slowly dissipate.

"This is Qaqavii," I say to Kitty. Qaqavii wags his tail and scoots over to her. "You can pet him."

Kitty steps out of reach before the dog is even near her. "Do they ever wash them? Or at least groom them?"

"Geez, Kitty! Just ... let it be, okay? The dogs don't care how they smell! Actually, they do. They roll in stuff *they* think smells great, and I can tell you it's not your strawberry-scented shampoo."

"Don't treat me like I'm stupid, Emmylou. I'm not saying to use shampoo. More like the flea stuff, you know ..."

"They don't have fleas! It's too cold here for fleas, but go ahead, Kitty. Give them a bath if that makes you feel better. You can use my towel." I stomp away and get the harnesses. I didn't have any intention of running dogs, not in this cold, but I'd rather be in a deepfreeze with my dogs than getting heated up about Kitty's stupid comments.

When the dogs see the harnesses, they perk up their ears and pace around their circles. Taqluk whines with excitement. If they're keen to go, it can't be too cold for them, can it? But I'm cold.

I warm my hands under Qaqavii's armpits. He licks my face and I quickly wipe his saliva off before it freezes on my skin.

"Do you really have to go out in that cold, Emmylou?"

I don't answer. Kitty follows me back and forth as I hook up the dogs. She's hugging herself tight now, rubbing her arms, wiggling her toes.

"Watch out, Kitty. You're gonna get tangled in the lines."

Kitty moves out of the way. She's not saying anything anymore. I know how she feels. If it's cold like that, you don't want to talk, don't want to let all that warm breath escape.

"I can do this on my own. I don't need you."

"I know. But I want to see you leave, at least." Kitty pulls her scarf over her mouth and nose.

By the time I hook up the last dog, the others are all curled up in one big ball, huddling together for warmth.

"Shall we?" I ask. The dogs don't move, which is for the better anyway. Because I still need to pee. I don't know why, but it happens every time, when all the dogs are hooked up and we're ready to go. It's become a ritual now. Just before we go for a run, I quickly squat down amongst the dogs, hoping no human will see me, and then Qakuq will pee on the same spot as soon as I'm done, and then, flinging yellow snow into the air, he'll scratch up our pee spot. It's embarrassing, but what's even more embarrassing is that I'm not even grossed out anymore. At night I sniff my clothes and I like that they smell of dog.

Today is different, though, with Kitty being here.

"Can you sit on the sled and put your foot on the snow hook, so they can't pull it out?"

"What? Why?"

"I need to pee."

"Now? Why didn't you do it back at the lodge? Where would you even go? Do these people even have toilets? Don't tell me you're going to sit on a frozen outhouse seat?"

"Never mind." I stomp the snow hook in and walk to the front of the team. They don't look as if they're going to take off without me today, but I'd rather not take a risk. So I pee right in front of them and Kitty.

"Emmylou! Don't you have any self-respect? What's wrong with you?"

"What's wrong? I needed to pee, Kitty! What can possibly be wrong with that?" I stomp back to the sled. My fingers hurt from the short time it took me to unzip my pants. I fumble with the zipper, holding my mitts with my teeth.

"Ha-ii," I call, the moment I'm back on the sled, pulling out the snow hook. Qakuq stands up, and then they all throw their weight into their harnesses and we lunge forward. I rub my mitts together as fast as I can. My hands hurt badly now, but the last thing I want to do is turn around.

Usually, the dogs never listen in that first mile, mile and a half. It's like their need to run just overwhelms their minds in those first few minutes. All their energy is focused on one thing: Run. I dread those minutes. It's like I'm not even there.

That's when the dogs run wild, like they're driven by an ancient instinct to run in a pack, just for the joy of it. I'm not in control and the dogs know it. Later, when they settle down and listen to my commands, I feel we're a team, we're working together, but those first few minutes remind me they only accept me as their leader because they want to.

Today is different, though. They settle right into their even-paced trot, as if they know, on a day like today, being out on the land does not allow for mindless mistakes. My focus is with the dogs now. Kitty and my anger stay further and further behind.

It feels good to leave the town behind. Not just because of Kitty. It's also because of that book I read. I have a hard time not thinking about what happened in Churchill. Every time a tourist leaves half his dinner on a plate, I want to yell at him, "Don't you know that only forty years ago, there were children here who had to scrounge food out of the dump?"

The other day, a guest complained about his room being too small, and I had to bite my tongue not to say, "Try living with ten people in it for a bit and it won't feel so small after that." But then I felt all hypocritical, because that had been my first thought when I saw my room. Too small to share it with Kitty, and certainly I would not like to share it with a bunch of other people.

I take a deep breath. The cold air stings, but in a good way.

Everything looks different in the cold, quieter. There are sundogs around the sun today. I saw them last winter in Calgary, but it's nothing compared to what I'm seeing now. The sun has a halo around it in a big glittering circle, and two sundogs on either side cast their light into the sky. There's no warmth from any of the three suns, just this strange and beautiful light. Mysterious and magical, even though I'm sure some scientist would have some logical explanation.

The sky looks bigger today. It's a pale yellow near the horizon but, higher up, it turns into a faint blue, almost as if you could see past the sun into the night sky. The air prickles in my nose, freezing the tiny hairs inside. The dogs' fur is frosty, and the ice crystals catch the light of the rising sun. Everything is still, like life itself is holding its breath. And yet, it's hauntingly beautiful, the stillness, the light.

The river flooded a couple days ago and the new ice is slick as a skating rink.

Qaqavii runs with the other dogs like he's never been afraid of slippery ice. The only one who is afraid is me. The dogs run full speed and the sled skids sideways. I try to slow them down with my hook, but it won't hold. I am scarily out of control.

Finally, we reach the other side. There's enough snow here to stop the team. We take a break, and Taqluk bites snowballs off from between his paws. The rest just look at me, waiting for my command to get going again. Not even Qaqavii is rolling in the snow.

"Let's go then!" I call. The dogs always understand *that* command. It doesn't matter what I say: "Ha-ii," "let's go," "shall we?" It's the slowing down or stopping that's a lot harder to teach.

I scan the bay for polar bears. All clear. I'm relieved but also a little bit disappointed, because there was something so powerful about the bears we saw, something ancient that awoke something ancient in me: the feeling of not being on top of the food chain, of simply being part of nature's law of survival of the fittest.

I wonder what it felt like for the Sayisi Dene when they finally made it back to the land after seventeen years living in Churchill. I try to picture them on their way north. They would have come by here, where I am now, and then gone up that river where Qaqavii and I learned to run on slippery ice. North Knife River.

And from there they went west, to search for a place where the caribou would pass and where they could rebuild their community. They found that place at Tadoule Lake, surrounded by sandy eskers and beautiful beaches.

I feel lighter now, hopeful even. And although it's bitter cold, and the hair in my nose is all prickly, and I have to keep rubbing my cheeks, I feel more comforted than I was under my blanket the other night. I take another deep breath and all the dark and heavy feelings slip away, and I'm just in the here and now—just me and my dogs under a vast Arctic sky.

I watch the dogs running, making sure they're not tangled or limping. I watch the sky for changes in the weather. I watch myself, making sure I'm warm. I watch for gray snow revealing unsafe ice and for tracks in the snow revealing bears nearby. And I watch the sun telling me how much daylight I have left.

Then, suddenly, the sled jerks, and the dogs turn and pick up speed. A little white animal scurries behind a rock. A rabbit! What's he doing out here on a cold day like this? The dogs chase him out of his hiding spot; the rabbit zigzags across the tundra, the dogs in pursuit.

"Whoa," I yell, and then I try to imitate the guttural sound that Old Ipilii and Barnabas use. "Wooh! Wrrah!"—almost like a dog growling. Too late! We hit a rock so hard that the dogs are stopped dead in their tracks. At the same time, I hear a loud cracking sound. The sled is wedged onto a rock.

I drag the qamutik off the rock and untie the caribou skins, so I can see the damage. Two crosspieces stick into the air like broken ribs. What now? Maybe I can just take the two broken pieces out? I try to pry one of the crosspieces loose, but it's hard to get out because of the notches in them that hold the rope that ties everything together. That's when I realize, if I did pull those pieces out, the whole sled would fall apart. I need to tie the broken pieces together, but with what?

What would they have done in the olden days if this happened? I remember seeing a historic picture of a sled made from caribou antlers and whalebones and walrus tusks. But that doesn't help. Where would I get any of those things? Wait! I know where there's a caribou antler. We went by one just past Button Bay where the trail goes back onto the land. They're scattered all over, Old Ipilii said. Left behind when the caribou shed their antlers or after a hunt. I've only seen one—it wasn't big but it will do. For a second, I'm all excited, but then I realize how stupid that idea is. It's way too far to walk there, and I'm not even sure I could find it again. Plus, I can't leave the dogs. I just need something to hold the pieces together, so they can't drag in the snow. Maybe the caribou skins will work? I hold the pieces in place and wrap the caribou skins tightly around them. Then I use a spare tug line rope to tie everything together. That'll work.

I turn the dogs around and when we run back, I realize it's not as calm as I thought. An icy breeze bites my cheeks and, no matter how much I rub them with the backside of my mitt, I'm losing the battle with the deadly cold. I slip my mitt off so that

I can rub warmth back into my cheeks, until my fingertips hurt.

"Let's go, puppies! Hurry, hurry, hurry!" I try to sound as encouraging as I can, but it's hard when the air bites you inside your lungs every time you open your mouth. Nevertheless the dogs understand. They pull faster and the air feels even colder.

I can see someone in the dog yard, walking toward the river now. Did Kitty wait for me? Is Barnabas back? I wave and the person waves back, slowly raising his hand just once. Old Ipilii!

The dogs see him now, too. They pick up even more speed. We run toward the old man, the fan splits and half the dogs are on Old Ipilii's left, the other on his right.

"Whoa!" I yell.

Old Ipilii jumps over the tug lines as if they were skipping ropes.

"Whoa! Wooh! I mean it!"

The dogs stop and crouch down.

"I'm so sorry. It's not like that all the time." I'm mad at the dogs but, even more, I'm mad at myself for nearly running over the old man with his own dogs.

"Ii." Old Ipilii says, but I don't think he understood.

"I ... uhmm ... I broke your sled," I say and glance at the makeshift fix.

"Ii." He rests his arm briefly on my shoulder. "Pitsiatutit.

Qimmiit illingnik naalaktut," he says, and smiles. "Qimmiujatuluatuq, taimana taitarnialiqtagiit."

Something tells me that he's proud of me, but there's nothing to be proud of. Didn't he see I broke his sled? Old Ipilii turns to his dogs. The dogs crowd around him, wagging their tails and sniffing his legs. He strokes over their sides feeling their ribs. Then he turns to me with a big smile.

"Good," he says. "Qimmiit good!"

Without saying any more, we unharness the dogs and tie them back in their houses.

"Where is Barnabas? Is he here?" I ask.

Old Ipilii shakes his head. "Barnabas Arviamiituq."

"Barnabas stayed in Arviat?" Does this mean we won't run the dogs together anymore? Isn't he going to race with his grandpa? I thought that was what this was all about. Getting the dogs ready for the race. I thought we were a team, Barnabas, Old Ipilii, the dogs, and me.

"Barnabas qaigianiatuq maqaitinik piqatiqarluni Arviamiutanik. Kuugjualianiaqtuq skidoo-kuut." The old man grips the air as if holding a handlebar. "Vroom, vroom."

"Snow machine?" I ask.

"Ii." Old Ipilii points northeast across the river, showing me the shadow-hand figure for caribou.

I shrug my shoulders. "I don't understand."

"Barnabas," he says. And then he imitates shooting a gun.

"He's ... dead? No!" I shake my head in disbelief.

The old man nods. "Tutusiamiat. Tuktu."

"Caribou?"

"Ii."

"I don't understand! Elisapii? Is she here?" I ask.

The old man points to the house.

Elisapii is lying on her bed. She's pale, almost gray, like she's slowly fading away. She smiles when she sees me and sits up in her bed, but I can tell it takes a lot of energy.

"Emmylou, qanuipit? How are you?"

She sounds tired, her voice is raspy as if speaking pains her. I rearrange the pillows behind her. "I'm good. You?"

"Good, good," she smiles weakly.

"Where is Barnabas?" I ask.

"Barnabas Arviat. Qaikanirnialiq. Tunilaupara titiqamik ilingnungaujumik." Elisapii points to a bag by the door.

"Is he okay?"

"Ii. He okay." She motions to me to bring her bag.

Elisapii's hands are shaking and I help her to unzip the

front pocket. She pulls out a letter with my name on it. Emmalu.
Emmalu.

How are you? I left Arviat by skidoo, so we can bring dog food but we have to hunt it first. Then I come to Churchill. Can you look that my grandparents have all they need? My uncle works at Harbor Inn. You can ask him for help.

I hope you and the dogs are well.

Yours truly, Barnabas

"He's coming by skidoo," I tell Elisapii, but of course she knows.

"Do you need anything?" I ask.

Elisapii smiles and shrugs her shoulders.

"Do you have food?" I pretend to eat.

"Ii." She points to the grocery bags on the table. They are full of dried caribou meat, smoked char, lard, and homemade bannock.

"What about water? Do you have water?" I pretend to drink.

She points to two blue 18-liter water bottles. Both are empty.

"I'll get you some," I say, happy that I can do something for the two old people.

★

My arms feel like they're being pulled out of their sockets by the time I manage to shove the two 18-liter bottles out the door of the Northern Store. Should I get Barnabas's uncle? I don't even know his name. I roll one bottle and then go back to get the second one. It's going to be a loooong way back.

A skidoo stops next to me.

"You need a ride?" A boy maybe a bit older than Barnabas grins at me. A qamutik is hitched to his skidoo. The sled is huge compared to Old Ipilii's dog sled.

The wheels in my head are turning full speed. Yes, I need a ride. No, I'm not going on a skidoo with a stranger. But he doesn't seem to be a stranger. He's got the same friendly smile as Barnabas—including a missing tooth. He's wearing a black anorak with bright fur trim all around the hood that makes his face look even rounder. But the coolest thing are his pants. They're yellowish-white with long thick fur.

"Are those polar bear pants?" I ask and then bite my lip. I hope he doesn't think I'm rude or something.

"My first bear," he grins. "My grandmother made the pants for me."

"Cool. You're from here?"

"No, Arviat. Just here to go shopping."

"Shopping? There are no stores in Arviat?"

He laughs. "Two stores, but they are expensive. And some things we can't buy. My cousin went on the train to Thompson, buying stuff there and sending a Jeep up for his family."

"But you can't drive to Arviat, I thought."

"That's why I brought the sled." He leans back on his skidoo, smiling at me.

"Wait, you're going to haul the car with the skidoo?" The questions just blurt out, but he doesn't seem to mind.

"Takes two skidoos to pull it. My cousin's and mine. We're still waiting for the freight train to come in with the Jeep."

"What about the jumble ice?" I try to picture a Jeep on the back of his sled making its way through the rough ice that's sometimes even tight for a dog team to squeeze through.

"Can be tricky at times. The Challengers will get through soon. Then we can just follow their trail."

"Challengers? What's that?"

"Like a big cat. The mines haul their freight in by cat train. They go all the way to Rankin."

"Mines?" I feel stupid for having thought that it's all untouched wilderness out there, just dog teams and polar bears.

"You need a ride now, or what?"

I nod.

"Where to?" The boy grabs one of the water bottles and

straps it to his skidoo rack. The other one he swings on the seat in front of him. The weight doesn't even faze him.

"Jump on."

I climb on the seat behind him.

"Where are we going?"

"The Flats. You know where they are?"

The boy turns around to me and looks me up and down. "You live there?"

"No, I'm ... I'm friends with Old Ipilii and Elisapii."

"How is Elisapii?" he asks.

"I think she's okay. But I'm not sure," I reply.

"They say she didn't want to come back to Churchill to continue her treatment. She wanted to stay home in Arviat, be with her family, and eat country food."

"I ... I didn't know that. What would happen if she doesn't get treatment?"

"She dies," he says as he starts his skidoo. "I'm Mike by the way. What's your name?"

"Emmalu. I mean, Emmylou."

Mike stops in front of Old Ipilii's house, grabs the two water bottles, and walks through the door. I follow him. He sets the bottles onto the table, pours water into the kettle, and lights the Coleman stove, all before he has said as much as, "Hello."

"Looks like they need fuel. Can is nearly empty. I'll drop some off later." Mike plunks himself onto the sofa and starts talking in Inuktitut with Elisapii. I don't know what they're saying and I wonder if I should leave, when I hear Elisapii say my name.

"She wants me to tell you that I passed Barnabas on the way down. They should be here tomorrow."

"Thanks," I say and feel myself blush. I turn away quickly. "I'll go feed the dogs."

"You want a ride back to town?"

"No, I'll walk."

"Emmylou, next time you can just get water from the river," Mike says as he nods toward the ice chisel by the door.

I feed the dogs quickly, rushing to get out of the cold. The wind seems even stronger when I walk back into town. I stop several times to rub my cheeks. Back at the lodge where it's warm, they suddenly hurt like heck. I go to the bathroom and check my face in the mirror. There's a white patch on each cheek, about two inches wide.

"Mom!" I yell.

Kitty doesn't answer. Right, she's in the restaurant. I put hot water on my cheeks, but it hurts even more. I stare at my face. The frostbitten cheeks make me look older. I like it in a weird kind of way. It's a reminder how quickly things can turn bad out there, but it's also a reminder that I was out there with the dogs in weather most people would never dare go out in. As if the Arctic had put her icy mark on me.

CHAPTER 20

It's still dark when I wake up. My cheeks are itchy and they feel leathery. I sneak to the bathroom. Where the white patches were, my skin is turning black and blistery and little pieces are falling off. Beneath it, new skin is forming already, slowly erasing the marks. I brush my teeth and then go down to the kitchen in my PJ's to get a bowl of cereal. I usually avoid getting out of bed before ten if I don't have to—which is on most days now. I only have to work to fill in if someone gets sick or wants a day off.

I finished my project on polar bears, which was depressing. I talked to the conservation officer, the one who gave me a ride at my polar bear non-encounter by the Cape. He said the bears are not endangered (yet), but they are a threatened species.

They depend on the sea ice to hunt the seals that den in the ice or come up through their breathing holes. Because of climate change, there is less ice and it freezes later and melts earlier. So the bears spend more time on the land and they're hungry, some of them even starving, and that's when they come into Churchill, looking for food—which ends badly for the bears more often than for the humans. I feel for those bears, sitting there waiting for the sea ice while all those tourists snap pictures of them—and then ending up in jail, because they came too close to the same tourists that were trying to get close to them in the first place.

Kitty is still sleeping when I come back with my breakfast. I feel my way in the dark to the coffee table by the window and stack my books to make room for my bowl of cereal.

I kind of gave up on my other school project, about the history of Churchill. I started writing about the Fort, Cape Merry, and the first trading posts, but all I can think of are the people left on the beach down by the Cape. Sometimes it's like I can almost see them: the crying children, the starving dogs.

What was their life like before? Before the Europeans came and took away their way of life, their homes, their children? What was it like to live out there, follow the caribou, hunt, gather, be outside all the time? How did they make their tents? Their dog sleds? How did they know where to go? That's what I really want to know. And I want to know more of the stories that Old Ipilii tells about when he was a young boy.

Then a horrible thought enters my head. How did Elisapii and Old Ipilii end up in Arviat? Did they choose to be there?

Kitty stirs in her sleep. She looks small, the way she's curled up under her blanket, hugging her arms to her chest. I dress as quietly as I can. She hasn't been sleeping well lately, so I don't wake her to tell her I'm going out with the dogs, but I leave her a note.

There's heat rising from the chimney of the cabin and I'm reminded that these are not "my" dogs anymore. I should ask the old man if I can take the dogs out. But it's still early, and what if he likes to sleep in? I grab the harnesses from the hook by the door. He wouldn't mind, would he?

When I arrive at the dog yard, Old Ipilii is already there. He's standing with Qakuq. Both are looking across the river. The sunlight has reached the top of the land on the other shore; river and jumble ice are still in the shadows. When the old man sees me with the harnesses, he walks to the qamutik and begins to untangle the lines, laying them out in a widespread fan. Has he been waiting for me?

I run back and forth to bring the dogs, and Old Ipilii puts their harnesses on and hitches them up.

We leave as the first rays of the sun are reaching the frozen river. The light catches the dogs' breath, turning it into golden steam. Further out, fog is hanging in the bay as golden as the dogs' breath. Our long shadows are growing shorter, making room for the light of the day. And then the fog dissipates, while the magic still hangs on.

We don't talk—there's nothing to say. We just watch the dogs, the sun, the trail.

A flock of white wings shoots into the air. Ptarmigans. I blink against the rising sun and watch them fly, until they disappear in a flutter of wings and light.

"Nanuq," I say and point to the polar bear tracks leading out to the floe edge. The old man has already seen them. If I was alone, I'd be scared, but there's nothing that shows worry in the wrinkled face of the old man, so I don't worry either. I wish I could ask him about my polar bear research and find out what he thinks about climate change and all that.

Button Bay looks different today. The sky turns from a pale yellow into glowing orange, which reflects on the glare ice. You could almost mistake the jumbled ice and snow-covered rocks for clouds, the dogs running into the sky. When the sun rises above the horizon, the red sky fades into pink, then a purplish blue.

I blink into the bright light. Old Ipilii pulls out a pair of super-cool sunglasses with orange lenses. I wish I had remembered to bring mine—fancy or not. I'm shielding my eyes with my mitt against the sun and the glaring snow. Every day the sun is a bit brighter. Even the sky has a different blue now. Darker, more intense.

"Qimmiujatuluatuq." The old man nudges me with his elbow, holding his sun glasses out to me.

I shake my head, but he insists, so I put his glasses on. It's instant relief for my eyes.

"Matna," I say and wonder what it means – qimmiujatuluatuq, I mean.

The trail is getting rough again. The ice heaves are at least a foot thick and, where the sheets have pushed up, they've left cracks of open water. Some of them wide enough that the dogs have to jump across. Where is Barnabas? Shouldn't we see him soon? I get nervous at the thought of seeing him, but in a good way, and I realize I miss him.

"Taikaulipuut," says Old Ipilii and points to the left ahead of us.

In the distance, there are black dots moving, maybe five or six. Maybe more. What am I looking at? Caribou?

The old man calls to the dogs. We change our direction slightly, running toward the dots. They are definitely moving in our direction, but we don't seem to get any closer. And then suddenly they change from dots to shapes—skidoos! The hunters. They must have seen us, too, since they're now changing their course.

The dogs are running toward a small rise. The wind has blown the snow away, exposing pebble-sized rocks and scattered driftwood. Is this a beach in summer, I wonder?

"Ha-ii," Old Ipilii calls when the sled hits the gravel. The dogs strain into their harnesses. The runners make a scraping sound like sandpaper grinding over wood, only louder.

"Whoo," Old Ipilii calls. He slowly gets up, holding his hip. Old Ipilii waves me away with his hand, like you would shoo a little child or annoying kitten. Does he want me to go without him?

"Ha-ii," he calls and his dogs take off. I guess that answers the question.

I turn back to make sure that this is what he wanted. He waves once and then turns to climb down to the gravel beach.

The skidoos are speeding up and someone is waving. Behind the skidoos, an orange vehicle with round windows on the side follows. It looks a bit like how a kid would draw a car, except it's got skis in the front and tracks in the back.

The skidoos stop just a short distance ahead of me. I can see now they're pulling qamutiks full of dead caribou. The frozen hooves are sticking out under the snow-covered tarps. The dogs are pulling hard despite me dragging the hook.

"Whoa!" I yell as we reach the first skidoo, but they pull

right past to the first hunter's sled. He's yelling something at me that I don't understand, but I get that he's not impressed. A second later my dogs are tearing into the meat. Now several people come running, their rifles slung on their shoulders, yelling at the dogs and me.

I run up to the dogs and grab the first one that comes in my reach. Aupaluk growls at me, but I don't let go. He snaps at Pamiuluk. She snarls and sinks her teeth into Princess. Suddenly, there's snarling and growling all around me. I'm in the middle of a dogfight.

"Emmalu, get away." Barnabas is suddenly there and, with the help of the other hunters, he commands the dogs to turn, helping with a boot if they don't listen.

Just as suddenly as the fight started, it's quiet again. Someone says something in Inuktitut and someone else laughs. Soon they're all laughing. Even Barnabas. The only word I understand is qallunaaq.

I stand frozen, not knowing what to do. I wish they'd all leave so I can turn the team around and go back while no one is watching.

"Why did you come out here all by yourself?" Barnabas's voice doesn't sound at all proud of me, like I pictured it. Well, I hadn't exactly pictured there would be mountains of dead caribou piled on sleds, either. In my imagination, I had left out the whole dead animal part of the hunters returning.

"Old Ipilii is not far," I say, and I'm upset that he let me run the last few hundred meters on my own. Surely he must have known what was coming. "I'm sorry about ..."

"It's okay," Barnabas says, and then, "Nice sunglasses," which makes me feel even worse.

A guy wearing industrial-style bib pants walks toward us.

"That's the one who looked after your dogs?" he asks Barnabas.

"Ii. This is my cousin, Christopher." He turns briefly to me and then back to Christopher. "This is Emmalu."

"Nice to meet you, Emmalu." The cousin shakes my hand. "Maybe you should feed your dogs more often," he says and grins.

I don't know what to say back, so I point to the weird orange vehicle.

"What's that?"

"You never seen a Bombardier?" Barnabas asks.

"No."

"Well, it's ... a Bombardier," he says. "A snow bus."

"Do you have lots of those in Arviat?" I look at the odd vehicle with its round hood and round roof. Like someone tried to put a skidoo, submarine, and Caterpillar all in one machine.

"Only two. For freighting. This one here is picking up a truck."

"Another one?"

"Where you come from, you have more than one truck, no?" Christopher asks.

Barnabas laughs.

"Show her," Christopher says and walks back to his own snow machine.

Inside the Bombardier are brown fake leather benches, shaped in a U around the three walls in the back. There's a photo tacked to the wall of a short man holding up a fish nearly his size. A Coleman stove and a blackened teapot are lying on the floor, a parka and a sock on one of the benches. It looks more like someone's living room than the interior of a bus, except it smells of gas, and the driver's shirt and hands are covered in black grease.

"You wanna ride?" the driver asks, pouring himself a cup of tea from his thermos.

"I'm here with the dogs," I say, thankful for having an excuse.

"I take the dogs and you ride here," Barnabas says.

"It's okay. I can take the dogs."

"Is warmer here," he replies, and I can't help thinking he doesn't want me to run his dogs.

I pass Old Ipilii's sunglasses to Barnabas. I won't need them.

Despite all the windows, it's dark in the Bombardier. The dog team leaves first. By the time we pass it, Barnabas has already reached Old Ipilii. Turns out Old Ipilii doesn't need his sunglasses, either. He's wearing a new pair, made of driftwood. Instead of lenses there's a slit carved into the wood to see through.

I kneel on the back seat so I can watch them as they slowly fall behind. It's neat to see them from a distance. The dogs' movements are matched, like they're running to music only they can hear.

It's hot inside the Bombardier. At first I'm glad for the warmth and the cushioned seat, but then the gas smell gets to me. I feel sweaty, have trouble breathing, and the engine sound is a constant noise in my head. I try to focus on the landscape outside, but it's just a blur of white.

I long to be back outside, listening to the rhythmic tap-tap-tapping of the dogs' feet instead of the groaning and moaning of the Bombardier as it labors its way across the land. I want to ask the driver to open the door and let me out, but I don't know how to ask, so I curl up instead, concentrating on my breathing, willing the sickness in my stomach to go away. The engine's groaning turns into a chant: qal-lu-naaq, qal-lu-naaq, qal-lu-naaq.

CHAPTER 21

Kitty sets a bowl of oatmeal on my bedside table.

"Kitchen is putting away breakfast, so I brought you some up here." She pulls the curtains and opens the window. The air is cold but also refreshing. I pull the blanket over my head.

"Trouble with that boy?"

"Kitty! I'm not even interested in him. I mean, that way."

"So what is it? How come you're moping in bed?"

"I'm not moping. I'm just … trying to sleep in, but you made sure that's not gonna happen."

"Don't blame your problems on me."

"I don't have a problem. Besides, it's got nothing to do with you, Kitty."

"Exactly, so don't make it."

"*I* don't. *You* always make it about you." I throw my cover off and glare at her.

"Let it go. Move on." Kitty moves towards the door.

"Move on? Like pack my suitcase and leave? Is that how I'm supposed to deal with my problems?"

"What problems?"

"I don't know. You tell me. You're the one who's the expert in that field."

There's a moment of silence. "You're just like your father. You ..."

I pull the cover over my head and plug my ears. I hear her voice, but not her words; muffled, but still stinging. *Go, Kitty, please go*, I silently plead under the stuffy blanket. The door slams. And then I wish she hadn't left.

"You're just like your father." She'd said it again.

Truth is, I don't know what my father is like. I do remember them arguing. Dad's voice always calm, Kitty's always Kitty's— shrill, edgy—and Dad asking me: "Who's crazy, Emmylou? What d'you say? Me or your mom? Say it, because she won't listen to me."

And I did. I said it was Mom. I know it wasn't right what he did—making me pick sides. But what if it's true? What if Kitty is crazy and Dad isn't as bad as Kitty makes him out to be? What if I'm more like him than Kitty? Would that be so bad?

I imagine my dad is coming to get me. I imagine he's a musher in Alaska. I'd have my own dogs, and I'd only have to go to town if I wanted to. I'd spend all day with my dogs and at night they'd sleep in my bed—or at least one of them would. In my imagination, that dog looks like Qaqavii.

I miss Qaqavii and how he looks me straight in the eyes, like he can see who I really am, but Qaqavii is never going to sleep in my bed, and I don't have a dad who's a musher in Alaska. I have a dad who's never bothered writing me a birthday card and a mom who thinks I'm one big mistake.

I haven't daydreamed about my dad for so long that I thought I was over it—the stupid fantasies. I miss my Paddington Bear sculpture. What if it really was from my dad? What if he'd sent me birthday presents all along and Kitty threw them out? So what if. A porcelain bear isn't gonna change that he wasn't in my life since I was five. I don't even want to see him. I want ... I don't know what I want.

I want to go see Qaqavii and run dogs with Old Ipilii and Barnabas like before. Before yesterday, when my dogs tore into the caribou carcasses on the hunters' sled and they all laughed at me. Even Barnabas.

I resist the urge to suck my thumb and bite it instead. I bite hard and the pain feels good; it quiets the thoughts in my head. When the pain begins to fade, I bite harder, and then I pull my covers away so I can investigate the tooth marks I left on my skin. They look deep and mean, but quickly fade. I get up and have a shower.

★

The dogs are gone when I arrive at the Flats, but I don't feel like going back to the lodge. I knock on the door, and then open it without waiting for an answer. I still haven't got used to just walking in without knocking.

Elisapii is sitting on her bed, slouched against the wall, her hands resting on caribou skins, a sewing needle in her hand. She's sleeping, but it doesn't look comfortable.

I grab the pillow from the couch and tiptoe to her bed. Elisapii opens her eyes as I try to wedge the pillow behind her head. Her black pupils move searchingly and then they focus on me. She smiles and lifts the caribou skins to make room for me to sit next to her.

"For dog race," she explains, stroking the skins. "Arctic Quest."

I nod, although I'm not sure what she's making. So far, it's just a bunch of skins sewn together into a big rectangle. Elisapii puts her hands under her cheek and pretends to be sleeping.

"A sleeping bag?" I ask.

"Ii. For sleep," she replies. We both smile and then sit in silence while I watch her sew.

Elisapii shows me how to make the stitches and then passes the caribou sleeping bag to me. She climbs out of bed and lays out a pile of fresh caribou skins on the floor. She strokes the fur, then turns the skin over to check the undersides. She shakes her head in disapproval and shows me an oval bump on the skin.

"Aarlungajuq," she says and motions a zigzaggy flight line with her finger while she makes a buzzing sound. And then she carefully scrapes the spot with her knife and pulls out a fat white larva. She holds it out to me and, when I recoil, she laughs and pops it into her mouth.

"Eww!" I say and then quickly hold my hand over my mouth to hide my disgust. Elisapii rubs her tummy.

"Candy," she smiles and holds out another one to me. I shake my head and pull a granola bar out of my pocket instead. I offer half to Elisapii.

"Eww!" she says and covers her mouth. And then we both laugh.

The sound of feet crunching snow makes me go quiet. There's a thud on the front step and then the door opens. It's Old Ipilii.

The old man sits on a chair and puts his feet on the bed. Elisapii leans forward, grabs his black sealskin kamik and pulls. They laugh and tease each other when the boot doesn't want to come off.

"Emmylou," Elisapii motions me to pull and, just when the three of us get the first kamik off, the door opens. Barnabas.

There is an awkward silence, and then Elisapii and Old Ipilii go to work on the other boot.

"Emmalu, good to see you," Barnabas says. "We just came back from the river. Too much slush ice. Old Ipilii got a booter."

Elisapii massages Old Ipilii's wet foot and I wriggle my way off the bed, not knowing what to do or say.

"I'm going to feed dogs. You wanna come?"

I nod and follow him around the house. I watch while he chops caribou meat into pieces.

He glances at me once in a while and we both look away when our eyes meet.

"So … ah … how was your time in Arviat?" I ask to fill in the silence.

"It was good. I spend lots of time in my cousin's garage, fixing up his skidoo, making it faster. We went hunting, too. I caught a wolf, but no luck with seals. My little brothers talk now. 'Anaana, ataata, and twenty-two.' They be great hunters one day." He smiles.

"What does it mean?"

"Anaana and ataata? Mom and Dad."

"And twenty-two?"

"Is my older brother's gun. He takes them hunting rabbits and small game. The twins always run around with their stick. Play hunting." Barnabas imitates his little brothers pointing an imaginary gun at imaginary rabbits. "How about you, Emmalu? My grandpa says you take the dogs out on your own?"

I nod.

He looks at me, kind of different, like ... I don't know. Like I wasn't just his little sister.

"Christopher said I was lucky to have a girlfriend that likes to run dogs and is pretty, too, he said."

I look down at my toes, my hands suddenly sweaty.

"I told him, you not my girlfriend, and he says then I'm stupid. But I think I'm lucky. Is fun running dogs with you, Emmalu. Too bad you can't come with us on race day."

My thoughts turn a hundred miles a minute and I don't know what to say. All I know is, his cousin, who had made fun of me, doesn't really seem to mind me, and Barnabas, who I thought just thinks of me as a stupid quallunaaq, likes to run dogs with me, and maybe he doesn't think I'm so stupid after all. What if ... what if he did want me to be his girlfriend? I feel the heat rising to my cheeks.

"Do you want me to take these to the dogs?" I pick up the chopped meat and drop it in the canvas bag.

"It be a good idea unless you wanna eat it all by yourself."
Barnabas grins and I throw a chunk of meat at him. And all
of a sudden, the anxious feeling is gone and we both smile at
each other. I carry the meat to the dogs and, as I go around each
circle, the dogs dance around me until I give each of them their
chunks. It doesn't take long, and they're all crunching happily
while holding the bones between their feet. I couldn't imagine a
better sound in the whole world right now.

CHAPTER 22

I've missed my deadline for my January progress report by more than a month already. Kitty doesn't know yet. I mean, she's the one who has to officially send it in, but I'm the one who messed up. The deal was I'd "self-direct" my learning and, instead, I directed myself to hang out with Barnabas and the dogs.

"I don't care what you do—it's you throwing your life away," she'd said. "But we can't have a truant officer knock on our door, is that clear?"

Is that what happens if you don't hand in your report? I need to find out, but the last thing I want right now is to talk to Lisa. I know she'll be disappointed in me. I just delivered the proof that I'm not as smart as she thought I was. In fact, I'm not even as smart as *I* thought I was.

But then an idea enters my head that gets me all excited. What if we moved? To a different province? Then nobody would really care what I did the four months we've been in Manitoba, would they? I could start fresh somewhere new, leave behind all that schoolwork that has piled up and start with a clean slate. Lisa wouldn't even need to find out that I messed up, despite all her help. That would work.

But then I think about Qaqavii and Barnabas and Old Ipilii and Elisapii and leaving them, and that's the last thing I want.

The stack of books stares accusingly at me, and finally I grab them and walk to the library.

★

"All done with those books?" Lisa asks.

I nod.

"So what's your next project? Shall we look at your outline again?"

I bite my lip. Here it goes. "I haven't finished the assignments and we didn't send the progress report in, either, and …. What's going to happen now? Will they send someone who'll force me to go to school?"

"Whoa, slowly now. Let's start at the beginning. What have you got?"

"I did a few pages on that math program you found for me, but … "

"But?"

"It's not the numbers that are confusing but the words. Polynomials and monomials and inequalities and …" I sigh.

Lisa laughs. "Good grief, Emmylou. That sounds horribly complicated."

"It is!" I say, smiling now. "And there are also exponents and variable bases and …"

"And addition and subtraction and multiplication?"

I look at her, not sure if she's mocking me, but she's serious.

"Sorry," she says, smiling apologetically. "Math isn't my strength. That's all I can contribute to complicated math terms."

I feel a ton lighter. A ton to the hundredth. Maybe it's not so bad that I don't know all these things.

"So what about your ecosystem project, focusing on the polar bears?"

"I have that." I pull out my thirty handwritten pages with quotes from people I talked to and resources I found at the train station and in library books. I even added graphs and cut out pictures from flyers and such. I'm actually kind of proud of it.

"That looks great, Emmylou. How about social science?"

I shake my head.

"You had so many questions. You couldn't find any answers?" she asks.

"It's not that," I say, and then I tell her how I started learning about Churchill, and how the history just seemed to start with the first explorers, "discovering" a land that was already someone's home, and how I wanted to know more about the people that live here, rather than how many furs they supplied to the trading posts and what treaties they signed.

And I tell her about reading the book she gave me, and how I can't get out of my head how the government saw nothing wrong with what they were doing, and how the young girls … how they're still suffering today, even though they're old women now, and their children and even grandchildren have a hard time, too.

I tell her about Old Ipilli and the stories he told me about when he was a young boy, but then he says nothing about the time later, and that I'm scared the same thing that happened to the Dene happened to Old Ipilii and Elisapii, only further north, and …

"How could it? How could people let that happen?" I interrupt myself.

"Come here, Emmylou." Lisa says reaching out to me.

I hesitate, but Lisa simply pulls me into her hug, and the moment she does, I can't stop the tears from falling.

"I'm so sorry I messed up and disappointed you, and … "

"You didn't disappoint me, Emmylou. Not at all. I'm proud of you. Really proud of you."

I sniffle real hard and pull away from Lisa, because I'm scared I'll get snot on her beautiful wool sweater.

"What you learned in that short time is really amazing. You learned where to find resources and to question the ones you do find. But most importantly, you're beginning to understand that we need to look at our past and rewrite Canadian history."

"Thanks," I say, not sure how to take her compliment. Thing is, I'm not rewriting history; I'm not writing anything.

"Now, about your progress report. How about we phone the Homeschooling Office and ask how best to proceed?"

I feel like someone just dumped a couple of heavy boulders into my stomach.

"Can you phone and maybe pretend you're just asking in general, so they don't know you're talking about me?"

"I could do that," Lisa says, and I listen to her as she describes my situation to a lady in Winnipeg. I pretend to look at the books in the Young Adult section, but I hear snippets here and there.

"… exceptionally bright student … missing parental guidance … self-directed learner … great growth in short time … but no written essay as planned …"

I smile. Listening to that, even I wouldn't guess Lisa is talking about me. Missing parental guidance. Ha, I wish! True, Kitty isn't really involved in my schoolwork, but other than that, not a day goes by where I don't suffer from Kitty's parental "guidance."

Wear purple; it suits your skin color. Do something with your hair. Take a shower; you stink like a dog.

"Okay, Emmylou. Sounds like you have two options." Lisa walks up to me.

"You don't need to worry about the January report for now. But your mother has to submit the annual notification form, and when they process that, they'll need your January and June progress reports, or you won't be a homeschooler."

"Meaning?"

"Meaning you just dropped out of school, which is illegal at your age."

"What do they do? Put me in jail?"

"Well, they first notify the school division, and then their truancy officer will follow up with your family."

Just the words "truancy officer" give me a heavy feeling in my stomach. Never mind the idea of one actually knocking on my door.

"So what are my options?"

"Ask your mother to write the January report and mention what you achieved and how that led to new questions that you will show answers to in your June report."

I'm not exactly fond of this option. I can't imagine Kitty getting excited about me not having produced a paper, because I wanted to know more about the people Kitty calls "those people" and "the people not from here."

"What's my other option?"

"You could enroll in regular school."

Definitely not fond of this option, either.

I leave the library and walk by the Duke of Marlborough School. I never really paid much attention to it, other than imagining Barnabas looking out the window as I walk by. It's a school like any other, a brick building, fairly new, fairly small compared to schools in the city. Lots of concrete. Concrete staircase, concrete walkway around the school. Nothing special, really, but when I look at it today, it looks more like a prison, with the chain-link fence around the schoolyard.

I turn and walk down to the Flats instead, where the dogs are silhouetted against the blue-white of the river ice, sitting under the vast sky.

CHAPTER 23

Every time I visit Elisapii now, she's working on a new sewing project. She's finished two beautiful caribou sleeping bags, but she's not happy because they're made from late-winter hides. The hair is thick but falls out easily, and she's had to mend holes from the warble fly larvae nesting under the skin. She has made the most amazing mukluks, using the different-colored hides to make a pattern, and then she made a felt liner for inside, like a big sock with decorative stitching on the top. Now she's making spare harnesses. Old Ipilii is a good hunter. He's always provided well for her, so he deserves good clothing, she says, and she sews as if she's running out of time.

Barnabas translates when we're inside the cabin, but when we're outside with the dogs—Old Ipilii, Barnabas, and me—we understand each other without many words. I haven't had the heart to ask about Old Ipilii's past. Maybe I don't want to know. All I want is just to spend time with him and the dogs.

The dogs are strong and run forty miles without a break. Barnabas talks a lot about winning the race, often urging the dogs to run faster, but Old Ipilii always slows them down. It's a long way to Arviat, he says ... better to go slow and steady.

★

The days are longer now and, when I shelter my head from the wind, I can feel the warmth of the sun on my face. It feels good after the long dark winter. Before I know it, it's March. Only a couple more weeks to the start of the race.

Today, Old Ipilii and Barnabas are taking the dogs out for an overnight run. I didn't ask if I could come. There are only two caribou-skin sleeping bags. I help to load their gear onto the qamutik. Canvas tent and poles, the Coleman stove and teapot, dog food, spare clothes. It's a big load, neatly wrapped in a canvas tarp and tied with rope. Last, Barnabas slides their two rifles under the ropes.

"Maybe we catch a seal. The dogs are going skinny from only caribou meat," he says. Old Ipilii seems livelier than usual; he doesn't hold his hip as often. The dogs are feeling the anticipation and seem more restless, like they know it's a special run.

I help Barnabas to harness the dogs, and just as they're ready to go, Elisapii walks down to us, carrying a tightly wrapped bundle. She's wearing a hand-knitted sweater and no jacket. The wind is blowing through her thin hair and the sun reflects in her watery eyes. Even though she stands hunched over, she appears taller than she does inside. The dogs crowd around her for attention. Elisapii passes the bundle to Old Ipilii and then turns to the dogs. She scratches each one behind the ears and bends over to give Princess a belly rub when she flops down on the ground, raising all four feet into the air.

Qaqavii behaves like he doesn't even know me. I can't help but feel a pang of jealousy, and then I'm mad at myself that I do. He isn't my dog, much as I would like to pretend.

Elisapii talks to every dog, and only when she's done do the men say their goodbyes.

We watch them weave in and out behind the towering jumble ice until they're nothing more than a small black dot moving across the river. The dogs are fast and strong, and I've helped them to become that. I feel I'm part of the team after all. I wonder if Elisapii feels the same. Without her, they wouldn't have the gear to survive the night outside.

Elisapii leans on me as we walk back to the cabin. She appears exhausted and she's holding her right side, but she smiles through her pain.

"They ready," she says. "They good qimmiit. Good dogs."

★

The sun is shining and I don't feel like being inside. I walk down Main Street and stop at the bakery to buy a cinnamon bun. It's soft and sweet and just perfect. I walk past Sleepy Bear Lodge and then I'm on the edge of town. I turn toward the cemetery.

The white crosses glitter in the sunshine. I don't know what pulls me here, why I have the urge to go back, but I feel drawn to the names and dates on the graves, as if they could reveal the stories that were buried with the people. It's quiet here. Peaceful. I'm among people but no one bothers me.

A family is picking up garbage along the chain-link fence. A dog runs around the little girl and then chases a grocery bag that's taking flight. Did we ever do that? Go for a walk together, visit Grandma Millie's grave? I can't remember, can't even remember the cemetery she's buried in.

I put the last piece of cinnamon bun in my mouth and lick my fingers. It feels safe inside the chain-link fence, like polar bears wouldn't bother me here. It's funny that I'm more worried about them here, close to town, than when I'm out with the dogs. Maybe just because people here worry all the time, but the people down by the river who go out on the land, don't. Or, at least, not the same way.

I should just go to the ocean. Sit on the rocks, look out over the bay. As I leave the cemetery, an old woman walks along the trail. Is it …? Yes, it's the same woman I saw before. My heart skips a beat as I'm trying to think of something to say to her. She walks by me and I quickly look down.

"Hi," I mumble too quietly for her to hear. After she's past me, I turn and look back. A lonely woman, stooped over by age, making her way to the monument.

The cinnamon bun sits heavily in my stomach.

CHAPTER 24

"How's Princess?" I ask as I harness Qaqavii.

"She's not favoring her shoulder anymore." Barnabas hooks up Qakuq and gives him a quick gentle stroke on the head. The old leader sits in his spot, waiting for the rest of the team. It's the dogs' last long run before the race.

"Is she coming?" I ask, holding her harness. Princess wiggles her head through the harness's collar. "I didn't ask you." I laugh and pet her behind the ears.

Barnabas and Old Ipilii have a quick conversation.

"She come, and if she's good today, she can race."

Princess shifts her weight from one front paw to the other, prancing as if in her mind she's already running. She hasn't been training with us since she came back from Old Ipilii's and Barnabas's overnight camping trip with a limp. That was two weeks ago. She made it all the way to their campsite just south of Nunalla, near the halfway checkpoint of the race. On the way back, when they were running over rough ice, she tripped and hurt her shoulder.

I hook up Princess next to Qaqavii and she can barely contain her excitement. She's turning in a tight circle, licking Qaqavii's face and rolling over.

"Princess!" I scold her. "You're behaving like a puppy."

Princess's ears lay back and she ducks down, but her tail is still wagging, making a half-circle in the snow.

Old Ipilii and Barnabas sit in the front of the sled, and I climb on behind them. I watch the dogs run, keeping an eye on Princess, but she's keen and eager and shows no sign of her injury. It's cloudy and it's hard to make out the trail. There's no contrast of light and shadow in the snow, and I'm surprised more than once when we hit a bump that I didn't see.

Then the sun breaks through the clouds, and I watch the light ahead of us spread out. When it reaches the dogs, the color of their fur intensifies. Aupaluk looks a lot redder, and the yellow in Qakuq's and Grumpy's white fur comes out. At the same time, the dogs' shadows become distinct, running alongside the team. I watch our shadow team gliding across snowdrifts. The shadows of Old Ipilii, Barnabas, and me are impossible to tell apart—as if out here, it doesn't matter who you are. Us, the sled, the dogs are all just one. One shadow traveling across the frozen bay, like millions of other shadows that traveled before us. When the sun disappears behind a cloud, our shadows fade into nothingness.

"Qimmiujatuluatuq!" Old Ipilii says quietly and points toward a fair-sized boulder, half-covered by a snowdrift. Sheltered by the drift is a white creature watching us curiously with round black eyes. A fox! The dogs haven't seen him yet and the wind is blowing from behind. We draw nearer, and the fox walks a few steps away. He hesitates. Then runs back to where he was sitting, grabs something white and feathery, and runs across the tundra as fast as his legs will carry him.

"He caught a ptarmigan," Barnabas says.

Qakuq spots the fox and leans harder into his harness.

"Nauk! Ha-ii." Old Ipilii calls before the team can change direction. The dogs listen, but they're pulling with new enthusiasm, like the fox has awakened their instincts. Like they were a pack, on the hunt together.

"Tiriganiatsialukauq," Old Ipilii says.

"Ii." Barnabas nods. "My grandpa used to trap foxes. Lots and lots of them."

"Uhmm … your grandpa, he calls me Qimmiuja…"

"Qimmiujatuluatuq?"

"Ii. I mean, yes. What does it mean?"

"One who speaks dog."

I feel all fuzzy inside for a second, but then I wish I hadn't asked. I know nothing about the dogs compared to Barnabas and his grandpa. Certainly not how to speak dog. Now I'll always be worried that he'll find out I'm not as good with the dogs as he thinks. I fiddle with the caribou hide, feeling all self-conscious, but there is another feeling, too. One that feels good. Qimmiujatuluatuq. One who speaks dog. I'd like to be that person, and maybe I am a little bit already, and Old Ipilii saw it before I even knew it myself.

I watch the dogs for a while and then let my eyes glide over the vast expanse of Hudson Bay. Somewhere out there to the east are the bears, stalking seals until the ice retreats. I haven't seen any fresh tracks lately, but I'm sure they're out there, belonging to the arctic landscape, like the ice, the water, the sky.

"Did you see any bears while you took the dogs camping?"

"Only with binoculars from far, but in the morning, there were fresh tracks over our old trail."

"It's sad that they soon will be gone."

"The bears?"

"I mean, with climate change and less sea ice, and all the bears having a tougher time. It's not going to get easier. I read up on it. Looks pretty grim, the scientists say. Even here in Churchill, they counted fewer bears."

"Maybe those scientists don't know where to look for bears. There are lots of bears in Arviat. Even our Elders say they seen more than in the past. But the wildlife people, they say there's less, so they take away our hunting tags. We only allowed to kill in emergency situation. Is bad. Bears are coming to town and breaking into our dog food shed. Sometimes they take a dog. My sister was chased by a bear in front of our house. She doesn't go out anymore after dark, but bears come, even in daylight. Is bad when the ice breaks loose and the bears have to wait longer for sea ice at freeze-up. They hungry and hang out at the dump."

So much for me thinking my assignment on polar bears is done ... I guess I can start over again. "Are there as many bears as in Churchill?"

"More than that."

"But ... why is Churchill the Polar Bear Capital of the World?"

"I don't know. Because they put up a sign?"

"So, what do you do with all the bears? Do you have a bear prison like Churchill?"

"No prison, but we get their prisoners when they release them. We are right on their migration route. We have a polar bear patrol, but bears are sometimes not so easy to chase away. And they gave us electric fences for dog yard. With solar power. Not much good with two hours of daylight in winter. Is scary, because you don't see them, and then you walk around a house corner and there he is. I think they get braver because we hunt them less now. People down south, they don't really know what it's like."

"What is Arviat like?" I imagine Barnabas's little sister nose to nose with a bear that could kill her with the swipe of a paw, but I can't get a picture in my head of the town itself.

"Lots of fun. There are lots of children in Arviat. They everywhere. In summer, my family goes out on the bay, setting nets for Arctic char and hunting seals and beluga. In spring and fall, we hunt geese, and when the caribou come through, we hunt them, too. Sometimes in winter, I go far with my cousin and we hunt muskox."

"So you hunt a lot. And what do you do for fun?"

Barnabas laughs. "Hunting is fun. In winter, we do ice fishing derby, too. For the whole family. And dog team races. Just about every weekend there is a fun race. Helps us get ready for the big races like Arctic Quest. And sometimes we have community feasts and dances and fashion shows. La laa. Hey! Qakuq! La laa." The dogs turn around a big chunk of jumble ice.

"Fashion shows?"

"Some of the women, they like to sew. Make beautiful parkas, and amautiit, and kamiit. Better than Toronto fashion show."

"Have you been there?"

"Toronto? No, but I know they don't make clothes you can take hunting."

"Sounds like a neat place. Arviat, I mean."

Barnabas is silent for a while. "Is not all good. Lots of problems, too. Bigger than bears."

"Like what?"

"Like drinking and suicide. Is not easy, if you don't have money for ATV, and boats and guns and all that. Then you stuck. But my grandfather says is not only that. Is we must remember how to make a human being—inunnguiniq. That's why he teaches me Inuit Qaujimajatuqangit. It's what Inuit have always known to be true."

Old Ipilii turns around when he hears the Inuktitut words. He talks to Barnabas while the dogs pick up a skidoo track and follow it without needing another command.

"My grandpa says we have to remember the old ways; they are still important today. Maybe even more important. The qallunaat teachers, they too try to make able human beings, but is not the same. Too much math and not enough running dogs." Barnabas grins and then translates. Old Ipilii laughs.

"Ii. Ilitisivalirnaqtujuit qimmiit."

"What did he say?"

"The dogs are good teachers."

"How do you mean?"

"I don't know. Ask the dogs."

I sigh and shake my head. But then I think about what I did learn from the dogs. They're so content with little things. Just the sight of a harness turns them into a tail-wagging, happy mob. They never criticize and they always see the good in me. They taught me that, in a team, I can go places I could never go on my own. They taught me to always look after the weakest, because we'll never go any faster than the slowest dog. And they taught Qaqavii how to become a sled dog just by showing him his place in the team.

"I don't know how to explain Inuit Qaujimajatuqangit." Barnabas fiddles with the caribou hide he's sitting on while he talks. "There is so much to know about our way of life and our laws, and how we learn about all that, that it's hard to understand one thing without the other. But in the end, is rather simple. A lot is about respect for people and animals and the land, and about helping each other instead of always wanting more."

"But that's how all people should live, isn't it?"

"Ii. Qallunaat didn't think that when they came here. They took over the education of the children, didn't think our ways are important in a modern world. That's why we need people like my grandfather, who remembers and can teach us before we forget."

"How does he teach you?"

"Like this."

"But he isn't saying anything."

"There is no lessons like in your school, Emmalu. I learn from being with him, learn how he does things and why, and how to share, and listening to his stories and spending time on the land."

Barnabas falls silent. I don't know what to say. We never talked like this before, and I begin to understand how special the relationship between Barnabas and Old Ipilii is. Not everyone gets to go out with their grandfather and learn to run a dog team. But I also understand how urgently Barnabas is trying to learn from Old Ipilii and Elisapii before time runs out, before the old way of life is lost.

I wish I could speak Inuktitut and could go to Old Ipilii's school.

CHAPTER 25

"This is good, isn't it?" Kitty takes a bite out of her cream cheese brioche. "Nice to have a change of scenery as well." Kitty's eyes wander around the bakery, scanning the crowd of locals and tourists sitting along the long wooden tables on brown plastic chairs—the crowd of male locals, I should say.

"Sure is," I say, looking past her at the wall where an Arctic Quest poster announces the race. A dog team of all white dogs is running through spindly trees under the halo of a sundog. I wonder who the mushers are. Their dogs are beautiful, their sled skinnier and shorter than Old Ipilii's. The two mushers are wearing caribou clothing nearly as light as the dogs themselves.

"Only three more days before the race starts," I say.

"Good. Then all this training business is over and you can have a real life again."

I feel my brioche sit heavy in my stomach like a pile of rocks. How could I not think of that? This is it now. The dogs are resting before race day. We're done training. And even if we do take the dogs out after the race, it'll be April and just a matter of time before the snow melts.

Real life. I don't even know what that is anymore.

"There's a party tonight at the Harbor Inn nightclub. You should come with Marie and me."

"Reminder: I'm only sixteen."

"Geez, Emmylou. If my mom had taken me to a nightclub, I for sure wouldn't have protested."

"For real? You and Grandma Millie at a nightclub?"

"Come on, Emmylou. Don't compare me with Grandma Millie. She was old already before I was even born."

"Did Grandma ever talk about her parents and about life when she was young?"

"Kind of. 'When I was your age, I didn't get to lie around in bed till noon—I used to milk the cows before breakfast.' 'Don't throw that out. There might be use for it later.' That kind of thing."

"She grew up on a farm?"

"Her brother sold the farm when their parents died."

"What was it like growing up on a farm?"

"Lots of work, I imagine. Grandma used to sew clothes, can food, make meals for the workers, the whole nine yards. I'm sure glad she didn't marry a farmer."

"Did she teach you?"

"What?"

"Things from the olden days. Like sewing and canning and ... how to become an able human being?"

"An able human being? Where did you get that from?" Kitty laughs. "I figured that out on my own, but looks like you might need some help. So, are you coming tonight?"

"No, thanks. Wanna come and help me chop up some seal meat for the race?"

Kitty rubs her temple as if I'd caused her physical pain. "You're kidding me now, right? Please tell me you're not clubbing baby seals."

"Mom! That's totally not ..." She just doesn't get it. "Yeah, I was kidding. We feed them chicken wrapped in Styrofoam and plastic."

Kitty sighs. "Just go."

I walk to the door but, as I leave, I feel the sudden urge to turn around. Can't we ever just not be upset with each other? I'm trying hard to think of something nice to say, when I catch a guy wearing a red ball cap and a thick gold necklace wink at Kitty. I only see him for a second, but he already gives me the creeps. Please, Kitty, just ignore him, but the guy is already moving toward her table.

The qamutik is laying upside down. I can see where Barnabas repaired the crosspieces I broke. The wood hasn't grayed yet. Now he's doing something to the white plastic screwed to the bottom of the runners. I give Qaqavii a quick pet before I join him.

"Hey," I say.

"Hey," he says.

"What are you doing?"

"Filling in the screw holes," he says and melts a piece from a plastic bucket handle with his lighter. Melted plastic drips onto the runners, covering the screw holes and scratches. "To make it go faster."

"Are those from hitting rocks?" I let my fingers glide over the deep gouges in the white plastic.

"Ii," he says and carefully shaves the plastic with a hand planer.

"Looks like lots of work."

"Not as much as icing the runners," he grins. "Before plastic, they used to coat runners with mud and ice. You warm water in your mouth and spit it on the runner. When you hit a rock and the ice busts you have to do it all over again."

"Do you sometimes wish you lived at that time?"

"I dunno. I like dogs, but I also like my skidoo. And my gun. How about you?"

"Me?" I never thought about that. In the Itsanitaq Museum, I wished I could have met the Inuit living in camps and seen what life was like before European contact, but would I want to live in igloos and tents my whole life?

"I could do without guns and skidoos," I say.

Barnabas shakes his head. "You would not like Arviat. Lots of guns and skidoos."

"How's Princess?" I ask.

"Good." He feels the runners with his hands and planes a couple more spots.

"Are you nervous about the race?"

"Nah. You help us at the start line?"

"Sure."

"We'll hook them up here and run to the start. Is right over there, where they ploughed out the parking lot. But we go on the river. I don't want to scratch up my runners on the gravel road. My uncle come with his skidoo and help. You remember Mike? The guy who gave you a ride? He will be there, too."

"What about Elisapii? Will she come, too?" I'd like that. Not being alone after they leave.

"I don't know. She is not feeling well."

"What's the matter?"

"Maybe the flu."

"Old Ipilii is okay?"

"Ii." Barnabas flips the sled over. There's nothing left to do, but wait.

"I see you at the start, then?"

"Sound good."

"See you."

"See you, Emmalu."

I turn away quickly and bite my lip. Qaqavii shoots out of his house when he sees me, but I hurry past him. I don't even know why I'm suddenly so sad, but I know I wouldn't hold it together if I stopped. It feels like a goodbye and I'm not good at goodbyes.

CHAPTER 26

When the polar bears moved out onto the sea-ice, the town went quiet, almost as if the locals were hibernating after the busy tourist season. Today, it woke up. The Arctic Quest teams from down south just got off the train. You can easily tell the mushers from the few tourists and reporters that arrived with them. Their clothing looks well worn, black and greasy from handling dogs, but they also look comfortable, not scared of the cold. And it's cold today, the few warm days we had blown away by a strong wind from the northeast.

The racers' dogs arrive two hours later on the freight train. Crates, dog sleds, and gear are all stacked in a semi-trailer that's unloaded at the train station and driven to the makeshift dog yard.

I watch as the mushers unload the dogs. As soon as the trailer doors are opened, the dogs go nuts. They bark, whine, scratch their crates, and howl. The noise gets louder each time a dog is released from its crate. I know that sound. "How come he got to go out and not meeeee?" they seem to say. And then: "Pick me, pick me," as the mushers go to the next crate. It's the same complaint Qaqavii makes until it's finally his turn to get harnessed. Except these dogs' barks are a lot more desperate, and I quickly find out why. They all need to go to the bathroom in the worst way and the snow near the trailer is turning a dark yellow.

The dogs look a lot different than Old Ipilii's. Less furry, longer legged, and skinnier. You can see their muscles underneath their fur—they look like real athletes, not like our heavy-boned balls of fur. The mushers tie the dogs out on long chains that are strung between stacks of pallets and packed with snow. The town's snow plough made windbreaks in between the rows of dogs by piling the snow up like walls, but the wind is funneling down the passageway. Some mushers put dog coats on their dogs after feeding them with a thick soup of dog food and hot water.

Peter Patterson is talking to a musher with a wild beard that's full of snot icicles. "Snotcicles"—I wonder if that's a word. His gear is spread out next to his sled. Dog food bags, sleeping bag, tent, socks, a rusty cooker made out of a five-gallon pail, booties. How is it all going to fit in that red sled bag? It's a beautiful wooden sled with a raised bed made out of wooden slats curled up at the front. But the runners are skinny. Nothing like the two-by-sixes our sled is made of.

"That sled is gonna be kindling before he crosses the river."

I look to my side, surprised to see a man next to me, his hands in the pockets of his heavy down parka. I've seen him before—he's an older guy from Churchill—always smiling despite his black nose that looks like it's seen frostbite a few times too many.

"Those guys have no idea what they're getting into," he says. "You know what it's like out there. It's rough."

How come he knows that I've been out there? I never saw another dog team.

"Are you in the race?" I ask.

"Me and my buddy. We've been in this race since the first year. It's going to be a cold one this year."

"Where do you train your dogs?"

"I stay in the bush most of the time. My arthritis doesn't like the cold. But I took them to Nunalla last week, so they know where the trail goes. You gotta teach them males to pee without a tree." He says it totally seriously, without a grin, so I have no idea if he's kidding me. "I watched you guys. You got good dogs."

I feel a tingling in my stomach. He said you have good dogs, as if I'm part of the team.

"I'm Garry," he says and we shake mittened hands. "Gotta go and look after my own dogs. Bet they're wondering who all these strange barkers are in town." He nods further down the road, where his dogs must be, but I can't see a dog yard from here. When he leaves, I wander among the southerners' teams.

The dogs are running around in circles on their long chains. There are black ones with white noses and paws, gray and white ones with floppy ears, brown ones with yellow eyes, and a lot with all sorts of colors mixed. Some look scared and huddle down at the end of their chains, furthest away from people and other dogs, while others surf on the end of their chains, trying to play with their neighbors. A lot of them bark every bark imaginable: high-pitched yips, deep slow barks, and short fast outbursts more like a snapping into the air. Some just stand and stare like they're wondering if they're in some strange dream. I follow the rows of dogs that reach almost to the cemetery. The cemetery! The dog yard is not where Camp 10 used to be, is it?

I see someone in the cemetery. Is it the old woman?

"You can go pet my dogs if you want, just not that gray one. He can be a bit snappy at times." A man with a brown parka that looks like an oldie from a secondhand store smiles at me.

"Oh. Yes. Thanks. Um. Actually, no. I have to go. Sorry. Later, maybe."

I wave to him and then run toward the cemetery as fast as I can. Which isn't very fast. I don't want to breathe through my mouth, it's too cold for that, so I try not to get out of breath.

I can almost stay on top of the snow, but once in a while I break through the crust, which slows down my progress. The woman is still there when I get there. I slow down, not knowing what to say to her.

"Lots of dogs down there, eh?" The old woman's voice startles me and I nearly jump.

I nod. Say something, Emmylou!

"I remember lots of dog teams here in Churchill. My parents had dogs, too, when they came here. But I don't remember that. I was a baby then."

I nod again. "Where did you come from?" I ask, although I have a feeling I already know.

"From up north."

"Was that in the fifties?"

She looks at me. Suspicious, it feels like.

"I … uhm, I read about the history of the Sayisi Dene …" I nod toward the plaques.

Silence. Then she gently slides her hand over a woman's name. "My sister," she says. And then two more names. "My cousins. And this here is my aunt."

I touch the plaques with my own hand.

The old woman doesn't look at me when she speaks again. "Is still there in my head. The nightmares. After all those years.

Now they talk about settlement. Radio comes, and TV, and ask lots of questions. They say it was wrong now, but where were the people that cared back then?"

I bite my lip. I don't have answers. So I say nothing. We sit in silence. Well, as silent as it gets with all the dogs' excited barking.

The old lady sighs. "Is not bringing them back, all that money."

"I wish ... there was something I could do."

"Listen to our stories," she says. "Not many people listen, but is important to know what happened. Is not over yet for our people. We are still struggling."

I nod, not knowing what else to say. And then the dogs below the cemetery start howling. First one lonely howl, barely audible over the noisy dog yard. But then all the other dogs stop barking and join into a long, sad howl. Then it's quiet.

We sit for a while in silence and then—on impulse—I put my hand over the old woman's hand. Her skin feels cold and rumpled, like Elisapii's. Like Grandma Millie's.

"I'm sorry," I say.

"Marsi chogh, my child." The old lady gets up, leaning heavy on my shoulder until she regains her balance. I watch her walk away, her back bent, her feet moving slowly, each step an effort.

MIRIAM KÖRNER

I don't feel like talking to anyone, so I just walk quickly past the row of dogs, but Garry is there and, when he sees me, he waves me over.

"Here come the Nunavut teams." He points toward town. I stop to watch.

A train of skidoos is coming down the main street, pulling big plywood boxes on heavy sleds. The first one is an open box filled with straw. I count ten dog heads craning their necks over the rim, straining on their chains, unable to contain their excitement as they near the dog yard. The other three boxes are closed in, with breathing holes in the shape of dog paws on the sides. The racing sleds are stacked on top.

"There are three teams from Arviat. That red dog box in the middle belongs to two brothers from Rankin. Gotta watch out for those guys. They won three times."

I wonder if he's the one with the all-white dogs, the one that's on the race poster, but I don't feel like asking. I just want to go home and curl up in my bed.

The teams are pulling into the dog yard, and the dogs tied here already are going crazy. There must be close to a hundred dogs here now and they're all barking. I cover my ears. The last team is pulling in. Someone sitting on top of the dog box waves at me. It's Barnabas.

"Emmalu!" He jumps off the box before the skidoo stops, landing gracefully in the snow, and sprints over to me.

I wish I could tell him about the old lady, but I know he's got other things on his mind right now.

"I was looking for you all over. Elisapii was medivac'd to Winnipeg." Barnabas catches his breath.

"Is she okay ... what happened?"

"Her kidney is making problem. Bad infection. But is okay. They can help her in Winnipeg. She had that before."

"Oh, good," I say.

"There is other problem. Old Ipilii, he go with her."

"Old Ipilii isn't here? The dogs, they won't race? All that hard work for nothing?"

"Maybe not for nothing." Barnabas rubs his feet together and then he looks straight at me, like he's considering something. "Old Ipilii is okay with you and me racing together."

"Me? Race?" This is what I've dreamed about, traveling with the dogs, seeing Nunalla and maybe even caribou, and I get all tingly and excited, but then I think I won't see anything in the dark, not even a bear sneaking up on me, and I'm getting so scared that I suddenly feel like I can't breathe.

"What ... what do you think?" I finally manage to ask.

"I think it be okay. I run the race before and you are good

with the dogs." Barnabas doesn't sound sure at all. I don't know who he's trying to convince, himself or me.

"We have to ask the race marshal to change the team. You need better clothes. You can wear Old Ipilii's parka and pants. His kamiik may be a bit big, but you can wear extra socks."

Now that Barnabas is actually making plans, it sounds so simple. Just pack some stuff and go.

"What about food?"

"Is packed already," Barnabas grins. "But maybe you prefer your junk food?"

I know he means my granola bars that I always have with me. Fermented caribou stomach isn't really my thing.

"It's not junk food," I defend myself. "There's nuts in them and oats and ..." I don't list the sugar and chocolate and peanut butter.

"Junk food," he says.

Arguing with Barnabas about our food choices calms me down. As if squabbling about granola bars protects me from polar bears.

"What about Kitty?" I ask.

"What about her?"

"Won't she have to sign some sort of waiver or something?"

"We can bring her the papers."

Kitty won't allow me to go, but I don't tell Barnabas because I've made up my mind. I am going to be in this race. No matter what the price.

★

"MOM! Please! It's no different than the training runs we went on." Only five times as far. And overnight. But I don't think that information will help my cause.

"Had I known this is where it's all ending up, I wouldn't have let you go in the first place. You always want more, more, more." Kitty paces up and down, not knowing where to turn in the cramped space of our small room.

"What?" I bite my lip. This is not going well. Focus, Emmylou! Don't let her turn this into something else. It's about the dogs. The race.

"Tell me one reasonable reason why I can't enter the race?"

"Just for starters, that guy who gave us the sled ride ... what's his name? ... Peter Something ... he said no woman has entered this race before. It's a test for man and beast. Men, Emmylou, not girls."

"Are you serious? Remember when I wanted to be on the soccer team and there was no girls soccer? You were the one who said just play with the boys. 'Never let anyone stop you just because you're a girl.' Those are your words."

"We are talking about grown men here, Emmylou. Adults."

"Barnabas is not an adult and he's in the race."

"Good point. There isn't even an adult with you. Just two kids in this … this frigging wilderness."

"There are eleven teams out there! And all the checkpoint people. And we even have a satellite phone."

"I'm not discussing this. I'm not signing this waiver and you're not going in this race. This is the Arctic, Emmylou. I wouldn't even know how to start looking for you if something happened. You could *die* out there and then what?"

"For someone who didn't want me in the first place, you should be happy at the off-chance of getting rid of me!" I slam the door behind me—or at least that's what my intention was. The heavy wooden bedroom door screeches and comes to a halt just before it closes shut. I help with my boot. The bang makes the desired effect but it doesn't feel good.

I stop in the entranceway and pull the waiver from my pocket. I scribble down my last name in small angry letters on the empty line for guardian. Leroux. From today on, I will be my own guardian.

CHAPTER 27

Breathe, Emmylou. Just take a deep breath in and out, I tell myself. It doesn't help. The sick feeling in my stomach is getting worse.

"I'll be right back," I whisper to Barnabas as I squeeze by the rows of mushers and handlers listening to the race marshal reading the rules.

"The race covers approximately four hundred kilometers of arctic barren land, much of it along Hudson Bay's unforgiving coast. There are four checkpoints along the trail, manned by the Canadian Rangers and other volunteers. At no time are racers allowed to accept outside help or seek shelter in the Rangers' tents ..."

"Excuse me," I say, trying to get the attention of the Quebec musher with the crazy beard, who's blocking my way to the bathroom, while *not* drawing the attention of the fifty or so other people crowding the bakery.

"You're quitting already? They shouldn't let you race,

anyway. You're not even a half-size portion for a polar bear," he says and the mushers that hear him laugh. I glance at Barnabas. He shrugs his shoulders and gives me a half-smile. It can't be helped, and I have more urgent matters on my mind.

I hold onto the white porcelain sink in the bathroom, but the bile is staying in the back of my throat. I let cool water run over my wrists and splash my face. I turn the tap off and sit on the toilet seat, straining to hear the race marshal's voice.

"While the trail crew tried their best to put in the trail, due to the extreme weather conditions in the Arctic, there is no guarantee there will be a broken trail or trail markers. The intent of this race is to be self-sufficient. You will need ..."

Our gear is already packed. I know what we need. I know what the first thirty miles look like out there and yet, hearing the race marshal talk, it finally sinks in. We're on our own out there. Four checkpoints in two hundred fifty miles, nothing in between.

I find an empty chair near the back of the room, close to the washrooms, and watch as the mushers brood over tidal charts, punch the checkpoint coordinates into their GPS, or mark them on their maps. The air is thick with a mix of anticipation, worry, and fear. I feel like I'm watching a movie, not yet getting that I'm part of the cast. Dropped dogs, emergency procedures, vet check, mandatory rest, lost teams—the words are spinning in my head, but all I can really think of is that when it boils down to it, it's just us and the dogs.

I glance at the clock: 9:20 PM. We still have to draw our bib numbers. Kitty's off at ten. If I'm not in my room, pretending I'd never been at the mushers' meeting, that would be it. No race for me.

"If there are no more questions, Parks Canada will provide a package to each team, with letters from kids in Churchill to kids in Arviat in commemoration of the historic trading route this race will follow—and then we'll come to the bib draw," the race marshal announces.

I glance around the room. No more questions. Barnabas receives our mail parcel and then draws a number out of a hat. Number seven. There are eleven teams altogether. We're the seventh team to start, right after the Quebec team—the guy who calls himself Jay the Sleigh and his partner, whose name I already forgot. The race marshal hands me a red bib with a big white seven. I stuff it into my backpack with my spare clothes and hand it to Barnabas. The entrance door opens. I hold my breath. It's one of the southern team's handlers. Not Kitty. The meeting is over at 9.45 PM. I will be in my bed in time.

I wake up in the middle of the night from my own scream. I dreamed I was running our team in the race. I'm on my own, my dogs are all white, but I don't find either fact odd. And then I come across this place, a village with a few log cabins, dog sleds parked in front of white canvas tents, but it's all deserted, nobody's there except an old woman wandering among the tents. She looks familiar but, when I come closer, she becomes faint and then disappears altogether. And then the dogs' butts become wider, their tails shorter. Only when the leader turns around do I realize I'm running a team of polar bears. The lead bear charges, my head is inside the bear's mouth and then, all of a sudden, it's dark, the smell of rotten-fish breath overwhelming. I push the covers off my head.

"Emmylou, are you okay?" Kitty's voice, sleepy, warm, soft.

"Just a dream," I say, wishing she would come, hold me, make my nightmares go away.

I hear her turn over, then the deep, heavy breathing of her sleeping. I toss and turn, worried I might sleep in and miss the start, and then hoping I will.

CHAPTER 28

"Ready, Emmalu? We are next team after them."

I stroke Qaqavii's fur from head to butt, head to butt, head to butt, as if my life depended on it. Dogs are barking, mushers are yelling, reporters are running with cameras into the middle of the action. A megaphone announces the names of the mushers: "Jay Dube and Marcel Herbert from Saint-Michel-des-Saints." The team ahead of us moves to the start line. It's Jay the Sleigh and his partner.

Ahead of us lies the river, across the river, Seahorse Gully and the spit of land that separates us from the Hudson Bay. *You've been here. You've done this*, I tell myself.

It takes five high school student volunteers to keep the team ahead of us from crossing the start line too soon. I feel my whole body tense while I watch the Quebec team under the red banner. ARCTIC QUEST, it says in bold white letters. I shouldn't be here.

"Six … five … four …"

The dogs in the Quebec team ahead of us are going nuts. The barking gets unbearably noisy.

"Three … two … one … GO!"

The team takes off in a cloud of whirling snow. Then all eyes turn to us. I scan the crowd for Kitty. She's not here.

"Emmalu!" Barnabas calls.

We're next. I know.

"Emmalu! We have to go!" There's a firmness to Barnabas's voice I haven't heard before.

"I need to pee."

Barnabas looks at me as if I just lost my mind. Which I kind of fear I actually might have. "Later. We can stop on the other side of the river."

I want to move, but my legs won't. I'm staring at Barnabas and the sled like it's the first time I ever saw a dog team.

"Team number seven. Barnabas Ulayuk from Arviat, Nunavut, and Emmylou Leroux from Churchill, Manitoba. This is the youngest team to ever enter the Quest." A tinny voice crackles through the megaphone. Barnabas Ulayuk. I never knew his last name.

"Ten … nine … eight …"

"Emmalu." Barnabas leads me to the qamutik. "It's okay. Don't be scared."

I sit in the hollow amongst our gear. Barnabas's uncle leads Qakuq by his collar to the start line.

"Seven ... six ... five ..."

The countdown voice is yelling right into my head.

"Four ... three ... two ... one ..."

The noise, the barking, the tension—it's all too much.

"GO!"

The volunteers let go of our dogs and we shoot down the start chute. "Good luck," someone calls, and I have the feeling I could need lots of it.

As the dogs take us across the river, a picture flashes in my mind. A lone figure staring at my dog team, becoming smaller and smaller. I imagine how Kitty loses sight of me in the jumble ice. Her daughter gone. What if something happens and I don't come back? My back turned on her—our last goodbye?

"You still need to pee?"

Barnabas's voice snaps me back to the now. Suddenly, the world around me is more in focus than I have ever seen it before. I hear the tapping of the dogs' paws on crunchy, cold snow; I hear their breathing, each dog's panting creating the rhythm that carries the team forward. The air flows through my nose, clear, crisp, slightly seaweedy. The wind carries the barking of the dogs at the start line to us, but it's faint like the thoughts in my head. There is no room for them out here.

Like the dogs who turned their focus on the trail ahead, the second we left the start line, my focus turned to the now, leaving everything else behind. For a second, I even forget we're in a race. It's just us and the dogs.

"Are you okay?" Barnabas's eyebrows are big question marks.

"Yes," I reply. Ahead of us, two hundred and fifty miles of dangers I don't know yet, and still I feel okay. More than okay.

"And I don't need to pee anymore." I grin as if that's the best news since the invention of chocolate. We run across the river, following the trail markers to Seahorse Gully. Once up on the peninsula, Button Bay stretches below us.

"You see the dog teams ahead?"

At first, I don't see them. Then I catch movement. A dark silhouette against the brightness of the ice. From a distance, it's hard to tell each dog apart. They're all mingled into one, a forty-legged creature. And then further ahead, two more teams, tiny dots in a vast ocean of frozen water. It's neat to see them, to get a perspective of what we must look like—small, like ants crawling over a white sheet of paper.

I lose sight of the teams once we're down in the bay. And then, suddenly, there's a team appearing and disappearing between blocks of ice.

"Are we catching up?"

"Ii." Barnabas says and then, "Pick it up, pick it up."

"Easy!" I protest. "Remember what your grandfather said. It's a long race. If we go too fast too early, the dogs will be very slow in the end."

"You tell the dogs," Barnabas replies.

"Easy!" I call. The dogs look at me for a second and then speed up. We still have some language issues, the dogs and me. Or maybe it's just selective hearing.

We're long past the "crazy mile" but the dogs are still loping in their fast gear, running faster than ever before. I can now read the bib number of the team ahead. Number six. Jay the Sleigh looks back when he sees our team approach and then starts pedaling with one foot to stay ahead.

"Those stand-up sleds are no good. Can't even drink tea while you are driving," Barnabas jokes.

"I hope your dogs had breakfast this morning and aren't going to eat mine," Jay the Sleigh yells as our team approaches. I can't tell if he's joking, but I try to smile anyway. Then suddenly our fan splits—eight are now on the left side of the team ahead, Qaqavii and Princess are passing on the right. Our qamutik aims for the middle.

"Maudit tabarnac!"

I don't speak French, but it doesn't take a language expert to know that he's mad. Barnabas yells at the dogs. I close my eyes and brace myself for the crash.

The cracking noise of shattering wood interrupts a series of French swearwords. I open my eyes. We're right next to the Quebec team. Qaqavii and Princess still on the other side.

"Wooh!" Barnabas yells. The hook scrapes over the snow and, when it grips, it brings the sled to a sudden stop. The Quebec team's leaders are looking back, then pull around to visit our leaders.

"Mouse!" Jay the Sleigh yells. "Your job is to keep that line tight and only stop when I tell you to. Is that so hard to understand?"

Mouse—whoever she may be—does not respond. Crazy Beard jumps off the sled and grabs the leaders, pulling them away from our team. I grab Qaqavii and Princess and lead them back to our dogs.

"You okay?" Barnabas asks the Quebec team.

"We were until you came along." Jay the Sleigh waves a piece of wood, maybe a foot long, at us. His broken runner.

"Haw, guys, haw!" A voice from behind.

Shit! Another team. No, two! "What now?"

"Wait till they pass us?" Barnabas says. It sounds more like a question than a plan.

The first team swings wide around us. It's Garry and a younger man I don't remember seeing at the mushers' meeting. "I told you that sled is gonna be kindling before the race is over," he yells as he passes us.

"I always wondered why you need two effing runners, anyway," Jay the Sleigh yells back. "Hey, Brownie! Don't touch that neckline. And don't chew your harness. Is that too complicated for you?"

Team Number Nine is a fan-hitch. They swing wide around all teams, passing first us and then the other team. The Quebec team's dogs start barking; two dogs are jumping like crazy into the air; a third one grabs the gang line with its mouth, pulling it back and then releasing it. The jerk pulls the sled forward. "Brownie! Don't touch that line!"

Qakuq whines and strains his line. Then they all start barking. It's the race start all over.

"Can we help you?" Barnabas yells over the noise.

"Yeah, by getting out of my sight, before I lose my mind," Jay the Sleigh yells.

Barnabas looks at me. I shrug my shoulders. I'm still not sure if he's just kidding around or serious.

"Ha-ii." Our dogs take off. Chasing after the teams ahead.

"He was mad," Barnabas says.

"Well, yeah, we broke his sled."

"But I offered to help and he was still mad."

I turn around and look behind us. Crazy Beard sits on the overloaded sled, balancing precariously, while Jay the Sleigh is riding with both feet on one runner. We're slowly pulling away, our dogs still going way too fast.

"They have race fever," Barnabas says as if he read my mind. Intoxicated by the scent of the dog team ahead, our dogs are trying their hardest to catch up. My hand is cramping from holding on so tight to the sled. We're just leaving Button Bay, about twenty miles into the race. I'm not sure I can do this for another 230 miles.

Just then the switch happens. The dogs settle down into their more relaxed trot.

"Better now," Barnabas says, and I'm sure he doesn't just mean the speed of the dogs.

I loosen my grip on the sled and shake the cramp out of my hand, but I still feel far from relaxed. The feeling of "just us and the dogs" is gone. There are other teams to watch out for. I don't really care if we win or not. I just want to get to Arviat, but I realize it's a tall order. There's no sign of the Quebec team or any of the other two teams that must still be behind us, but there's also no sign of any of the teams ahead of us, either. And yet, they're in my head. Is the Quebec team still in the race? Are we catching up or falling behind? We only started at three-minute intervals apart, but if we're all traveling close to the same speed, we're a long ways apart from each other—which I don't mind if they're all crazy and out-of-control like Jay the Sleigh's team.

"We must be getting close to the checkpoint." Barnabas nods ahead. The trail markers lead us toward shore. We run up a rise and, in a flash, we're at the checkpoint. It isn't really much of a checkpoint, just a red flag stuck into the snow. I crane my neck. The roof of a weather-beaten building peaks over a high bank of the North Knife River. Is this one of the Dene houses, the ones that lived by North Knife River? No, it's too new for that. But that's the river they followed inland in search of a new home. It's strange to actually be here. If I didn't know what had happened, there's nothing here to tell their story, except the rocks and the wind and the river itself.

Skidoos and a blue Bombardier are parked near a canvas-wall tent. There's a team parked right ahead of us. Checkpoint volunteers are gathered around him.

"That's Fast Tommy. From Arviat. He has good dogs." Barnabas waves to him, but Fast Tommy doesn't notice us. He's showing the checkpoint people his mandatory gear.

Two Canadian Rangers in army pants and red parkas rush over to us, writing down our time: 12:08 PM. We left at 9:21. Thirty miles in under three hours!

"Can I see your mandatory gear?" a young guy holding a clipboard asks. Barnabas pulls out the items as the checker reads them off the list:

- ✓ Two cold-weather sleeping bags
- ✓ Snow knife
- ✓ Cold-weather tent
- ✓ Cooker and fuel
- ✓ Booties for each dog
- ✓ Dog food
- ✓ First aid kit
- ✓ Emergency food for the mushers
- ✓ Satellite phone
- ✓ Parks Canada Mail Parcel

"You're good to go," the checker says.

"Thanks, we snack the dogs and then go," Barnabas says, already throwing a piece of seal meat to the first two dogs. They catch it in mid-air, gobble it down, and sniff the ground for scraps.

We're pulling out of the checkpoint as the team behind us pulls in. It's not the Quebec guys, though. It's already hard to keep track of who is where. What was the order on the checker's clipboard? Team two is in the lead ahead of team one. Teams four and five have passed team three. Team eight left four minutes ago. Team nine is just pulling out now. And then it's us—we passed one team and were passed by two others. We're in eighth place, but the starting times still need to be adjusted. So we might be further ahead. I guess we'll find out at Nunalla, which is the halfway checkpoint. There's a mandatory rest of six hours and our times will be adjusted there. Because the last team left 33 minutes behind the first team, the first team has a mandatory rest of six hours and 33 minutes and so on. And then whoever is first to the finish line wins.

Our dogs leave the checkpoint with new enthusiasm, catching up to Fast Tommy's team. Their sled is skinnier and shorter than ours and both mushers lie down to cut down on the wind resistance. They glance back at us and then whistle at their dogs, who pick up speed. It's hard to guess their age, with most of their faces covered by the fur on their hoods, but I think they're younger than the other racers. Maybe in their twenties.

"Are we passing?" I ask.

"We can try." Barnabas calls the team to go left. This time

all the dogs are on the same side, and we're slowly pulling ahead, but we're not getting past the other team's leaders. Our dogs lope flat out now, their backs arched, their tongues lolling. Saliva freezes white and foamy on their whiskers and fur. We run side by side for a while and then our team falls back.

"Nice looking dog, that one behind the leader," Fast Tommy calls. "Who is it?"

"The one with the stumpy tail? Pamiuluk. Out of Qakuq, that white leader, and one of Old Philip's females. The one he got from Rankin last spring."

"How old is she?"

"Four."

"I wouldn't mind a litter of pups from her," he calls as his team slowly pulls away.

Barnabas nods and then turns his attention back to the dogs.

"You know all the parents of your dogs?" I ask.

"Ii. Parents and grandparents. If you breed your dogs, you want to make sure they're good dogs, all the way down the line."

"It must be fun having puppies around."

"Lots of fun," Barnabas smiles. "My sister, she always, always plays with them. Even carries them around in her amauti."

I try to picture her with the puppies, squirming and wriggling, fuzzy and warm, but I can't get a picture in my head.

It all feels so foreign. Like I'm learning about the dogs and life and everything just now. At least Barnabas and most of the dogs have been here before.

I glance down at my red bib with the white number seven, just to make sure it's really real. I'm racing in the Arctic Quest. The red of the bib stands in contrast to the grayish brown and white of my caribou parka. My snow pants are tucked into the felt liners of my sealskin kamiks. I barely recognize myself and yet I love what I see.

I try to imagine what it would have been like growing up here when Old Ipilii was young and dog teams the only way of winter transportation. The cool thing is it probably wouldn't have looked so much different—once we leave the checkpoints behind. Our dogs, the sleds, the clothing—it's almost like traveling back in time.

Fast Tommy's team slowly but steadily pulls away, until it becomes a small black dot and then disappears altogether. I look back, but there's nobody behind us. The sun is as high as it will get today, the snow so bright I forget I'm wearing sunglasses. And then, slowly, our shadows move to our right, becoming longer, and the harsh bluish whiteness of the snow becomes softer, turning into a warmer white.

"Wooh, wooh!" Barnabas suddenly yells. The snow hook

makes a screeching sound as it scrapes over ice. The trail suddenly ends in fast-flowing water. A river on top of the ice. Steam rises above the deadly water, its color an icy turquoise. The dogs fan out, running along the edge, looking for a way to avoid the water. The snow hook doesn't grab on the glare ice and the sled slides ahead, passing the dogs.

My heart beats violently while the rest of my body freezes. We're sliding towards the deadly river.

The sled comes to a halt, just inches from the water. I hear a strange sound, a bubbling and gurgling, like someone is speaking in a language that's not human, and it takes me a second to realize it's the water flowing through the ice making that sound. There are holes in the ice and the water runs down in a swirl like a toilet being flushed. I feel hot and cold at the same time.

"Where are we? What's happening?"

"Seal river. Is tidal overflow."

"What now? Do we have to wait till the tide goes out?"

"Nah, we can go through. See the trail marker over there? And then up there?" Barnabas points to a piece of wooden lath stuck in the middle of the river. The water is flowing fast around the marker, a crown of white on the turquoise waves. I follow the line of markers until I see one far in the distance. Teasing us from its spot on dry land.

"What if the water is too deep? What if the ice isn't safe? Did you see those holes?"

"Is only overflow. We can go around to stay out of the deep water."

"Around where?"

"Always out to the sea-ice, my grandfather teach me."

I stare to our right. Barnabas might be right, the water is slower over there and maybe less deep, but my eyes are drawn back to the swirling holes sucking down the water, and suddenly there's an image in my head—us swirling to the bottom of a green-blue ocean and, above us, a ceiling of turquoise-white ice, beautiful in its horrible deadliness.

"I'm not going there. I don't want to die," I say.

"The other teams are all gone through. We be fine."

"What if we get wet feet?" I ask. "Our toes will freeze."

"You wear sealskin kamiik. You won't get wet. Help me." Barnabas grabs Qakuq and leads him to the right toward the sea ice. The ice is glare and Barnabas struggles to stay upright, but once Qakuq understands where we're going, he straightens out the line. The other dogs follow. Except Qaqavii. Whining, he turns in tight circles, staying put where he knows it's safe. His breathing is too fast, his tongue hanging out despite the cold, his eyes bulging. He's terrified. I know how he feels.

Barnabas grabs Qaqavii by his collar, but Qaqavii won't budge. Barnabas pulls harder and slips on the glare ice.

"Emmalu. Get Qaqavii. He trust you."

I take a deep breath and then another one. If Qaqavii can sense how scared I am, it will only make things worse. I tighten my hands into fists, willing them to stop shaking.

"It's okay, boy," I say as I walk carefully toward Qaqavii. "We're going around the river and back to shore. It's just a little detour. We'll be fine. You might get wet feet, but that's all, okay? I promise." It's like I'm talking to myself as much as to Qaqavii. There's a tail wag, ever so slight.

"Come here," I coax him and he slinks toward me. As soon as he reaches me, he rubs against my legs, his tail wagging wildly. He paws my leg and, when I bend down to give him a rub, he licks my cheek.

"Jump on, Emmalu."

I shuffle back to the qamutik and Qaqavii takes his position in the team. The dogs are keen to keep moving and Qaqavii forgets his fear. We run east toward the sea along the overflow of the river, and when Barnabas tells them to turn north, they don't hesitate to plunge into the river. Their paws fling water in the air and a million tiny drops glitter in the sunlight. It's almost magical—if it wasn't for the constant fear of falling through the ice. The water only reaches up to the dogs' wrists, and when we pass the holes close by, I can see we're on two feet of ice, but the fear does not subside until we reach the shore on the other side.

Barnabas stops the team to let the dogs roll in the dry snow. Even though the snow wicks away the wetness, the water freezes so fast that ice clings to the dogs' coats, freezing their harnesses to their fur. I feel the sweat on the back of my neck cooling and start to shiver. I jump off the qamutik and rub the ice off the dogs with my mitts, warming them and me at the same time.

"You cold?"

I nod, not wanting to talk, not wanting the cold air to fill my lungs. Barnabas gives the dogs snacks, and as soon as they're done eating, they curl up in the snow, tails tucked under their noses. Barnabas pours me tea from his steaming thermos. It feels good, the warmth, even though it cools quickly.

"Eat, Emmalu—you stay warmer that way."

I fish out a cereal bar, but when I try to bite into it, it's so hard that I'm afraid my teeth will break.

"Give it to me."

Barnabas takes my cereal bar and stuffs it under his parka. He cuts himself a few slices of fermented something. I'm too cold to even ask and refuse when he passes me a slice. Barnabas gives me my cereal bar back. It's still cold but I can bite chunks off now.

"I make more tea," Barnabas says and gets his Coleman stove out. Just then, team number ten passes us, making a wide berth around us. Our dogs jump to their feet and strain their lines, all signs of tiredness gone.

"Suluk and his son Jonah. They got good dogs," Barnabas says, and then quickly packs the Coleman stove away. My throat is scratchy from breathing in too much cold air, and my mouth is dry after eating the cereal bar, but I guess there's no time for more tea. We chase the team ahead of us until we catch up, and then our dogs slowly pass. There's an old guy on the qamutik, older even than Old Ipilii.

"Takuniaqpapsi Nunalla-mi," Barnabas calls. "Tuktusiuq-tailigitsi."

"Ii," the younger of the two grins and pats a rifle next to him.

I turn around and watch their dogs chasing our team. They're running so close to our sled that I could reach out and pet their leader. He's black, except for his white nose and the white dots above his eyes. His fur is long and matted. It's frosty around his muzzle, but between his ears, it stands up. His mouth is open as if frozen in a big smile. He looks me in the eyes while he's running.

"Atta good boy you are," I say and he tries running faster, but soon the team falls behind. Suluk sips his tea, smiling at us. He looks so comfortable, sitting with his legs straight out, like he's spent his whole life sitting on dog sleds and igloo floors.

"Suluk was born at Nunalla. Sometime in the forties," Barnabas says.

"There was a community there?"

"Just a trading post, but people camp there."

"He was born in an igloo?" I ask.

"If it was winter. You have to ask Suluk. He know better."

"Where was Jonah born?"

"In a hospital," Barnabas replies, like it's the most obvious thing in the world. Which it is, I guess. I look at father and son. Suluk in his shiny caribou outfit, Jonah wearing a once-red Canada Goose parka, now faded into pink from years of sunlight. Suluk wears caribou kamiks, Jonah clunky black Sorel boots. Suluk born on the land, Jonah in a town. Their worlds seem far apart but, out here, they're still the same.

Barnabas waves as our team pulls away. "We'll have tea for you when you come to Nunalla, but hurry or it will be frozen," he teases.

I watch them until I feel dizzy from looking back. There's less snow here and the trail is rougher. We cross windswept ponds with snowdrifts hard as rock. The dogs swerve around the bigger drifts, causing our sled to whip sideways. Then we're on land again, and soon after, on another pond—the land is like a patchwork quilt of blue-gray ponds and white snow-covered tundra.

Ahead of us, another team. They're stopped, feeding the dogs, but when they see us approach, they quickly pack up and leave before we can pass. It's Peter Patterson and a guy wearing a matching red down parka. I feel the sudden urge to call up the dogs, be faster than them. 'That's no world for women out there,' he had said back then on my dog cart ride with him. It feels ages ago now. "Pick it up, pick it up," I call to the dogs, but then I feel stupid. They wouldn't care what Peter had said, so why should I? The other team slowly pulls away from us and then we're alone.

A wispy white cloud floats in the sky like a feather. On the horizon, more clouds hanging low with a pastel-colored sky above. We travel in silence until I can't remember if we left hours or days ago. The shadows are becoming longer, the light more intense as if trying to keep the night at bay. How many hours of daylight will we have left?

★

"There is Long Point Checkpoint." Barnabas nods toward a square shape in the distance. It takes a few more miles before I realize they're buildings, and then—only a minute later—we're there. Three guys in camouflage snow pants and red parkas rush toward us. One is clumsily holding a clipboard and pencil with big black leather mitts.

"Are you camping here?" the one with the clipboard asks as he's checking our gear.

There's no sign of other mushers here. They all must have pushed on to Nunalla, another forty miles away.

"Can I see the time sheet?" Barnabas asks.

I lean over Barnabas's shoulder as he's studying the times. They don't mean anything to me. Just that the other mushers are faster, but I already knew that.

"Fast Tommy is in the lead. He's only an hour ahead of us. The last team left thirteen minutes ago. It's a close race. I think we go on," Barnabas says and looks at me. "Maybe we can camp with Suluk and Jonah when they catch up."

"Okay," I say, caught in race fever.

"You're better off to stay here," the checkpoint guy says. "We were checking the weather forecast with headquarters in Churchill. There's a bad storm coming." There's a note of authority in the checker's voice that makes me feel like I'm in the principal's office.

"You can put up your tent over there." He points past

where the skidoos are parked and then walks back to the cabin. When he opens the door, a shimmer of warm light escapes the building, making it feel even colder and darker out here.

Barnabas is looking at the sky all around us. The sun has set, so we'll only have a short period of twilight and then it will be dark.

"Let's camp here," I say. "At least there are people and a cabin close by."

"I don't see a storm coming. The other teams all left."

"But they heard it on their radios," I argue.

"The weather forecast lies all the time," Barnabas says, but I can tell he's unsure himself. "We should go," he says. "Travel while we can."

"What if Suluk and Jonah don't catch up to us?"

"We camp on our own."

That's what I wanted, wasn't it? Traveling for days, camping on the tundra. But now that I feel the weight of the approaching night, I want to duck away, crawl into a warm building.

"We should stay ..." I say, "... please."

"Maybe we rest the dogs and then go with Suluk." Barnabas sounds relieved. As if I had given him an excuse to stay. We feed the dogs and ourselves, and then sit on the sled, watching the night approach.

"There's a headlight!" Barnabas jumps up. "Suluk is here."

But as the team approaches out of the darkness, illuminated by the headlamps of the mushers, I can see that the dogs are running side by side and not in a fan.

"Merde, how do you train for a race like that? Take your dogs to the local swimming pool? Chase the effing Zamboni around the skating rink?"

One of the checkpoint people laughs.

Barnabas and I look at each other. Where is Suluk? Weren't they right behind us?

"Maybe Suluk and Jonah camped?"

"You could ask Jay the Sleigh," I suggest.

"You could, too," Barnabas replies.

Neither of us moves.

We watch as the Quebec team puts up their tent in the light of their headlamps. It's pitch black now. Their dogs curl up immediately. Our dogs watch the other team for a while and then dig themselves beds in the snow.

"I'm cold," I say.

Barnabas gets the tent out and we silently set it up. There's no sign of Suluk, no sign of a storm. I feel bad that I messed up Barnabas's race, but not bad enough to want to head out into the night.

I walk a few steps into the dark, close to the dogs, switch off my headlamp, and quickly pee. One of the dogs gets up, shakes, and then turns in tight circles, settling back into the bed he's melted into the snow.

I crawl into the tent. Barnabas lays out our sleeping bags, leaving a six-inch gap between them. I pull off my kamiks and then crawl into my sleeping bag with all my clothes on. I'm cold. Can you freeze to death while sleeping, I wonder?

"Are you warm enough?" Barnabas asks.

"Um ..."

"You can come closer. Is warmer that way," he says.

I shuffle over an inch or two with my back turned to Barnabas. Barnabas, too, inches closer until our backs are pressed against each other.

"Better?" he asks.

I nod, even though he can't see me in the dark.

"Good night, Emmalu," he says.

"Good night," I say.

It's silent. So silent that it's almost noisy, if that makes any sense. I lie in the dark, looking up at the canvas walls of our tent. The dogs are resting a few feet from us. Once in a while, I hear a dog shake. And then a different sound, like water being poured out of a cup. A dog peeing. I stifle a giggle.

"Are you sleeping?" I whisper, real quiet.

Barnabas doesn't respond. But I know he's not sleeping, his breathing is too quiet.

Our dogs suddenly all get up and then there's barking.

"Wooh!" I hear a voice.

"That's Jonah!" Barnabas bolts upright and fiddles with the tent toggles. He pulls his mukluks on and runs out in his shorts, pulling his parka over his naked skin as he stumbles behind the team in the dark. I watch from the tent opening, still wrapped in my sleeping bag. The team pulls out of the checkpoint before Barnabas catches up to them—two headlights shining on the silhouettes of the dogs, illuminating their breath like white fog rising into the dark night.

Barnabas comes back, crawls in his sleeping bag but doesn't lie down. He sits with his arms slung around his knees, thinking.

"I'm sorry," I say. "We could go, if you want." Neither of us is sleeping anyway, and the night isn't any darker if we're out there or in our tent here, I try to rationalize. But I'm relieved when Barnabas says, "We leave at first daylight. Let's sleep for a few hours."

I wake up with a start to the sound of snow crunching. Something is out there. Walking around. Sniffing. I hold still, trying not to breathe. Please don't come here. But it does. It's pushing against the canvas walls. I fumble for my headlamp with one hand, shaking Barnabas with the other.

"Barnabas! Barnabas!" I whisper, my whole body trembling so badly I can barely talk. "There's something outside," I say.

Barnabas slowly turns over, shielding his eyes from my headlamp light. "What is it?"

"I don't know. A bear?"

The dogs are barking like crazy now, and not just our team. I hear barking from further away.

"Go look," Barnabas says. "You got the headlamp."

"Me? You look. You got the gun."

"Is in the sled," Barnabas says. "I didn't want it to get condensation."

I hear something brush against our tent.

"Do something!" I scream. "What if he comes in the tent?"

"Who?"

"Wake up, Barnabas! There's a bear!"

Barnabas sits up and wipes the sleep from his eyes. I pass him the headlamp and he opens the bottom toggle on the tent flap. As soon as he undoes the second toggle a white snout with a big black nose pushes its way through the gap.

I scream and grab onto Barnabas. The bear hesitates for

a moment and then pushes his whole body into the tent. A slobbery tongue licks my face and I hear a familiar whine and Barnabas's laugh.

My whole body shakes violently and it takes me what feels like an eternity to realize: a) I'm still alive, and b) it's not a bear. I let go of Barnabas and shift back.

"Qaqavii! How did you get loose?" I pant, my breathing a total mess. Qaqavii plunks himself onto my sleeping bag.

I ruffle Qaqavii behind the ears, forcing my breathing to slow down. "Can he stay?"

"If you let me sleep then." Barnabas closes the tent flap.

I curl up with Qaqavii. The tension is slowly easing out of my tired muscles.

CHAPTER 29

"The storm is coming now. Better to have traveled last night."

Barnabas takes down the tent while I harness the dogs. There's a faint glow of yellow shining through a thickening layer of gray sky. An eerie stillness is in the air, as if the land is holding its breath.

There's no sign of life yet from the Quebec team's tent. The race volunteers tell us the last team got lost only thirty miles out of Churchill and eventually found its way back last night. There's only ten teams left in the race now. Two teams made it to Nunalla, but that's already old news from a Ranger who phoned with his satellite phone around midnight. We're six hours behind Jonah and the other teams. If we stay ahead of the Quebec team, we'll be in ninth place, unless there are teams camping just north of the checkpoint. Maybe we can still catch up to those.

★

The dogs follow the trail of yesterday's dog tracks. They don't need trail markers. The sun is fading in and out as the clouds gather. When there is sun, the dog tracks are easy to follow in the contrast of light and shadow. When there is no sun, I have to strain my eyes until they hurt, and all I can do is trust that Barnabas and the dogs know where we're going. The trail markers seem further and further apart and are sometimes hard to see in the distance.

And then the wind sets in. Snow begins to drift, wiping out the trail we follow. The dogs fade in and out of the drifting snow. The tundra is suddenly alive, the drifting snow a moving creature with countless arms, constantly moving, clawing at my wind-battered legs. There is a strange beauty to it, a captivating power that won't let me take my eyes off the blowing snow— and yet I have the feeling that this is just the beginning, that the worst is still to come.

Barnabas urges the dogs on.

"How far to Nunalla?" I ask.

"Far," he replies, chewing on his lip.

We travel on in silence, afraid we won't outrun this storm. Barnabas at least knows what a storm in the Arctic looks like.

I have no idea. Maybe that's for the better, I think, as big heavy snowflakes begin to fall from the sky. Soon the snow falls more heavily, settling on our gear and the dogs' fur. Drifting snow and falling snow mingle in an uncoordinated dance until I can't tell the two apart. Snow swirls up from the ground, falls from the sky, and wraps tighter and tighter around us. All I can see is white.

It's impossible to make out any tracks or trail markers. There is no horizon, no shadows, no telling if we're traveling up or down, just white all around me. I don't know if we're traveling on the land or in the sky—or if both are the same. We're running north, further and further, and yet we don't seem to move. I never thought about what infinity looks like, but if you asked me now, I'd say it's a dog team running into a whiteout. It's the most beautiful thing I've ever seen. And the most terrifying.

I didn't think the wind could pick up any more, but it does, driving the snow horizontally across the land and into our faces. The dogs crouch low to the ground, pushing on against the wind. It feels like with every step forward we're moving one back. Within minutes, I can't see our lead dogs. I lean forward, touching the tangle of the lines that attach me to the dogs like a lifeline.

Snow clings to my eyelashes. As soon as I wipe them, they are a slushy mess again, until all I can do is turn my head away from the storm. I shield my face with my mitt, a short-lived relief, for now I can't see anything. The storm is so fierce that it sucks my breath away.

Once in a while, the dogs appear out of the whiteout, their bodies leaning sideways into the storm, their fur plastered with snow on the upwind side, their heads tilted downwind. I haven't seen a trail marker for a long time.

"We have to make shelter," Barnabas yells. The wind is so strong, he has to repeat himself twice before I can hear him.

"We have to call for help," I yell back.

"How?"

"With the satellite phone!"

"I don't have batteries."

"What?" I feel the blood in my veins grow cold.

Barnabas yells something but the storm carries his voice away.

The snow is drifting across the tundra, crawling under my parka, and burying the dogs, who curl up with their noses tucked tight under their tails.

"Help me!" Barnabas yells. He's standing next to the qamutik, tugging on my sleeve. My legs won't listen. I sit on the qamutik, hugging myself tightly, feeling the cold creep in.

"Emmalu! Move!" Barnabas yells. This is it, I think. We're gonna die. And then I have this horrible image in my head of

Kitty running toward me at the start line and me turning my back to her. What if she really was there and this was the last image she'll have of me? No, I'm not going to die. At least, not without a fight. But how do you fight a storm that has wiped out the world around you? A storm so full of rage that it drowns out the voice of your own thoughts?

I look around me. There is no sign of the sun, no telling where north or south might be. I already don't know anymore where we came from or where we're heading.

And then the strangest thing happens: a bird appears out of the whiteout. It's tiny, not bigger than a sparrow, flapping its wings fast and furiously. For a few seconds, it hangs still, right above me, and then—finding an eddy in the whirling wind— it dives forward, wings folded back, its tiny body streamlined against the current. One wing flap at a time, it pushes forward, falls back against the wind, regains the distance lost, and starts all over again until it's out of sight.

I force myself to get up. The wind pushes against me and I struggle to stay upright. I stretch out my arms like wings and let myself fall. The wind carries me, my weight balanced perfectly against the push of the blizzard. And then it eases off, just for a second, but enough for me to stumble forward, forcing me to hold my own weight again.

"What do you want me to do?" I yell.

"Flip the qamutik up, make a wind break," Barnabas yells.

I grab an end of the big heavy sled.

"No, the other way! Our gear downwind!"

We hunker behind the sled, catching our breath. The snow swirls around us, but where we sit, it's calmer.

"What now?" I ask.

"I need my snow knife." Barnabas digs in our gear and pulls out a knife with a thin, rusty blade as long as my arm.

"My grandpa's pana." Barnabas holds it up for me to see. The handle looks like it's carved out of antler. Barnabas hesitates for a moment, then he cuts the snow where he's sitting into two-foot squares.

"Not the best kind of snow," he yells against the wind as he pulls out the first block. It breaks into two pieces. Barnabas carefully stands them on their sides, and then cuts another block and another one, until we've made a circle around us, just big enough for us to sit in. The second row is trickier. The wind pushes the blocks over but, between the two of us, we manage to build a small igloo. Barnabas passes the blocks, and I hold them until they're wedged in and hold their own weight. The snow walls surround us like a cocoon.

Through the small opening, Barnabas passes me our

sleeping bags, the Coleman stove, the teakettle, and a bag with food. Then he crawls back out to fill the cracks between the blocks with snow.

I sit inside the igloo, surprised by the quiet and calm. It feels warmer than outside—or maybe that's just my imagination. When Barnabas comes back, he pulls a block of snow behind him to close off the entrance hole.

"What about the dogs?" I ask.

Leaning on his elbows, Barnabas looks outside. "They're fine." He pulls the block of snow into place, leaving just enough of a gap that I can still peek outside if I hold my head just right. Qaqavii is the only dog I can make out in the blizzard and even he is barely visible, so much white snow is clinging to his fur.

"They're getting buried in snow! How can they be fine?"

"The snow insulates them. They dig down and let the snow cover them. They know."

"Not Qaqavii. He's not digging down." Even from here, I can see he's sitting up shivering miserably.

"We'll cut him a few snow blocks later. But we look after ourselves first. If we're not okay, we can't help the dogs … okay?"

"Okay," I say, but feel anything but okay.

Barnabas lights the Coleman stove and fills the kettle with snow. The fumes of the stove sting my eyes, but the heat doesn't reach my chilled bones. Barnabas passes me a piece of dark dried meat. I'm not hungry. Just cold. I chew on it just to give myself something to do. The more I eat, the more I feel warmth flare up inside my stomach, spreading to my hands and toes. When the water has boiled, Barnabas pours strong black tea into a chipped enameled mug and passes it to me. I hold onto the cup, soak up its warmth.

My eyelids feel heavy. The night before the race I barely slept, and last night wasn't any better.

"What about Qaqavii?" I ask before I fall asleep sitting up. I crawl to the igloo entrance. Drifting snow has closed our hole, so I push the snow block out of the way. The blizzard hurls flurries into my face, tears at my hair, and howls into my ear. I back up into the entrance. I can't tell Qaqavii apart from the rest of the dogs. They're all curled together into a big ball, drifting snow forming a hard-packed shell around them.

"Best not to disturb them," Barnabas says. "You don't want them to get up and shake the snow off. Let's try to sleep. Conserve some energy."

The igloo isn't big enough for us to stretch out, so we curl up like the dogs. Barnabas rubs my feet through my kamiks. The warmth thaws out my icy toes. It hurts—the warmth coming back—but eventually the pain subsides.

★

I wake up from a chattering noise close to my ear. It takes me a while to realize it's my teeth. I wiggle my toes. They feel numb.

"You okay?"

"I'm cold," I say.

"I'll get you more food."

"I'm not hungry, just cold."

"The food will warm you," Barnabas says and wriggles out of his sleeping bag. He lights the stove and puts on more tea. "Are your clothes dry?"

"My T-shirt is a bit damp, I think."

"Take it off then."

I hesitate. Won't I be even colder with fewer clothes?

"Give it to me. I'll dry it out for you."

I wriggle my hands under my shirt trying to take it off without taking my fleece off, but Barnabas isn't even looking my way, so finally I just take both off. I suck in my breath when the cold air touches my naked skin, but as soon as I have my fleece back on, I feel warmer than before. My T-shirt was a lot damper than I thought. I pass it to Barnabas and he stuffs it under his own shirt—to dry it with his body heat, he tells me.

"Here," he passes me tea and dried caribou meat dipped in lard. The first bite makes my mouth water and I realize I am hungry.

"How long did I sleep?"

"Long," he says.

"How's the weather?"

"Same. Not good." Barnabas shuts the Coleman off. "Better not to use too much fuel. We might be here for days."

"Days?" I ask, feeling the igloo wall moving closer. "How many?" I tug on my fleece, making more room around my throat. It feels tight all of a sudden.

"Until the blizzard stops. Is upinngakssaq. The season of new snow and spring storms. Not a good time to travel."

"Why do they put the race in April, then?"

"Maybe because of longer daylight hours? Is also warmer. I'm going out to feed the dogs. Want to come?"

We put on our parkas, bumping into each other in the small space. It takes Barnabas a while to dig out the snow from the entrance. The longer it takes, the more desperately I have to get out. I wriggle through our entrance hole and take a deep breath. Or at least I try. The wind is still strong enough to suck my breath away. Our sled is drifted over, the blizzard claiming it bit by bit. I'm glad for our tiny snow cave, glad that Barnabas knows what to do—and yet I wish I were home. Home. I don't even know where that is, but the picture that flashes in my mind is our room at the lodge, Kitty and I sitting on our beds, Kitty smiling at me, not mad, just glad I'm back.

I crouch down next to Barnabas, who slices pieces of seal meat for the dogs, using the runners for a cutting board. Only two heads poke up watching us. If it wasn't for the humps of snow and the odd ear sticking out here and there, you wouldn't know there were any dogs at all.

The dogs are waiting for us to place their supper in front of them; then they gobble it up, still lying down. Qaqavii doesn't touch his food. He looks so cold and miserable. I hunker down and break off tiny pieces of meat, holding them to his mouth. He takes a piece and chews. The snow at Qaqavii's butt end moves. A tail wag? I pass him another piece and then another. Qaqavii gets up and eats the rest and then pees where he stands without lifting his leg. Like a puppy.

"It's okay, you and I, we'll be fine." Qaqavii squeezes tight against me and I shield him from the driving snow and cold as much as I can.

"Can Qaqavii come inside?" I yell over the noise of the storm.

"Can I stop you?" Barnabas yells back.

Qaqavii dances around me as I crawl back into the igloo.

The other dogs are all up now, straining on their lines trying to follow Qaqavii in.

"If you let one in, you have to let everyone in," Barnabas says.

"Seriously?" I imagine us cramped into the tiny igloo, wagging tails and slobbery dog kisses everywhere. That would be so much better than knowing they're outside on their own.

"Only if you sleep outside," Barnabas grins. I show him my tongue.

Qaqavii settles in between Barnabas and me. I spoil him with belly rubs.

"Want some more tea?"

"Sure," I say. Not because I really want more tea, but because it gives us something to do.

"Hey, wait, I got something to go with the tea." I dig in my travel bag and find what I'm looking for. A chocolate bar. I break it in half and pass one half to Barnabas. I fill my mouth with three frozen pieces at a time, enjoying how the flavor unfolds as it thaws in my mouth. Chocolate in one hand, Qaqavii between Barnabas and me, the Coleman putting out heat; the waiting almost becomes bearable.

"What else do you have in your bag?"

I quickly stuff everything back into my pack. "Just clothes,

toothbrush, and a peanut butter jelly sandwich. Pretty frozen."
I say and feel myself blush.

"What's that furry thing?"

"Silly."

"What's silly?"

"My stuffie. From my Grandma." I slowly pull out Silly.
Her fake black and white fur is matted to her body, one eye has
come loose, and there's a hole in the seam by her belly. I quickly
stuff her back inside. I don't even know why I brought her.

"Let me see," Barnabas stretches out his hand, but I pull
away. We wrestle for the bag until Qaqavii joins in and pulls on
the straps with his teeth. I let go. Barnabas pulls out my stuffie.

"Hello, Silly." He holds her like a puppet.

"Where are we?" Barnabas asks in a high-pitched voice,
turning Silly's head back and forth.

It's not like I imagine Silly's voice at all, but then again, I
never heard her talk. Only in my head.

"In a big snowstorm conjured by an evil spirit." Barnabas says.

"Evil spirit?" Silly asks, hiding behind the caribou skins.

"Nonsense," I interrupt. "It's just a storm." I feel
embarrassed because I don't want my stuffed animal to worry.
It's just … I don't know. A habit, I guess. Grandma and me, we
always treated her like a living being.

"How did we get here?" Silly asks.

"That's a looong story," I say.

"Looks like we have lots of time for looong stories," Barnabas says in his Barnabas voice and puts Silly down. Qaqavii sniffs Silly and then tenderly chews her ear. I tell Barnabas how I didn't want to come to Churchill at all and how I was actually going to leave when I lost Qakuq. And then I met Qaqavii and I wanted to learn about dogs and going out on the land with him and his grandpa.

I tell him how I miss Grandma Millie and how Elisapii reminds me of her. I mean, she's different, but sometimes she makes me feel the same way my Grandma did. The words just come out and, while I listen to my own story, I realize it never was just about the dogs. And then it occurs to me that I never asked Barnabas about his parents.

"My parents? Which ones?" Barnabas asks.

"Do you have … more than one pair of parents?" I ask, confused.

"I have my birth parents and the parents who raised me. I have lots of family. Four parents and eight grandparents, but one grandpa died, and I don't see my birth dad very often."

"So you're … adopted?" I don't want to make him talk about things that might be hard for him to think about, but I'm curious, too.

MIRIAM KÖRNER

Barnabas stuffs his sleeping bag against the igloo wall, using it as a pillow

"My mother was just in high school when she had me and her oldest cousin was already married. They had just lost their baby, so my parents—I mean my birth mother's cousin—adopted me."

"I'm sorry," I say.

"About what?" Barnabas seems confused.

"Your birth mother ... she didn't want you?"

"Of course, she always gonna be my mother, but she was too young and in school, and her cousin was so sad about losing their first child, so my family decided I should go there."

My mind is racing a million miles a minute. Can you give up a baby, even though you love it? Or *because* you love it?

"How come you live with your grandparents now?"

"My parents have lots of children now, but my grandparents only have one son in Arviat. The other two moved back to Iqaluit. I always liked going out with the dogs, so I came with my grandparents when they needed me."

It sounds so simple. Like it doesn't really matter who you live with. As if everyone loves you just the same. But it's not so simple. Not for me. No one ever wanted me. Except Grandma Millie, maybe. I wriggle Silly away from Qaqavii's mouth before he chews her ear completely off. I hold her tight, thinking of

Grandma Millie, and thinking that if she was still alive, I'd look after her like Barnabas looks after Elisapii.

And then I think of how Grandma Millie always looked out for me and how, when you grow up, things turn around and you look after your grandparents. Except I don't have grandparents to look after.

Then the image of Kitty is in my head and how she always looks so hurt when we fight. I wish I could hug her right now. I bite my lip and try to change the topic.

"Your grandparents aren't from Arviat, you say?"

"Elisapii is, but not Old Ipilii. He's from Qikiqtaajuit. His mother moved to Arviat when Old Ipilii was little."

"Because they wanted to?"

"Ii. Kind of. Too many bad memories."

"What about his dad and the dogs? They didn't move with them?"

"Is a sad story."

"I guess we have lots of time for sad stories," I say, although I don't know if I really want to know this one.

"My grandpa be a better person to tell the story. I only know little." Barnabas says, fiddling with his tea mug. For a second, I think he won't say more now, but then he looks up from his tea as if he's found the story at the bottom of his mug.

"He was born on the land in a winter camp with lots of igloos, big ones for whole families, not like ours here. He always loved dogs, was always playing with the puppies. When he was seven, they moved to Iqaluit, the place of many fish. Frobisher Bay, the qallunaat called it, after some explorer who discovered the place where our people used to camp for longer than anyone can remember."

"Nobody made them move?"

"At that time, lots of people moved closer to the trading posts, worked for the Hudson's Bay Company and later for the government. They went back and forth between living in the community and on the land."

Barnabas takes a break in his storytelling and lights the Coleman stove. His voice sounds a bit as if Old Ipilii was telling the story himself.

"When they moved to Iqaluit, they came with all their dogs. There were many people and lots of dogs. Ipilii, too, had a dog. His first sled dog. He had already trained puppies, but this one was Ipilii's to keep, his dad said."

Barnabas pauses, stirs the melting snow in the teapot and adds more. His voice is scratchy. He takes a sip of water. And then he says, very fast, as if he'd rather not say it at all, "He wasn't meant to keep his puppy. The RCMP, they shot all the dogs."

"What? Why?"

"You have to ask them. The RCMP, they have their story. Inuit who remember have another story."

"What's Old Ipilii's story?"

"Sad. Real sad. When they came, his dad was not home. Old Ipilii hid his puppy under the doorstep and he watched as they shot his father's dogs. The dogs were running away, but they weren't fast enough for the bullets. Ipilii started crying, and then the puppy whined, and then the RCMP, they pulled out his puppy and ..."

I'm covering my ears. I don't want to hear what happened next, but I can't stop the image of a little boy appearing in my head. He's dressed in caribou clothing, so proud to have his first dog, but now he's standing there, his nose snotty, a dead puppy in his arms.

"What happened then? What did his dad say when he came back?"

"His dad never said nothing. The next day he left his government job and went out hunting. Without the dogs. He never came back."

Barnabas offers me a teacup. I shake my head. I can't swallow.

"Old Ipilii had nightmares, and finally his mother took him far away to Arviat. He couldn't be around dogs for a long time.

He was angry and nobody could make it go away. It's not good to be angry.

"When he grew up, he had a son and then two more. He wanted that his children grow up with dogs like him. Old Ipilii bought dogs. It was hard, but Ipilii wanted to teach his children the things his father had taught him. His boys liked skidoos better than dogs, but Old Ipilii, he kept his dogs.

"I liked going out hunting with the dogs since I was young. Way better than with the skidoo. Old Ipilii teaches me, so I can teach my children. I don't think his children will ever have dogs. Too expensive." Barnabas laughs. "They eat more than any skidoo."

We talk about the people in Arviat who have dogs and what efforts they take to feed them. And then Barnabas tells me how Inuit and their qimmiit did everything together in the past—way more than just dog sledding. The dogs were always with the families, helped hunt polar bears, sniffed out seal holes, and in summer they carried packs. Having a good dog team—well fed and strong—gave you lots of respect from everyone in the community.

While we talk, I keep wondering what Elisapii's story is, and I finally ask where she grew up. Barnabas says his grandmother was moved around a lot, but he doesn't know much because Elisapii doesn't talk about it.

"I tried finding out for myself, but I couldn't really understand it all. My grandmother's people lived at Ennadai Lake where hunting was good, but then the government moved them to Nueltin Lake, where there were no caribou. So they walked back. Took them many, many months, and once they got there, there was plenty of food again. But they didn't let them stay. Moved them further away to Hennik Lake. Again, they can't find enough game and people were starving. So they move them to Arviat—Eskimo Point it was called back then. By the bay, not inland like they used to be."

"Why?"

"I don't know," Barnabas says. "They never explained. Just told them to get in the plane. There was a radio station at Ennadai Lake, and quallunaat lived there, too. Maybe something to do with that?"

"There must be a reason," I say, but Barnabas just shrugs his shoulders.

"Maybe. All I know is that they had food, lots of caribou in stone caches, ready for winter. They had to leave it behind and go where there is no food. And they did not want to go."

I imagine Elisapii having to leave everything behind and not understanding why she has to move. How old would she have been? My age? Or just a child? I feel a lump in my throat, but I'm also angry. Angry at anyone who can just come and take you away to a place where you don't want to be. But why? There has to be a reason. Something that explains it to make sense of it all.

★

Barnabas and I talk until late into the night. Barnabas talks about his brothers and sisters and about growing up in a large family. And I talk about growing up without one.

"How about we adopt you?" Barnabas asks.

The thought makes me all warm and fuzzy inside, but then I think of Kitty.

"My mom wouldn't be happy," I say.

"We'll adopt her, too," Barnabas says.

I know he's kidding, but I wonder what Kitty would think. Grandma died when I was five. Kitty was only twenty-two. Her dad died when she was even younger, before I was born. Maybe she still needs a mom. Maybe it's not just me who grew up without a family, but also Kitty. The two of us is all we have.

"I feel sorry for my mom," I say, not sure why that came out, because really, mostly I'm simply mad at her. But here in this tiny igloo, as far away from Kitty as I could possibly be, I miss her and I'm sorry for all the arguments we've had. They suddenly don't seem so important anymore out here in the storm, where all we have to do is wait. Wait and survive.

CHAPTER 30

Sunshine is playing on the igloo walls when I wake up in the morning. I hear Barnabas chopping meat for the dogs. I crawl outside and blink into the bright light. The sky is so blue that the whiteness of the snow blinds my eyes. The dogs are lazily stretching their limbs in the warmth of the sun. It's so calm that the day before seems unreal, like a nightmare.

"Good morning, Emmalu." Barnabas smiles at me.

I smile back. We survived.

"There's tea in the thermos if you want." Barnabas pulls our sleeping bags outside, bangs out the frost, and packs our gear. I sit on the qamutik and sip my tea, enjoying the warm sun on my face.

Qaqavii and Aupaluk play-wrestle until Barnabas lays out the harnesses. Qaqavii noses his harness as if he's trying to put it on himself. When he's finally wearing it, he stands proud at the end of his line. I squat behind the igloo for a pee and then run to the sled. The dogs and Barnabas are already waiting. I sit next to Barnabas; our shoulders are touching but it doesn't feel strange. Just comfortable.

"Ha-ii!" Barnabas calls. The dogs take off with their usual enthusiasm, but this time it's not uncontrolled chaos. They're in tune with us from the moment we pull the hook.

The snow is hard and the trail rough. The wind has formed the snow into a pattern of frozen tongue-like drifts. It almost looks like an ocean of frozen waves. Or like a desert, except with snow instead of sand. Dunes on the move, ripples and drifts, snow devils and storms. It's impossible to describe, a world of snow and ice following its own rules that I don't understand.

"Do you know where we're going?"

"Back to where we lost the trail."

"How do you know which way we came from?" For all I know, it could be any direction in a 360-degree circle. There was no telling where we were going in the whiteout.

"Follow the tracks."

"Tracks?" I look closer. Our trail is visible again! The snow that hid our own tracks in the storm blew off, leaving the paw prints raised in the snow like perfect little snow carvings.

We backtrack our trail until we see trail markers and turn north. The fresh snow glitters in the warm white of the early morning sun, the shadows still long and blue. The air smells fresh, like new snow, cool and pleasant, not biting cold anymore.

"Caribou," Barnabas says, pointing at U-shaped hoof prints crossing the trail. The dogs have sensed them, too, picking up speed, chasing the scent.

"Lots of them!" Barnabas grabs his rifle and then grins sheepishly. "I forgot we are in a race."

I forgot, too. When we left, I felt rushed, hurried, always trying to figure out where the other teams were. Now it's just us, traveling at our own pace. The only goal is to get to Arviat—alive.

"Do you think the other racers are all in Arviat by now?"

"Depends if they got to Nunalla before the storm. But even then, they would have waited until now. Some might be still close to us. And then there is still one team behind us."

"Jay the Sleigh?"

"They probably got cold feet and went back, too."

I realize that even finishing this race is a big accomplishment, and I want to finish—not just survive, but finish the race.

"Emmalu!" Barnabas elbows me and then points to the east.

Caribou! A whole herd of them, running toward our trail. Their heads held high, balancing the weight of their antlers, their hooves barely touching the ground, like a dance captured in slow motion.

The caribou notice us at the same time the dogs notice them.

The caribou stop, staring at us; the dogs throw their weight into their harnesses and lunge forward.

"Easy, easy!" Barnabas calls, scraping his snow hook.

The caribou stand undecided. When we come close, they take off with great leaps, quickly disappearing to the west.

The dogs turn to chase after them and it takes a while before we have them back on the trail. Just then another group appears. Barnabas secures the snow hook and we walk up to the team, making them lie down, while we watch hundreds of caribou cross our path. I feel goosebumps on my skin. There's something strange that I can't quite understand. The caribou move steadily, setting one foot in front of the other, like they're in a long and slow procession, but they're not slow. It's almost like time runs differently for them. I don't know how to describe it. It's like I can see through a window into a world that runs parallel to ours. As if the caribou's presence here in our world was only temporary, a crossing place of sorts, where our world and theirs collide.

"Females with last year's calves," Barnabas says.

"How do you know?"

"Look at their antlers. They are small, and the calves are smaller than the females. They will chase them away soon, so they can give birth to the new calves."

"Here?" It's so exposed, there's no shelter at all.

"Further north. They go inland, way up to Qamanirjuaq Lake."

"What do they do in a storm?"

"I don't know. Maybe lie down, wait."

The last stragglers hurry behind the group. In the distance, we see a long line of caribou walking single file—ghostly in their silent procession. We walk back to the qamutik and I remember Old Ipilii saying that caribou are like ghosts. Appearing out of nowhere, filling up the land, and then disappearing again. I strain my eyes but, as far as I can see, there are no caribou.

"You see any trail markers?" Barnabas asks.

I look around once more. "No, you?"

"I guess the caribou ran them over. I'm not sure if we are on the trail. So many caribou tracks ..."

I feel panic rising. First the storm, now lost. I picture us from above—a tiny speck on a gigantic sheet of white paper.

"We just keep going north, stick to the coastline. Nunalla must be close."

"But ..." I start and then hold my breath. Out of nowhere it seems, a caribou appears right in front of us. And then another one. We're behind a small rise, and they don't see us until they're just about touching the lead dogs. Then there are dozens of them. The group parts as they run around us, nearly touching our sled with their big wide hooves as they run by. There is a clicking sound as they flail their legs, but it doesn't come from their hooves, it comes from inside of them, their own bones singing as they walk. The click-click-click is all around us, and yet it's strangely silent at the same time. No snorting or grunting, just clicking. The dogs go crazy, turning in circles, chasing caribou to the end of their line, then turning back to snap at another caribou.

And then the clicking sound is gone. They have passed us, and I watch them until they're out of sight. How can they disappear in a land that seems so flat? How do they know where to go? They have no trail, no map.

And then I understand. In the grander scheme of things, we can't get lost. To the east is the flow edge, to the southwest the tree line; the communities are along the coast. It's just a matter of traveling, of not giving up, of keeping calm and moving. But what if there's another storm?

What if we run out of food?

What if a polar bear finds us?

What if we break through the ice?

Too many what-ifs.

A caribou flies by us in a panicked run. A second later a dog pops up over the rise, followed by a whole team. It's Suluk and Jonah! Their dogs are welcomed by ours with raised hackles and growling. Barnabas and Jonah herd the teams away from each other, commanding them to lie down.

"You are going the wrong direction," Barnabas says.

"You didn't seem to be going at all, so we came to look for you," Jonah replies.

Suluk joins us and the three of them talk in Inuktitut, until Suluk walks back to the sled and unties a caribou carcass strapped on top of their gear.

"You sure you don't want any?" Jonah asks.

"We are okay."

Jonah takes a hindquarter and puts it on our sled. "You never know."

"Matna. We see you in Arviat," Barnabas says.

"We're not traveling together?" I follow Barnabas back to our sled.

"They camped not far from here last night and then, when they came to Nunalla this morning and learned that we hadn't come in, they turned around to look for us. Their dogs are tired, ours are still fresh. Suluk says we should go. Make it back before the next storm."

"But we don't know the way!"

"The dogs know. They can follow the fresh scent of Suluk's team straight to Nunalla."

I look over to Suluk. He's calmly untying his gear. Their dogs lie splayed out in the sunshine.

Barnabas senses my hesitation. "Is not far," he says.

"Not far" and "too far" are too close together for my liking.

CHAPTER 31

Manitoba's red flag flutters next to Nunavut's white and yellow one with the red inukshuk above the weather-beaten building with the hip roof. Gaping holes where doors and windows used to be leave the old trading post open to the elements. The snowdrift inside climbs over old tables and beds all the way to the ceiling.

So this is where Suluk was born? I try to picture the scene without skidoos, igloos instead of the three green army tents, dogs following little children, hoping to steal a treat.

A tent flap flies open and a race volunteer walks around the tent to a yellow spot in the snow. He is about to unzip his pants when he sees us.

"Team!" he yells.

Tent flaps are thrown back and race volunteers hurry toward us. A Canadian Ranger stops to check his wristwatch and scribbles our time on his clipboard.

"So, you made it. We were getting worried about you." The

checker holds out his clipboard for us to sign. The pen he passes me is frozen. I scratch my initials into the paper next to our time: 10:28 AM. I can't believe it's still that early.

"Are you staying or going on?" the checker asks.

"Don't we have a mandatory six-hour rest stop here?" I ask.

"Yeah, but you're the last team. You and Suluk's team. But they got disqualified. So they're off on their own."

"Disqualified? Why?"

"Went hunting."

"But they only hunted because they came looking for us and needed extra food, and they also gave us ..." I say, but Barnabas nudges me with his elbow.

"That's what the rules say," the checker says. "I didn't make them up. So are you going to go on or what's your plan?"

"Where are all the other teams?" I ask.

"The first three teams are in Arviat. The rest should be there by late afternoon."

"What about the team that was behind us?"

"They came back to Long Point in the storm. They quit there. We're taking them back to Churchill. We have to take that dog box down with all the dropped dogs. So if you want to go, we can get going."

I look at the dog box behind the blue Bombardier. Four dogs

are sitting next to the box on short drop chains. One of them is holding up his paw. I count the holes. Ten. Not enough room for our team, I catch myself thinking. There's nobody close by?

"Can I see the timesheet again?"

One team checked out about the same time we left the Long Point Checkpoint yesterday. The last team checked out this morning at 6:24 in the twilight just before sunrise, about the same time we left our snow shelter. We're not going to catch any of them. My fear of running in the dark cost us the race.

"The dogs can run another two hours or so before we need a break. We'll go," Barnabas decides. He doesn't tell the checker that they devoured a whole caribou hindquarter less than an hour ago.

We are barely out of the checkpoint when Qaqavii starts falling behind. Barnabas urges him on, but I know he has no more to give. His tail that's usually waving in the wind like a flag is tucked between his legs.

"Whoa!" I call, and when the dogs have stopped, "Qaqavii, come!"

There's nothing of his bouncy puppy gait in his step as he walks slowly toward me, his head hanging down. I pull him onto the sled next to me. "We made you go too far, didn't we? It's all right, buddy, you did fine. You're a good dog." He curls up and goes to sleep. I stroke his fur, swallowing the lump in my throat.

When the sun stands high in the sky, we stop and let the team rest. It's warm enough for us to lie in the snow with them. I turn my face into the sun. There's some heat to it now and I feel myself getting sleepy. I watch the dogs stretching their tired limbs. When my eyes fall on Qaqavii, he wags his tail and wiggles closer.

"Come here, boy," I say and he snuggles up to me. I pet him behind the ears and, as I promise him we'll be in Arviat tonight, a weird feeling overcomes me that I hadn't felt before. We'll make it, I hear my own voice in my head. We're a team and we'll survive. There's no room for doubt or fear, only a sudden determination, a knowing that things don't just happen to me. I can make them happen.

I wake up shivering. The sun has disappeared behind a cloud and a cool breeze crawls under my parka.

"We better get going," Barnabas says.

Princess is limping when we leave. Barnabas makes room for her on the sled. She sits next to him, licking his face, pawing him whenever he stops petting her.

"Hush, now," Barnabas says. "Or you can run in the team again." But he keeps petting her, and I can tell he doesn't feel good about her being hurt. Maybe she should have stayed home? But she wanted to come so badly.

We travel in silence, watching the sun arcing its way across the sky. I don't know how far we've come. Nor does it seem to matter what time it is. But when the sun nears the horizon, I feel the urgency of getting to Arviat before nightfall become stronger and stronger.

"How far do you think it is to Arviat?"

"One more sleep. The dogs are getting tired and I don't want to cross Big River at night."

We set up the tent in silence. This time I know what to do and, between the two of us, we have our shelter up in no time. Strange, how a little bit of canvas between me and the darkness of the night can provide so much comfort.

I wake up needing to pee. I wriggle my feet into my frozen kamiks and crawl out of the tent as quiet as I can. The Northern Lights are dancing, changing color from green to red to white. Silhouetted against the bright lights is another tent, a dog team resting not far from it. Suluk and Jonah must have arrived while I was sleeping.

I watch the Northern Lights slowly fading away, revealing

the stars blinking from an endless sky. And then the stars fade and a faint glow appears on the eastern horizon. I'm the only one awake—even the dogs don't stir in their sleep. I watch the night making room for the day, an ancient ritual as old as the earth itself. I feel grateful to be here, to see the magic in what is so easily taken for granted. When the sun's first rays reach the peaks of our tents, Barnabas wakes up.

We feed the dogs and then share my frozen peanut butter jelly sandwich. Jonah walks out of their tent in his kamiks and underwear, stretching his arms above his head.

"Ready to go soon?" Barnabas asks Jonah.

"You go ahead. Suluk will want his morning tea."

"We see you in Arviat then."

"We'll pass you way before that." Jonah grins.

I don't ask how far to Arviat, but I have the feeling it's close. Too close. I realize I don't want this trip to be over. Don't want to arrive somewhere that takes me back to fights and worries and new starts over and over again.

The closer we come to town, the more skidoo tracks cross our trail until there's no trail anymore, but Arviat is still not in sight.

"Have you seen any trail markers lately?" I ask.

"No."

"How do you know we're going the right way, then?"

"Is easy now. Just follow the landmarks."

"Landmarks?" I ask, looking around but seeing nothing but snowdrifts and rocks.

"See the rise there? Eskers always go this way." He imitates the lay of the eskers with his arms, but I have no idea how they can tell him where to go.

"I know a lot of the rocks, too. Like that big one that looks like a house." He points toward a big boulder in the midst of the white emptiness. It sits there, oddly out of place—like a marble dropped by a giant millions of years ago.

"There are inuksuit along the way, too. Just wait till we're by that ridge. You'll see."

Piles of stones in all shapes and sizes peek over the ridge.

"Cool. I've never seen a real one. I mean, like, out on the land like that. Why are they there?"

"Those ones? I don't know. These are old. You have to find someone who grew up here long time ago and still remembers from his parents or grandparents. Could be just to show the way or to make caribou run where you want them to go. All depends. They all have different names, too."

"What does inukshuk mean?"

"A stone person made to look like a human."

We pass by the ridge and now, looking back against the light, the inuksuit do look like people. I wonder what they have seen, those rocks, as they stand and watch over this ancient land.

CHAPTER 32

Strung between two poles, the red banner of the finish line waits for us like a gate into another world. Behind us, the land of ice and rock. Ahead, people, buildings, vehicles, noise. We stop our team under the banner, unsure of what to do.

"We're here," Barnabas says.

I nod.

Children are sliding on snow pushed up into piles. They are the first to see us. A little girl with a pink parka and a purple fur ruff runs over and pets Qaqavii. He puts his paws on her shoulders and tumbles her over. She giggles and rolls in the snow with him. Qaqavii rubs against her and she pets his belly. A boy of about four or five asks Barnabas which one is his leader. Soon Barnabas is surrounded by young boys wanting to know if we'd seen bears, why it took us so long to get here, and what the names of our dogs are. Some of the kids take off down the streets, spreading the news that our team has arrived.

The kids' voices, noise from the town, buildings, trucks, stop signs, movement, colors—suddenly, it's all too much. I want to tell Barnabas: let's turn the team around—but then what? Go where?

I put my arm around Qakuq.

"Thank you for leading us here," I whisper in his ear. Qakuq leans into me and licks my cheek. I hug each dog, quietly thanking them.

The way I felt this morning when I watched the sun rise is fading into a blurry memory. I wish I could hold onto it, still be out there. But I'm also relieved to be back, the fear of making a mistake—a deadly mistake—finally gone.

The girl in the pink parka climbs onto our sled.

"Go, go," she calls. "Good dogs!" She wiggles up and down and sideways as if the sled is on the move.

Qaqavii paws my leg and then puts his paws on my chest. I put my arms around him. His brown eyes look deep into me. He makes a quiet sound as if he's trying to say something.

"What is it, boy?"

The little girl comes back and Qaqavii's attention is diverted.

Qakuq sees Old Ipilii first. His ears perk up and he whines impatiently. Was he here the whole time, waiting for us? Old Ipilii walks toward us. Our eyes lock and the noise around me seems to quiet; everything slows down. Old Ipilii nods, just once, and I know he understands what I've seen and how I feel.

And then a voice all too familiar calls my name. I turn around.

"Emmylou!" She's running in the middle of the street, trucks and skidoos swerving around her. Her face is flushed, her usually tidy hair a mess.

How does she manage that? Show up at the most unfitting moment? But then I smile. For Kitty, that's fitting.

"Mom!" I run toward her.

"I was … so … worried," she gasps, trying to control her breathing and her sobbing at the same time. "They said they didn't know where you were and there was this horrible storm … and I …" She breaks up, holds me tighter, until I can feel her warmth through my winter clothes.

She releases her hug and looks at me, her eyes red and swollen. "I was so scared I lost you. I … wouldn't know what to do without you, Emmylou."

I feel that lump in my throat, but it's different this time. I think of something to say, but there are no words. Just a warm, fuzzy feeling. And then I see Barnabas waving me over and the moment is gone. There is a race official there now and Barnabas is signing something, while Old Ipilii is taking a bootie off Pamiuluk's paw.

"I have to go," I say to Kitty.

"Don't go." Kitty grabs my arm, panic in her eyes.

"Come with me, then," I say.

The checker passes me a piece of cardboard. Mushers' bib numbers and times are penciled on it.

"Sign here," he says. I glance at the times. The winner came in after 42 hours and 15 minutes. Our time is 78 hours and 46 minutes. One more signature and the race is officially over.

"We are so late, we missed the banquet," Barnabas says and grins.

"This is my mom," I say.

"Nice to meet you." Barnabas holds out his hand to Kitty. She doesn't take it.

An awkward silence hangs upon us.

"I help Old Ipilii to bring the dogs to the dog yard and then come back, okay?" Barnabas squeezes my hand and then immediately lets it go again.

"Whose dog yard?" I ask, even though it doesn't really matter. They're not my dogs; they never were, never will be.

"Our dog yard. The dogs are staying here. We're staying here."

"Elisapii?" I ask, suddenly catching on that Old Ipilii should be in Winnipeg with her.

"She's here, too. No more treatments."

"But …" I think of what it means if she's refusing treatment.

"Is okay, Emmalu. That's what she wants. Be home with her family. I pick you up; you can stay with us."

"Okay," I smile, relieved that this not a goodbye, but then Kitty bursts in.

"We are staying in the hotel," she says putting her arm around me, pulling me to her, away from Barnabas.

"Is expensive," Barnabas calls after us.

"I don't think that's your concern," Kitty snaps.

Barnabas looks puzzled. "See you," he says to me. It sounds like a question.

"See you," I say, not sure now if this is a goodbye.

I watch as the team runs past three gigantic satellite receivers next to a big, modern, red and yellow building—a school, maybe. They ignore the red stop sign with the Inuktitut syllabics and run down a street with blue houses built on stilts. Kids run behind the team or—if they are fast enough—throw themselves onto the sled so they can catch a ride. I wait for Barnabas to look back, but he doesn't.

We're the only ones at the finish line now. The sun disappears behind a cloud, dulling the colors of the houses that appeared so bright a minute ago. I suddenly long for my bed at the Sleepy Bear Lodge—or just any warm bed I can curl up in.

"My stuff is at the hotel," Kitty says, leading me down the road. Her arm feels heavy on my shoulder. I can't breathe. I free myself of her hug, that hug that I wanted so badly just a few minutes ago.

★

"Why, Kitty?" We're the only guests in the hotel restaurant. The smell of frying oil is too strong, but once my order of fish'n'chips arrives, I can't help myself from stuffing one fry after the other into my mouth. For a moment, I almost couldn't care about anything else but the hot, greasy food.

"Why what?" Kitty says.

"Why can't we stay in one place?"

"Who says we can't? We just have to find a place that's worth staying at. Speaking of which …" Kitty pauses, but I already know what's coming. We're moving.

And now I get it. Get that it's never going to change. She'll keep looking for a place where she'll be happy, a place without problems. Thing is, that place doesn't exist. Her demons will follow her. Follow us. But what are they?

"Why now? Why can't we stay in Churchill?" I ask, but then I remember that the dogs and Barnabas and Old Ipilii and Elisapii won't be there anymore.

"What's keeping us there? Don't you think I haven't noticed

the way people look at us? Do you think they don't hear our arguments? And then the parenting tips they give me? Marie doesn't even have children, but she figures she'd be a better mother. And then that boy you keep running to. That's not you, Emmylou. He's putting all sorts of ideas in your head that are pulling us apart. And it will only get worse, I can feel it. We need a fresh start. Both of us."

A million thoughts are buzzing through my head; like a swarm of blackflies, they seem to be everywhere at once. Barnabas putting ideas in my head? Didn't Kitty say the same thing about Maya? Tell me we didn't move because Maya and I were too close? Closer than Kitty and me. I feel panic rising. She wouldn't do that to me, would she?

"I don't want to lose you, Emmylou." Kitty reaches over the table.

Is that it? Is she so scared of losing me that she's lost herself? A teacher asking a question about our home life and she thinks social services will come and take me away? An argument between us and she thinks I'll hate her and run? Thing is, I just about did. Because I didn't get it, thought she didn't care. And then I remember the Paddington Bear sculpture. Did she throw it out because she thought my dad was trying to take me away? I feel sick to my stomach.

"What's the matter, Emmylou?"

I shake my head, trying to shake off the buzzing thoughts. One thing she's right about. We need a fresh start. Need to figure out how we can go on together.

"You don't want to lose me but you're driving me away. You …" I start but don't know how to finish. It's just going to end up in another argument. And truth is, I'll never understand her because I don't think like her. I think about Elisapii and all the people that were moved against their own will who never understood why. I had thought there must be a reason, something logical that explains it all, that would make it better in a way, but there isn't. There is no reason good enough, no reason that can take that pain away.

And then I get the whole irony of our situation.

If she doesn't want to lose me, she'll have to let me go. But how? And where to?

CHAPTER 33

Turn left by the Co-op, go down 3rd Avenue past the church, and turn left again on Seventh Street. House Number 298. I reread the instructions Barnabas has scribbled onto a piece of cardboard and left with the hotel manager. I squint against the sun, trying to read the street sign.

◁ᶜˢdᶜ 7th ST.

Good, I must be close. A skidoo passes me, the driver a young girl, maybe twelve. Behind her, a child is hanging onto the older girl's jacket.

"What's your name?" The child turns her head as they zoom past me.

Before I can reply, they're already out of earshot. I wave and the child waves back. Snow machines are definitely the major mode of transportation here. There's one parked next to nearly every house, some of them with big qamutiks attached to their hitches. I haven't seen a dog team since the end of the race.

I move to the side as a snow plough drives past. He's not scraping the snow down to the gravel, just pushing the drifts aside. The road is lined with snow piles on either side, and lots of the buildings are buried in snow up to the windowsills. An ATV sits buried in snow, just the headlights and handlebars sticking out, next to a house with weathered wooden siding. A path through shoulder-deep snow leads to the entrance. The street bends around a corner and I'm suddenly at the edge of town. A dozen or so houses shine bright in the midday sun. Past the houses, Hudson Bay stretches beyond the horizon.

The ocean looks different here than in Churchill—wilder, bigger, merciless. In Churchill, I couldn't wait to find out what was north, to see what the Arctic was like. But now that I'm here, it's too vast to wrap my mind around it. I'm not at the edge of the Arctic anymore, not flirting with unknown adventures. I'm in the middle of it, lost like a puppy that strayed from her mother's den. I shiver, thinking that I was out there just two days ago. And only now do I realize how lucky we were, how many things could have gone wrong.

A mother on an ATV passes by me, grocery bags dangling from the handlebars. A toddler, cheeks flushed red from the fresh air, peeks out of the hood of her amauti. Two children are holding onto the rack with one hand, clutching grocery bags with the other. They stop in front of a red house with white window trim and a blue tin roof. A raven picking at a garbage container caws before he lunges into the air and lands on a power pole nearby. He watches as the family unloads their groceries.

I love all the different colors of the houses. There's a series of identical green ones with small brown porches and, further down, a couple of blue ones. Rusty propane or gas tanks sit against the buildings and steam rises from the chimneys. Power poles stand tall along the road, and a crisscross of cables run to the houses. Some of the houses are almost buried in snow, reminding me of the blizzards waiting out there.

House Number 298 is an orange one. Where the snow has been blown off the roof, patches of silver tin roofing show through. I don't see any dogs and I wonder if I'm at the right house, but then I see a clothesline with our caribou-skin sleeping bags airing out in the sunshine. I walk up the wooden steps to the porch door and knock. No answer. I knock again and put my ear against the door. I hear noises that seem far away. I turn the door handle and peek inside the porch.

It's cold in here, just like outside. Two freezers are lined up against the wall, a seal carcass lying on one of them. The floor is littered with boots in all kinds of sizes. Giant black sealskin kamiks are lying next to red toddler rubber boots, and caribou parkas are hanging on nails in the wall, next to a girl's pink snow pants. Cardboard boxes are stacked in one corner, milk jugs containing who knows what in another. There's a familiar smell of musky animal, stinky boots, and something sweet.

I look for Barnabas's parka but it's not there. A trail of empty floor space leads to the entrance door. I hesitate. What if he's not home? What if he is? My palms are getting sweaty.

I hesitantly knock on the door and then open it. A big flat-screen TV is playing *The Lion King,* and three young kids are sitting on the floor, their eyes glued to the screen as the lion cubs enter the elephant cemetery. Two of them are boys—twins. A girl about eight or nine is playing with a puppy. She looks up when she sees me enter.

"What's your name?" she asks.

"Emmylou. Is … um … is Barnabas here?"

"Are you his girlfriend?"

"No, I … just … I came to say goodbye. My flight is leaving this afternoon."

"He's not here."

"Do you know where he is?"

She shrugs her shoulders. "Hunting or fixing skidoos. He's never here. Do you want to pet my puppy?"

"Um … sure." I'm surprised how soft he feels. He licks my

hand and it tickles. He looks like Qaqavii, only tiny. I relax a bit.

"What about Elisapii and Old Ipilii, where do they live?"

"You want me to show you?"

"Sure, but shouldn't we tell your mom?" I ask.

"Anaana!" She yells. "I'm going to see Anaanatsiaq with Barnabas's girlfriend! Come." She walks down the hallway, not to the porch as I expected. As we walk by the kitchen, a woman pokes her head out the door, wiping her floury hands on a dishtowel.

"Hello," she says.

Before I can say anything, the girl grabs my hand. "This way."

I follow her awkwardly. Shouldn't I stop and explain to Barnabas's mother why I'm here? I turn around but she's already back in the kitchen.

"What's your name?" I ask the girl.

"May," she says, struggling to open a door in the hallway, while at the same time holding the puppy. The puppy slips out of her arm and drops to the floor. It yelps and then scurries down the hallway, squatting down to pee.

"Oh-oh!" May quickly pushes the door open and then hurries after the puppy.

Old Ipilii is leaning over Elisapii, carefully holding what looks like a baby cup to her open mouth. Elisapii coughs and

Old Ipilii sets the cup down on a bedside table.

"Emmylou." Elisapii pats the mattress next to her. Old Ipilii moves to a chair and I sit on the bed. Elisapii looks weaker than I've ever seen her, but her watery eyes shine. I take her hand and she puts her other hand over mine. I want to tell her I'm so glad that I got to see her before we left, and how glad I am that I've met them both, and I want to thank them and tell them about the race and … and I don't know how to say any of it, so I just hold her hand.

I glance at the huge wall-hanging over her bed. It's a scene from a camp long ago. White figures are hand-stitched to the dark blue felt that makes the background. There are people, dog teams, igloos, and polar bears. The dogs have surrounded the bear; hunters with harpoons are closing in, and women come running out of the igloo. They all wear parkas with long flaps decorated with colorful stitching. But there are also shapes that don't make sense. Creatures that are neither human nor animal, and it makes me think about the voices I heard at Seahorse Gully.

The artist has stitched her name in syllabics in the bottom corner. I wonder if Elisapii made it, but even if she didn't, I'm sure she's seen it—the scene in real life, I mean. There's lots that I don't understand, but my eyes keep falling back to the dog team. Now that I've traveled across the tundra, sat out a storm, built an igloo, and come all the way here by dog team, I have so many more questions I want to ask Old Ipilii and Elisapii.

I wish Barnabas were here. But I know, even if he were here, there isn't enough time. I realize that this goodbye is forever. I wipe my eyes. Elisapii squeezes my hand and, when I can't control my sobbing anymore, she pulls me to her. She lets me cry, silently stroking my hair, and only when a coughing fit shakes her, do I sit up again.

"Bye," I say and slip off the bed. "And thank you for everything. Matna." I turn to Old Ipilii and he takes my hand.

"Qimmiujatuluatuq," he says and then he talks long and quiet in Inuktitut. I want to tell him I don't understand. But he knows that, so I look into his eyes instead and I see them fill up with tears. He's at a faraway place and yet he's here with me. I want to tell him that Barnabas told me about his dad and his puppy, and that I'm sorry and sad, but also mad at the RCMP, and ashamed what those people—my people—did to him, but I have the feeling he already knows. Old Ipilii takes a breath and I see a deep calmness in his eyes, and I feel as if there's a weight lifted off my shoulders, a weight I didn't know was there.

CHAPTER 34

The airfield isn't any bigger than the size of a schoolyard, the runway a patchwork quilt of black asphalt and white snowdrifts. There's just one plane parked outside the small airport building. Southbound. The plane's door is open, a metal stairway waiting for the passengers to board. The airport is full of people, young women carrying their babies in colorful amautiit, kids in hockey uniforms, an old man in a wheelchair.

Kitty keeps staring at the clock as if she's afraid we'll miss our flight. I keep glancing out the window toward the town, hoping with every opening of the door to see Barnabas. And then I'm kind of relieved when it isn't Barnabas, because I wouldn't know what to say.

I glance at the big airport clock. Only half an hour before boarding begins—twenty-eight minutes and fifteen seconds, to be precise. And then I see a red ATV pull up, a dog carrier tied to the back. Barnabas jumps off the seat and hurries to the door.

I run toward him but then stop. What if he didn't come to see me?

The door opens and Barnabas flashes his smile with the missing teeth at me. Gosh, I'm going to miss that.

"Emmalu!" He waves me toward the door. "Hurry!"

"I'll be right back, Kitty," I say, already halfway out the door.

For a second, I have the stupid picture in my head that I will jump on the ATV with Barnabas and we'll drive off into the sunset, sappy music playing in the background as the credits roll.

Barnabas opens the dog crate. He barely catches hold of the leash as Qaqavii jumps out and runs toward me.

"Qaqavii, you came to say goodbye?" I ruffle his ears.

Barnabas passes me the leash. "A present. From my grandpa."

"You're giving Qaqavii to me? Really? I don't know if I can …"

"He's always been your dog. He chose you."

Qaqavii jumps up on me, placing his paws on my chest, looking into my eyes.

"Emmylou, our plane is leaving." Kitty stops a few steps away from us, her hands jammed into her sides, but I hear the pleading in her voice.

"You got time," Barnabas says. "They are still de-icing the wings." He nods to the runway where workers are spraying the wings with what looks like a fire hose.

"Mom," I say. "Qaqavii is coming with us."

"You're kidding, right?" She looks from me to Barnabas for a hint that we're joking, but I've never been more serious about anything in my life.

"Even if I … we can't, Emmylou." Kitty looks at me, hands up, eyebrows raised.

"You can take the crate, too," Barnabas says. "Is no problem. We take dogs on the plane all the time."

He's missing the point, which is, Kitty doesn't want us to take him. I feel my fingers tighten into fists. It's Qaqavii and me or Kitty can go on her own.

"Kitty, I'm not asking, I …"

"Okay."

"What?"

"We'll take your dog."

"You're serious? Thank you, thank you, thank you." I throw my arms around her and then I hug Qaqavii. When I stand up again, there's an awkward silence. Kitty is looking at me, I'm looking at Qaqavii, and Barnabas is looking at his boots.

"I should go," he says.

"Uh … Mom," I say giving her a clue with my eyebrows.

"What now?" she asks.

Of course, subtle hints aren't exactly Kitty's thing.

"Could you ..." I make a shooing motion with my hand, hoping Barnabas doesn't notice. "Go away, please," I mouth.

"Right," Kitty says. "I guess I'll see about buying another ticket for our new passenger." She takes Qaqavii's leash and I watch her walk back to the airport, turning in circles as Qaqavii runs around her and the crate. She must hate it with all her paranoia about fleas—and yet, she took him. Just like that.

"I have a present for you as well." Barnabas holds out his hand.

I wipe my eyes and Barnabas places a caribou antler carving in my hand. A small bird, graceful in its simplicity. My fingers glide over its streamlined body, leaning forward as if resisting an invisible storm.

I look up from the carving in my hand. Barnabas is looking into my eyes. I hold his gaze and he reaches out for my hand. I take it and he pulls me closer. I lean forward to kiss him. Our noses rub awkwardly against each other before my lips find his.

"EMMYLOU!" Kitty is standing in the airport doorway. Behind the building, people are walking across the runway to board the plane.

I pull away from Barnabas, even though it's the last thing on earth I want to do.

"Bye, Emmalou."

No, I think, but all I say is: "Bye."

And then I realize I never asked what Qaqavii means. I turn one more time to Barnabas.

"Do dogs have name spirits, too? Who is Qaqavii named after?"

"He is named after Ipilii's puppy. The one he had when he was a boy."

It takes a second before I realize which one he's talking about. "The one that was shot by the RCMP?"

Barnabas nods and I chew on my lip to stop the tears from coming up. This is not the sunset movie goodbye I had imagined.

"What ... does his name mean?"

"One that wants to be loved."

CHAPTER 35

The plane's engine starts roaring, and within minutes we're airborne. I look for Barnabas as the airport becomes smaller and more and more houses come into view. There's a red ATV driving down the road from the airport into town. I wave, but I'm too far away to see if it's Barnabas. And then the whole community is in view, tiny houses scrunched together in the vast expanse of whiteness all around. I can see where the finish line was— it's easy to tell by the big satellite dishes—and I can even make out Barnabas's house at the edge of town. And then, around the community, I see tiny dog houses, smaller than match boxes from up here, lots and lots of them.

As we fly south, I see the ridge with the inuksuit that guided us into Arviat, and then I see a dog team, and then a second one—tiny black dots moving across the land.

And that's when I realize, it's still all there, the life I've been longing to find out about. It's there in those inuksuit and the dog teams traveling across the land, and a hundred other places I can't even imagine. I watch the dog teams until they become too small to tell apart from the land. And, as if on cue, a low sad howl erupts from the back of the plane where the luggage is stored. It's not the unmelodic yippyish puppy howl anymore, it's a beautiful sad song and, in that moment, I know exactly what it's saying. I jump up from my seat.

"We have to go back!" I yell.

"Emmylou, sit down. What's the matter? Did you forget something?"

"I can't take Qaqavii. He doesn't belong down south. He belongs to Arviat, to the land down there, to his team."

"What do you expect me to do? Tell the pilot to turn around?"

"No, Mom, but we have to bring him back."

"It's okay, Emmylou, we can send him back, I'm sure."

"Okay," I say, but I feel anything but okay.

Kitty and I had had a long talk in the hotel in Arviat. We talked like we never talked before. Kitty thinks all I want is to be as far away as possible from her. Sometimes I do feel that way, but only because I think I can never please her, that I'm not the daughter she wanted.

There are also other problems, too. Bigger ones. Things that I don't understand. Like her problems. I don't think Kitty understands them, either—or even sees them. But it's okay that I don't understand them. What's not okay are our arguments. I told her how tired I was of fighting. All I want is that she just accepts me the way I am. We both cried, and I feel a lot closer to her now, even though it's still in a messed-up sort of way that ends more often in arguments than in hugs.

For the first time, we plan our next destination together. In fact, she lets me choose, but it's not as easy as I thought. Now that I'm thinking of leaving, I realize how much I like Churchill. I like that you can walk out of town and be on the land. I've even come to like the tourist shops, with their artworks and knick-knacks of polar bears and belugas that remind me they're our closest neighbors. The people are friendly, too, but I don't want to stay in Churchill without Barnabas and the dogs, and I know it's not the place for Kitty. Too remote, too much wilderness, not enough city.

Kitty comes up with about fifty new ideas a day. Toronto, Montreal, St. John's, but I can't decide on one. So for now, we're going to Winnipeg, because that's the easiest way out of Churchill, and then we'll plan from there. Another "fresh" start—I'm kind of excited, but I can't get rid of the feeling that I've missed something important.

CHAPTER 36

"I came to return your book." I pass *Carved from the Land* to Rosemary and quickly turn, not wanting to talk to her or anyone.

"Oh, thank you. How was the race? I heard you made it all the way to Arviat."

Everyone in town has heard that I was in the race. Everyone congratulates me, as if I'd won, but all I feel is a sense of loss.

"What's the matter, girl?"

"Nothing," I say, and in a way it's true. I feel nothing since we put Qaqavii back on the plane.

I wait till I know Lisa is off work and then I drop my library books into the after-hours slot at the library. I've left her a thank-you note among the books, and that was already hard enough to write. I have one more stop to make before we leave Churchill tomorrow morning.

The old lady is at the cemetery when I get there. A short smile of recognition flits across her face. We sit in silence for a while. The wind is warm today, playing gently with the old woman's hair. It's sunny, and I resist the urge to close my eyes and hold my face up to the sun. It's so nice to feel the warmth returning after the coldness of winter.

"I like it here," I say. My eyes glide over the white crosses and I quickly add, "not here ... I mean, up there." I point north, past the town toward the river.

The old woman nods. "It's a good place, that land. Healing."

"I have to leave tomorrow," I say. Not sure why I'm telling her, not sure why I was hoping to see her before I left. I miss Elisapii.

"I'll miss going north with the dogs, and I want to see the river break up, and I want to know what the land looks like when it's not covered in snow, and I want to see the tent rings and places where people used to live, and ..." Then I remember where she came from and what she lost, and I feel real embarrassed. "I'm sorry. I didn't mean to bother you. I'm really, really sorry."

She pats my hand. "Is good you know where you belong. Don't let anyone take that from you, child."

I stare at her, and I realize why I'm not feeling okay. Finding a new place to live is not what I want. Kitty asked me where

I wanted to go, and I was looking for a place she might like, when, deep down, I already knew where my place was.

I jump up, feeling like a big weight has been lifted off my shoulders.

"Thank you!" I call to the old lady as I'm already leaving the cemetery. "Thank you so much!"

I burst into our room, gasping for breath. Kitty's clothes are spread out over both of our beds as she's folding them for her suitcase.

"What's the matter, Emmylou?"

"We're not going south tomorrow. We're going to Arviat." I'm so excited that I want to jump up and down on my mattress.

"We already booked the flights to Winnipeg. We're gonna …"

"… go to Arviat. I didn't want to stay in Churchill, but I didn't want to leave, either. It all makes sense now. It's not the town where I want to be. It's the land. The land with the caribou and polar bears and Old Ipilii who understands it and can teach me, and I'm even willing to go to school until I graduate, because if we stay in Arviat, I can learn everything I want to know just outside of school. And I can be with Qaqavii and …" I suddenly feel my face turn hot. And Barnabas, if he's okay with me coming.

"Easy, Emmylou," Kitty interrupts, but I'm going full speed and there's no slowing me down.

"It's where I want to be. You said I could choose."

"Yes, of course. But not Arviat. What am I supposed to do there, Emmylou?"

"We'll figure it out. Maybe you could work at the hotel."

"Geez, Emmylou, it's not just work. It's …" Kitty sighs, a deep exasperated sigh, and I'm feeling the all too familiar lump in my throat. Up by the cemetery, talking to the old lady, I was so sure about what I really wanted to do, but here with Kitty, it's different. What are we going to do in Arviat? What if Barnabas and Old Ipilii don't take me out on the land? Where can I go when the arguments with Kitty become too much? Where is Kitty going to go? But … I guess we'll have to figure that out no matter where we go.

"I need you to do this, okay? For me," I plead, but then I realize it's not just for me. It's for us. If she doesn't want to lose me, she has to let me go. That's how it has to be. Let me be the person I want to be, in a place I need to be.

Kitty sits for what seems like an eternity on her bed, without saying a word. Then her head nods ever so slightly and my heart starts beating like crazy. Is it a yes?

DISCLAIMER

While my own experiences inspired me to write the novel, and Churchill and Arviat are indeed real places, *Qaqavii* itself is a work of fiction. The characters are products of my imagination and any resemblance to real persons, dogs, or businesses is entirely coincidental. Sadly, the forced relocations of the Sayisi Dene and Ahiarmiut, as well as the RCMP dog slaughters, are real historical events. However, the dialogue around the events and Emmylou's understanding of them are fictional. They are not meant to be an accurate historic account, but to encourage the reader to do his or her own research. Likewise, Brother Volant is a historical real-life figure, but the conversation about him is fiction.

–Miriam Körner

DOG COMMANDS

Ha-ii – Go

La laa – Left

Haala – Right

Yaai – Easy

Wooh – Stop/Stay

Iiaaq – Quit that!

Annit – Get out!

DOG NAMES

Qakuq – White One

Taqluk – Patches

Qaqavii – One who wants to be loved

Pamiuluk – Stumpy Tail

Aupaluk – Red One

ACKNOWLE**D**GEMEN**T**S

This novel would never have been written had I not listened to CBC Radio reporting about the Hudson Bay Quest Sled Dog Race, one rainy afternoon in the spring of 2005. Two hundred and fifty miles of Arctic wilderness, blizzards, polar bears, caribou, and mushers in fur clothing on traditional *qamutiit*. Whose imagination would not immediately be captured? Within a year, my partner, Quincy Miller, and I had two dog teams ready to race in a place so harsh we would never have dared to venture out on our own, nor could we have afforded the logistics of getting us and the dogs to the edge of the Arctic. Although at the time I had no intention of writing a novel, I'd like to thank those who, in the end, gave me the opportunity to have the experiences that led to the writing of *Qaqavii*.

I thank all the volunteers and race organizers, especially Dave Daley, who arranged transportation for the "southern" teams. Both Gardewine North and Calm Air went out of their way to get us and the dogs safely to Churchill and Arviat, via train and airplane.

Jenafor and Gerald Azure offered us generous hospitality, not only during the race, but whenever one of our Arctic adventures brings us back to Churchill.

Lorraine Brandson and Diann Elliot patiently answered my never-ending questions on my visits to the Itsanitaq Museum (then Eskimo Museum) and introduced me to their archives.

In Arviat, my thanks go to Lynne Rollin and the Mikilaaq Center, who gave us shelter during our first visit, and the Tagalik and Baker families who shared so much with us in the following years. *Matna*, Shirley, Kukik, Darryl, Simona, Donny, Pud, Odie, Natalie, and, last but not least, *matna* to the late James Tagalik, who will always have a special place in my heart.

Along the trail, my deepest and heart-felt respect and thanks to the late Phillip Kigusiutnak and the late Jimmy Muckpah, who were such an inspiration for writing the character of Old Ipilii.

Matna, Peter Sr. Mamgark for believing in me, and for Qaqavii and the mitts, Moses Kigusiutnak for the extra clothing, Simona Baker for cheering me on, Andy Kowtak and Andrew Panagoniak for sharing stories, and Peter, whose last name I do not know, for guiding us to Arviat in the second blizzard.

Thanks to all the mushers who shared the trail with us and became friends.

Most of all, I owe the dogs for their trust, their endurance, their loyalty, and their unconditional love.

As I worked through several drafts of this novel, I am again greatly indebted to the Tagalik and Baker families. *Matna*, Simona Baker, for the translation into *Inuktitut*, and Kukik and Darryl Baker for the proofreading. A special thanks to Shirley Tagalik for taking the time to ensure that what my Inuit characters do and say rings true to Nunavut readers, and thanks to all her children, who helped to find answers to my questions.

Thank you to Lorraine Brandson who provided thoughtful feedback on the Itsanitaq Museum chapter, to Michelle Marchildon from Manitoba Education and Training Homeschooling Office, who cared about Emmylou's school issues as if she were a real protégée.

Marsi chogh, Ila Bussidor, for writing your courageous book and for answering my questions.

Thank you to my writerly friends who provided feedback throughout the many drafts of this manuscript: Sagehill Writing, Alissa York and the Shark-Tailed Grouse Gang—Rita Greer, Darla Tenold, Iryn Tushabe, Katherine Koller, and Becky Blake; Quincy Miller, Karsten and Zev Heuer, Leanne Allison, Jane

Kubke, Ella Tomlinson, Ashleigh Mattern, Mark Lafontaine, and Linda Mikolayenko.

Thanks to the Alex Robertson Public Library and the Saskatchewan Arts Board for their financial support through their Artists in Communities Residencies Grant.

Last, but not least, I would like to thank the team at Red Deer Press, especially my editor Peter Carver, who saw so clearly where my own story became intertwined with Emmylou's story and helped me to untangle the knots.

INTERVIEW WITH MIRIAM KÖRNER

What moved you to write this story?

It's a strange thing with stories. They seem to have a life of their own, and they suck you in as a writer until all you can do is succumb to the story and let it unfold. At the same time, it is no coincidence that this story chose me. Emmylou and I have more in common than I initially thought.

Questions of belonging, of finding my place in the world, of understanding where we all fit in are questions that I often think about. A lot of my answers I find on the land or in conversation with Elders who grew up on the land, and I was very fortunate to spend some time in the Arctic and get a glimpse of the traditional way of life there.

It's a fascinating place, and being there had such an incredible impact on me that I was looking for a way to share it with my young readers. Here, I hope to take them on a journey few of them will ever experience in real life—at least, not by dog team.

Photo credit: Hannah Taylor

Your own experience with sled dogs led you to take part in a race somewhat like the Arctic Quest you describe in the novel. What was that experience like for you?

The first time I competed in the Hudson Bay Quest, a 250-mile wilderness race between Churchill and Arviat, was in the spring of 2006. Only one musher per team was allowed and my partner, Quincy, and I ran ten dogs each. The older Inuit mushers

The author and her team in the 2008 Hudson Bay Quest.

in the race were wearing caribou clothing, and I immediately knew we were ill-prepared to travel in a land that allows for no mistakes. We were out of place and barely made it to the finish line that first year. What we were lacking most—next to proper clothing—was an intimacy with the land, which only comes from the knowledge passed on from generation to generation.

The following three years, Quincy and I took turns racing and, bit by bit, we learned the lay of the land and acquired skills needed to travel in the Arctic environment. The Inuit mushers always watched out for us—the *qallunaat* that knew so little. They made sure I was dressed warmly enough, told me where to cross the river, stopped with me on the trail when my dogs needed a rest.

I felt especially drawn to the oldest musher in the race— Phillip Kigusiutnak who was born on the land near Nunalla. Being with him always gave me the feeling that there was a direct link, almost tangible, to life in the past, when Inuit families lived on the land.

He has passed on since, but I've never stopped wondering what he thought when we reached Nunalla—the place where he was born—and the changes he had seen in his lifetime. Emmylou inherited my sense of wonder, and she asks questions that were born while I was racing along Hudson Bay's unforgiving coast.

You have said that the novel is a mix of fact and fiction. Explain.
Qaqavii is a novel, set in the real towns of Churchill and Arviat. Emmylou walks in and out of the real and fictional worlds. Sleepy Bear Lodge, for instance, is made up, while the Itsanitaq Museum, Cape Merry, the train station, the cemetery, and Dene Village do exist. But even though real places and events occur, sometimes they follow a fictional timeline, and sometimes fictional objects are added to real places.

Qaqavii is set around 2012. At that time, the Itsanitaq Museum was still called Eskimo Museum. (The name officially changed in 2017.) Some of the sculptures that Emmylou describes, you will find in the museum—like Antonin Attark's *Sighting of his First Airplane*—while others are fictional. The dialogue between Emmylou and Rosemary is made up, as is Rosemary herself, but Brother Jacques Volant is a historical figure, who indeed

Darryl Baker planing his runners while dogs are taking a break.

lived nineteen years among Inuit before he became curator of the Eskimo Museum.

The Arctic Quest—although inspired by my own experience of participating in the Hudson Bay Quest in 2006, 2007, 2008, 2010—is a fictional race modeled after Arctic dog sled races that allow two mushers per team. However, the landmarks in the novel are as I remember them from my actual journeys. Seahorse Gully, the rivers, the ruins of Prince of Wales Fort, and the old Hudson's Bay Company trading post at Nunalla (also spelled Nunallaaq or Nonala) are still there today.

A lot of my characters' experiences are—as in most works of fiction—experiences that have happened in a similar way to a lot of different people. Emmylou shares lots of my experiences, but also some of Quincy's.

Likewise, Old Ipilii's stories are not stories of one particular person, but inspired by stories of Elders like him. While his and Elisapii's names and biographies are made up, the historic events in their biographies are not.

Is it true, then, that the RCMP shot dogs in Inuit communities? And the stories of the relocations are true stories as well? How could young readers find out more about those events? It is true that the RCMP shot dogs in Nunavut and northern Quebec in the 1950s and 1960s. The question of what led to the shootings is not so easy to answer. As Barnabas says, Inuit have their truth and the RCMP has theirs. *The Qikiqtani Truth Commission: Thematic Reports and Special Studies 1950–1975: Analysis of the RCMP Sled Dog Report* is a detailed document that looks at this question. In the end, truth is what we believe and it's not up to me to be the judge of that.

Around the same time as the dog shootings occurred, the government forcibly relocated Indigenous peoples off their traditional lands and into settlements. The book *Night Spirits:*

The Story of the Relocation of the Sayisi Dene that Emmylou reads, does indeed exist and is one of the most haunting books I've ever read. Emmylou's summary of the events, however, is influenced by how she sees the world. *Qaqavii* is not a history lesson, but the coming-of-age story of a young girl who tries to make sense of the world around her.

As Emmylou learns the details about the Sayisi Dene relocations, I also wanted her to understand that, more commonly, we might never know the trauma that the people close and dear to us carry with them. Emmylou guesses right that Elisapii had to face similar struggles as the Sayisi Dene, but even Barnabas does not know Elisapii's story. Many Elders choose not to tell their stories, out of fear that the anger will be passed on. Likewise, the reader learns very little in the novel; but I want my readers to ask themselves: What happened at Ennadai Lake? Maybe they will do their own research. *Relocating the Ahiarmiut from Ennadai Lake to Arviat (1950–1958)* would be a good place to start.

Readers of your book gain many insights into life in the north. How did you learn about Inuit culture and language?
When I first came to the Arctic, I was immediately drawn to the way the people I met travel and understand the land and—being

The real Qaqavii, who inspired the title of his novel.

a musher myself—I was fascinated with the dog culture that's so deeply embedded in the history of Arctic peoples. I learned a lot in a short time, simply by spending time out on the land with our dogs, and later—as we became friends with some of the mushers and their families—on repeated visits to Arviat and Churchill. Like Emmylou, I always want to know what life was like when people lived on the land. The more I learned, the more questions I had. And like Emmylou, I was always welcomed with the generosity that is so inherent in northern communities.

Again, I want to caution, though, that *Qaqavii* is not a history lesson. What the readers learn, they learn through the eyes of a sixteen-year-old fictional girl, whose story is intertwined with my own subjective views and experiences.

The credit for the translations goes to Simona, Kukik, and Darryl Baker. I don't speak Inuktitut, but I like to get a feel for languages, and I either ask how to say certain words, or find sources that use Inuktitut words to explain cultural traditions and worldview. I believe language is key to understanding the soul of a culture, and therefore my knowledge will always be limited.

How much of the information you gained came from books and similar resources, and how much came from talking to people?
Both informed the other. I remember seeing a qamutik for the first time at the start line of the Hudson Bay Quest. It made me curious about how people used to travel in the Arctic and I talked with lots of the older mushers. But I also looked up historic images, watched early documentaries, and searched out interviews, diaries— anything, really, that would document life in the past in the voices of the people who experienced it.

Being out with some of the Elders on the land, I realized that this knowledge of life in the past is just as relevant today. When I understood this, my questions changed. It wasn't about a certain time in history of a certain culture anymore, now it was just as much about myself—there is so much to be learned that is relevant to our understanding of our place within this country and within the cycle of nature, and yet not only did we fail to seek out this knowledge, we nearly destroyed it. So I listened with a different understanding that came out of a mix of talking to people and reading about the impacts of colonization. And that changed, in turn, what people shared with me. Since I now knew more, they would share details with me they previously might not have.

At the time I was in the Arctic, I had no intention of writing a novel, but when I did, I couldn't have written it without help from friends in both communities—who not only translated for me, but also made sure that what the characters say and do rings true. One of them happens to be the co-editor of *Inuit Qaujimajatuqangit: What Inuit Have Always Known to Be True*, and I was honored when she offered to read through the manuscript, because it was in an early conversation with her that I began to understand my personal experiences within the bigger picture of the history of the people I met.

Quincy Miller at the start line of the Hudson Bay Quest.

Andy Kowtak's team at the finish line.

Though Emmylou is a stranger, Barnabas and his grandparents are generous to her when she arrives in their world. How does this generosity help Emmylou?

The generosity of Barnabas and his grandparents is embedded in their worldview, in which sharing is an understood and important part of human existence. I believe they would treat anyone like Emmylou. No strings attached.

Emmylou, whose mother always seems to have a selfish motive for acts of generosity, immediately feels drawn to the Inuit family.

As they get to know Emmylou, they accept her as part of the family and Emmylou—although she wants to be grown up and independent—allows herself to be the child that still needs a family.

It's the beginning of a healing journey for Emmylou that eventually will lead her to accept herself and move toward reconciling the complicated relationship with her mother.

There is another important focus in the novel: the relationship between Emmylou and her mother. Why was it important for you to explore this relationship?

The relationship between children and their parents is such an important part of growing up. No matter if the relationship is loving and caring, hurtful, or non-existent, it forms us in many ways we might not even be aware of. I could easily identify with Emmylou who is seeking to get away from a mother who causes her hurt, while at the same time craving her love and approval.

I had much more difficulty writing Kitty's character and rewrote her many times. She, too, wants her daughter to be close to her, but Kitty's love is not unconditional. She needs Emmylou to be dependent on her for her own self-worth, and she manipulates their lives in ways that isolate Emmylou from forming lasting relationships with others, but—and this is important—Kitty is not aware of it. Nor is Emmylou at the beginning of the novel. Their arguments derail and neither of them understands why.

I think that arguments with parents are quite a common experience of growing up, and as we get older, we might seek to understand what causes them, but we might not always find answers—and even if we do, it does not mean it will solve the conflict.

I believe that a lot of arguments between children and parents happen because one party, or even both, fails to accept the other as they are. I also believe the same accounts for our relationships outside of the family, at school, at work, in the community we live in, but also on a more global level. I think this is why it was so important to me to explore this relationship in so much detail, because a lot of it centers on accepting others for who they are—or what happens if you don't.

What do you think is the most important aspect of Emmylou's personal story for young readers to think about?

Emmylou begins to understand the world around her in a more complex way, sees that there is more than one side to each story, and struggles to figure out how she fits into this world she increasingly becomes more aware of. On the one side, she craves independence, and yet there are times where she longs to be loved and cared for like a child. As she's trying to find herself, Emmylou has to overcome outside challenges, but also challenges within herself. I'd like young readers to think about what those challenges are and how Emmylou overcomes them. Who is Emmylou at the beginning of the novel, who at the end?